IT CAN'T SEE YOU IN THE DARK

FEROZE ENGINEER

ISBN (PAPERBACK) 978-1-0687836-0-9
ISBN (E-BOOK) 978-1-0687836-1-6

Book cover by Zainab Karachiwala

Prologue

Kasim had told himself the old crewman was sick and wouldn't have made it past the next few years anyway. But that was a lie; he would have fed his own mother to the beasts, to keep them alive.

The old man hadn't screamed when they locked him in the cage with the animals. Perhaps it was the fatalistic attitude of a man who had led a long life at sea, or perhaps it was the rum they had given him. Either way, Kasim could not help but feel a pinch of admiration surface over the guilt when he saw the man facing his demise with steady feet, despite the alcohol and the sway of the boat.

Just a few days ago, Kasim could not wait to leave the shores of Africa. He was tired of the daily routine – greasing the palms of local officials and then looking for large quantities of fresh meat to feed the ill-tempered cargo.

They had travelled from Kenya to Somalia by truck and then transferred the large container onto a ship at Mogadishu. As soon as he was on board, Kasim realised he couldn't wait to be on dry land again. The sea had been rough, which didn't bode well with the shipping container's occupants. And the smell! Oh, the smell was revolting. It had seeped into their hair, their clothes, their very being. Then, when things couldn't possibly get worse, the refrigeration units on the ship had broken down and all the meat they had bought in Mogadishu was spoiled.

Refrigerator or no refrigerator, the cargo had to be fed. If he reached Baghdad without any of the three monsters in immaculate condition he would be shot on the spot, after which they would turn their attention to his family.

It had been a logistical nightmare, even though Mamello – the owner of the illegal farm in Kenya –had told them there would be no problems. Things would be easier once the convoy touched Iraqi shores – bureaucracy and rules no longer mattered there – all he had to do was show them the letter with the presidential seal and he would be extended every courtesy.

By the time they reached Baghdad two weeks later, night had already fallen. The convoy made its way to the presidential palace. The mammoth iron gates were opened for them – they were expected.

Once inside, they drove past the main palace, the gardens, the fountains, the peacocks, the stables and the 20-car garage. They only stopped when they reached the second palace. The garish façade of the ostentatious building looked especially ugly in the fading light.

The staff had been forewarned of their arrival. A forklift crane stood in the courtyard. A servant with a blank expression stood beside it, holding a donkey by a string attached to its neck.

Kasim was sure the servant did not know why he had been told to bring a donkey and a forklift to the palace at midnight. He was equally sure the man hadn't given it a second thought

– they were all used to strange orders from above. Kasim himself was a mechanic. Transporting wildlife had not been in his original job description.

Kasim dismounted from the cab of the massive truck and went about supervising the unloading of the cargo container.

When the containers were safely on the sprawling front lawn, he finally lit his first cigarette of the day. He had barely exhaled when a loud, pink Ferrari blaring even louder gangster rap sped down the drive of the palace. It screeched to a halt, narrowly missing the large cargo container.

A man in his thirties emerged from the Ferrari. He was wearing a pink suit, exactly the same shade as the colour of his car. He was over six feet tall and had neatly manicured stubble. Mirrored Ray-Ban sunglasses were perched on his head. They misted and de-misted slightly every time he exhaled from the long Cuban cigar lodged in his mouth, just to the left of his two large, protruding front teeth.

He strode briskly towards them, his haste failing to mask the arrogant swagger with which he walked. 'Where are they? Are they here?' he shouted almost like a spoilt six-year-old asking for his Christmas present.

As soon as he was within four feet of the containers he recoiled and shouted, 'Fuck! What is that smell?' Then, composing himself, he said 'Kasim? It's you, isn't it? Did you shit your pants again, you ugly fuck?' He laughed uproariously at his own joke.

Kasim stubbed out his cigarette – no one was allowed to smoke in Uday's presence. He smiled politely at the joke, though it was unlikely Uday was even looking at him; he never looked at his inferiors, only shouted at them.

Uday removed the lit Havana from his mouth and tossed it carelessly behind his back. It bounced off the hood of his

Ferrari in a shower of sparks. He didn't care – he had a new toy to play with. Three new toys, to be precise.

'So, are they inside?' he said beckoning to the containers. 'Come out, come out, wherever you are,' he sang and kicked the side of the container with his patent leather shoes.

A roar erupted from inside.

Unfazed, he continued. 'I swear to god, Kasim, at least you could have shampooed them or something before you brought them into my presence. That stink is almost unbearable. Did they come with accessories?'

'Accessories, your Excellency?'

'Everything I need, you fool – especially collars for their necks. What good are they without studded collars?'

'I'm sorry, your Excellency.'

'You can't do one thing right can you, Kasim? I should have you shot right now, you bloody faggot.'

'I'm sorry, your Excellency. Please.'

'It's OK. It's fine.' Uday sighed as if he were doing a great act of charity by putting up with the errant servant. 'Just get them ready for tomorrow.'

'What is tomorrow, your Excellency?'

'Tomorrow is the big game you fool – Iraq versus Qatar. As Sporting Minister of Iraq, I wish to have the lions at my feet. It will remind the players of their fate if they don't score any goals.' He smiled. Kasim did not have a shadow of a doubt that Uday was being deadly serious.

'Your Excellency, the lions are not trained yet. They can be dangerous.'

'You dare to lecture me? I wrote my thesis in biology. First class from Baghdad University!'

Kasim doubted that Uday had even read the title of the thesis that a team of academics had been hired to write on his behalf. But if Uday was killed by the lions, his father, Saddam, might hold him responsible for bringing them to Iraq in the first place.

'Your Excellency, please, I am merely afraid for your safety.'

'Don't you know anything, Kasim? In Egypt, the kings always had lions with them. Also that king in that movie, he had one. What's the name? Oh, never mind! Anyway, if those skirt-wearing Egyptian fucks can have a lion at their feet, why the fuck can't I?'

As he couldn't think of a suitable reply, Kasim decided to keep his mouth shut. Uday was not a king. He was merely the arrogant first-born child of Iraq's president and dictator, Saddam Hussein. However, Kasim did not want to be the lion's first meal. He excused himself and went about the sordid affair of feeding the lions with the live donkey while Uday watched gleefully.

1. Abdul

There was no getting away from it – the heat was everywhere. A radio in the corner of the dusty auto-repair garage announced that Iraq was losing to Qatar in the football, but Abdul wasn't really listening.

He reached out for another cold Farida, the local brew, from under the bonnet of the ancient Jaguar he was working on and smiled as he thought of the new posters that had blanketed Baghdad: a picture of Saddam Hussein with his family, all studiously absorbed in a large Quran laid out on a stand in front of them. A quote that translated to 'Religion is the backbone of our society' was plastered on it in large, pink Arabic script. In the picture, Uday, Saddam's eldest son, looked suspiciously hungover.

Just then, Abdul heard a horn sound from outside the door of the auto-repair garage.

A polished Mercedes E-Class stood in the dust outside – standard issue for the more elite circles of Iraq's ruling Baathist Party. Abdul could see a driver in the front and a girl in the back seat, her head buried in a book. He walked out of the garage as the driver rolled down his tinted window. He looked worried.

He told Abdul that strange sounds had been emanating from under the bonnet, and he wondered if Abdul could have a look.

They opened the bonnet while the young lady, who had scarcely looked up, sat in the air-conditioned luxury of the car, and continued to read.

Abdul brought out his father's old toolbox. Despite owning several newer and lighter tools, he still preferred to use the worn-out old set - each ratchet, spanner and socket bearing countless scratches. One for every car they had fixed, Abdul liked to think.

He picked up the adjustable spanner, remembering the first time he had held it.

Abdul's parents had both been physicists, researching and teaching at the University of Baghdad. Although well respected amongst Iraq's polite society, academics were not very well off. One of his father's few luxuries was an old Morris Minor, which he had managed to keep running since he had acquired it third-hand, just after Abdul was born.

Admittedly, however, the car had broken down often.

As he had no money for repairs, the professor spent hours hunched over the bonnet of the car trying to figure out its most recent mechanical failure. Lacking a television or properly functioning radio to keep himself entertained, the eight-year-old Abdul had often sat around watching him work.

The professor, like many who instruct a classroom, enjoyed having an audience. He would think aloud when trying to fix the car, almost as if he were explaining its inner workings to a class, which helped him to understand it himself. He knew this was for his own benefit, never expecting his adolescent son to pay much attention, much less understand what he was saying.

'Now let's see… what do you think the problem could be today, Abdul? The car simply isn't starting. Let's approach this systematically. First, the ignition system…'

And so it had continued, with Abdul's involvement extending only to occasionally fetching a tool for his father from the box in the corner.

That's when Abdul's parents first started noticing things.

The toaster, which had been lying in the corner, broken for months, suddenly seemed to work again. The ancient radio, which had only ever been able to pull in stations from within Iraq's boundaries, was suddenly able to relay the news from Africa and Europe. The ice cream maker, which had never quite worked since they purchased it from a street vendor in Hiwa Market, suddenly produced the creamiest, smoothest delights.

Abdul's father simply assumed that his wife had gotten the items repaired, and she, in turn, assumed that her husband had finally gotten around to fixing something other than his precious automobile.

One day, when all three of them were in the car on the way home, the Morris emitted a loud grinding noise, slowed down and stopped in the middle of the busy market road in old Baghdad.

A few passers-by had helped them to move it to the side so that the traffic could continue to weave through the stalls, pushcarts and street vendors. The bonnet was opened, and much discussion ensued about what the problem may be. The vegetable seller suddenly became an expert in automobile repair, and the local traffic-policeman a consummate mechanic. Abdul's father tinkered for almost an hour. But no one could get it to start again. Eventually, Abdul's father was forced to walk to the nearest garage to fetch someone who knew what they were doing, dreading the accompanying bill with every step.

Abdul had stood on the side of the road with his mother, watching the hullabaloo. Once the vegetable seller and the policeman lost interest and wandered away, and his father had left for the garage on foot, he quietly opened the trunk of the Morris and removed the toolbox.

He then commandeered a discarded old wooden crate and pushed it to the front of the car so that, when he stood atop it, he was tall enough to open the bonnet.

His mother watched him with interest. She smiled as he removed a spanner from the toolbox and made a few adjustments before returning it and shutting the bonnet, just like the adults before him. Her smile turned into a frown when she noticed the grease all over his hands, no doubt thinking of how she would have to scrub them clean when they got home.

Finally, his father returned with the mechanic. After throwing the bonnet back open, the man instructed his father to try starting the car while he watched the engine in a bid to identify the problem.

But to their surprise, the car started the moment Abdul's father turned the key.

At first, they were convinced it must be some kind of fluke. But they tried again and again, and each time the car never faltered. If anything, the engine seemed even more responsive to the key than it had been before.

After the irritated mechanic had been placated and dispatched back to the garage, the family got back into the car. Abdul's father stroked his beard, wondering how on earth the car had worked.

Abdul's mother seemed lost in thought all the way home – uncharacteristically quiet for a woman who was normally very talkative.

The next day, Abdul's father left home early for his morning lectures. Abdul sat at the family's kitchen table, uniformed and ready to start his day, waiting only for his mother to tell him it was time to go, at which point the two of them would get the bus together. He would head to school, and she would do some shopping before returning to grade some physics exams.

But that was not to be.

'Where are we going mama?' Abdul asked as they set off on foot in the opposite direction from the bus stop.

'Wait and see,' she replied.

After twenty minutes of walking, Abdul realised they were walking towards a garage. Piles of discarded tyres lay in a heap outside. Some cars were parked inside the building, but the majority overflowed onto the pavement and even spilt out onto the road. The smell of fuel and grease was strong in the air. A man emerged, wiping his hands on what looked like a very dirty rag. Abdul immediately recognised him as the same fellow his father had returned to the car with the day before. He never forgot a face.

In fact, he never forgot *anything* he saw.

The mechanic no longer seemed irritated, but rather amused. 'Is he the boy? I hadn't even noticed him yesterday. Salaam, young man. Your mother seems to think you can fix cars. Today we are going to find out.'

The trio walked to the corner of the garage where an old Mitsubishi truck was parked.

'So, little man, this car does not start either. Granted, it's very different from your dad's old banger, but the problems are similar. What do you think it could be?'

Abdul walked around the truck, peeping into the cabin. The bonnet was already lying open. He noticed a stool in the opposite corner and fetched it. He stood atop it for a few minutes, just looking into the engine with his hands by his side.

The mechanic grinned.

'Would you turn the key in the ignition for me, sir?'

'Sure.'

The engine coughed but did not turn over.

'Again?' asked the mechanic, still grinning.

Abdul did not reply. He did not hear the mechanic anymore.

Everything aside from the bonnet of the car had receded into the background, almost as if the focussing ring on a camera had been twisted in his head. He was no longer privy to the various sounds and smells of the garage. He could not hear, see or smell anything other than the inside of the Mitsubishi. And he did not want to. If he had been dragged away, he might have had a breakdown. Over the next few years, he would learn to control this feeling, to live with it.

Immediately, his mind associated various parts of the car with the ones he was familiar with in the Morris; they looked different but he knew they did the same kind of thing. Next, he noticed all the new and different parts, immediately inferring their utility depending on what they were connected to.

He got off the stool and went over to the other side of the garage, the mechanic and his mother following behind, watching intently. Without hesitation, he walked directly to the rack of spanners on the wall. He had noticed them when they had first walked into the garage, along with the hydraulic jack, the vehicle lift, the oil drain and caddy, the air compressor, the battery charger and jumper cables, the brake lathe and the strut compressor. If you asked him, he would not have been able to name the items, but instinctively he seemed vaguely aware of all their functions just by glancing at their structure and position in the garage.

He dove back under the hood of the Mitsubishi for a few minutes. Then he pulled over the rolling dolly that enabled one to slide underneath a car to work on its underbelly.

'Hold on,' said the mechanic. 'The problem with this car is not one you can fix there, young man. The problem is under the bonnet.' He seemed almost relieved. He had frowned for a moment when the boy seemed to have retrieved exactly the right size of spanner from the 30-odd variants on the rack. Luck, he guessed.

Abdul had rolled back out from under the car, poking his head out from under the chassis.

'Oh. I've fixed the ignition already sir. I'm just curious about how the … um… I think it's called transmission... works,'

The mechanic jumped into the cab of the truck and turned the ignition.

As the V6 engine roared to life, Abdul's changed forever.

As he worked on the Mercedes, at age 23, he was considered one of the best mechanics in the city. Even Saddam's chief mechanic and secretary, Kasim, had once come to him with a problem that involved a heavily modified Lamborghini. Despite his abhorrence for the Hussein family, he had not been able to resist working on the car.

The voice of the driver of the black Mercedes brought Abdul back to the present, as he set to work with the spanner. He seemed to be a chatty, if slightly nervous, fellow. He said he was taking the boss's daughter back home from the prestigious Baghdad College for Girls, as he did every day. Her father was a big shot in Saddam's government. He would go crazy if he learnt that the driver had brought his precious daughter to a lowly auto-repair garage, especially in a poor, Shi'a-dominated area. With all of the unrest that had been stirred up against the government in recent weeks, the driver insisted that Abdul fix the issue quickly so that they could be on their way.

As he finished replacing the jammed bearing in the cooling pump, he caught a glimpse of the girl in the back seat. She looked about his age. The long black curls of her hair fell over her face as she focused entirely on the book she was reading, lost to the world. The intensity of her expression contrasted sharply with the delicate features of her face – dusky skin, a small pert nose and her mouth slightly ajar in concentration. Somehow, he knew this was not a person who did things by half measures. He recognised the novel; he had read it during the year he had spent studying automotive engineering in Austria on a full scholarship.

Since his return, he had gotten his hands on more than a few books by Western authors – even the ones that had been banned in Iraq. What started with a couple of novels, had become a lifelong love affair with literature – allowing him to escape from the dust and darkness that characterised the unfortunate point in time and space he found himself in.

When the driver ran off to the toilet, he tapped on her window.

The girl looked up at Abduls grinning face, taking in his grease-stained coveralls and goatee beard – popular amongst the young men in Iraq. She lowered the window cautiously.

'It's good, isn't it?' he said.

'Eh? What? What's good?'

'The book you're reading. Stephen King. He's one of my favourite authors.'

'Really? Which one's your favourite?' she asked, raising her eyebrows.

'*The Stand,* of course. But they are all good really, aren't they?'

'*The Stand,*' she repeated, pulling out a ballpoint from her satchel, and scribbling it down on the palm of her hand. 'Do you read a lot of horror?'

'Yes, I read the newspapers every day.'

She cracked a lopsided grin, which lit up her face. Now that she was looking at him, he noticed her startling eyes – they weren't of any particularly unusual colour, but they sparkled with the same intensity as the rest of her features. Abdul wondered what she would look like if she laughed.

Their conversation showed no sign of abating as the driver returned and started pacing up and down anxiously. Clearly, the boss's daughter chatting with the mechanic hadn't been in the plan.

She had been introduced to fiction in English by the daughter of a US diplomat who had attended her prestigious school, she explained. Of course, the girl and her family, like most Western families, had long since left the country due to the impending war. The topic of conversation worked its way, as it inevitably did when book lovers met in Iraq, to the distinct lack of current literary output in their own country.

Hesitatingly, she asked him if he had heard of an Iraqi author called Whistler.

Abdul smiled while furrowing his eyebrows, pretending he had never heard of the man. Whistler was indeed an unusual literary choice for the daughter of a prominent Baathist Party official. He would have to be cautious. 'Who's that?' he asked.

'Oh, he's not very well known. He writes a blog – like an online journal – the only one in Baghdad. Never mind. What are you reading at the moment?'

Abdul noticed how quickly she changed the subject, but he had no objections. He got very nervous when people started talking about Whistler.

The person in question had become rather infamous in some circles, Abdul knew. When Whistler first emerged online, he became known among locals for his essays and poems about Baghdad, which were often laced with irony and sarcasm. But the dark humour in his writing attracted an international audience, providing an unbiased view of life on the ground in Iraq as the country became of more and more interest to the world's journalists. Soon, he had more readers abroad than in his homeland.

As time passed, his writing became more political. Unlike many other Iraqis, he publicly criticised the Saddam regime, but he was equally sceptical about US intervention and the reasons behind it.

Inevitably, this outspokenness drew the attention of the mainstream media. Articles were written about him in newspapers around the globe. Still, despite this newfound fame, not a soul knew his true identity. It was a miracle he hadn't suddenly disappeared, like everyone else who displeased Saddam. The Hussein family's reach was long, and they had spies at every level of society.

Abdul was happy to change the subject and tell her all about what he was reading. It was best to pretend he did not know who Whistler was.

They were still swapping names of their favourite books when the driver finally interrupted them, 'Madam, your father will wonder where we are. It would be best if we returned home now. If he comes to know that I brought you to a garage and let you speak to a stranger, however helpful or nice he may be' – he glanced at Abdul – 'I will be made into a sheesh kebab'.

She nodded. Grabbing a sheet of notepaper from her bag, she scribbled down the names of some books and handed it to Abdul before the tinted windows went back up. As the car pulled away, and Abdul was left in a cloud of dust, he realised he had forgotten to ask her what her name was. He sighed deeply, cursing his forgetfulness, and started packing up for the day.

He took a deep breath. For some reason, the aroma of the pine trees that lined the Tigris strengthened when dusk arrived, just as the birds sang their final song. The last fading rays of the sun lingered hazily in the air while the muezzin began his melancholy call to prayer from the minaret of the Mosque nearby. For a short while, the heaving metropolis always seemed to slow down and relax.

Abdul took off his oil-stained coveralls, hung them on a peg behind the door of the garage and made his way up the stairs to the small studio apartment on the first floor. Rugs covered the floor. There was a bed on one side and a desk that held his prized computer on the other. Books on shelves covered every square inch of the wall. He switched on his computer and made himself a cup of tea while he waited for it to boot up.

It had taken a while for Baghdad to catch up with the world when it came to technology. Not because of any economic or cultural barriers, but purely because the Mukhabarat, Saddam's feared secret police, were ill-equipped to monitor the vast landscape of cyberspace. Indeed, these were the same reasons that satellite TV and mobile phones were not permitted – wireless communication is hard to monitor in a developing police state. However, Baghdad was eventually pulled, kicking and screaming, into the 20th century due to the demands of commerce and, more importantly, because Uday Hussein wanted to watch internet pornography.

Finally, when his computer had finished booting up, Abdul sat down at the keyboard and went through his security routine, loading up software that would mask his digital footprint. This was always a time-consuming process on the shaky dial-up connection.

Finally, he glanced at the front door to ensure he had locked it, then loaded up his blog – said to be the only one in Baghdad – and typed in his username: Whistler.

2. Ava

Ava crouched in the darkness.

She wore a black turtleneck, black jeans and black shoes. Binoculars were glued to her eyes as she sat in the shrubbery, spying on the house on the moor.

Ava had been late because she couldn't bring herself to wear the black turtleneck.

It was just too much of a cliché. She might as well have brought along a big brown sack and worn a black eye mask. She stifled a giggle in the moonless night as she looked out at the big house.

Ava could recall a time when she was scared of the dark. She had many sleepless nights as a child. When she did sleep, she often had nightmares of monsters under her bed. Ava would wake up sweating, often finding she had wet the bed. Mummy didn't like to be bothered at night. She wanted Ava to be strong. And so, because she was a brave girl, she suffered alone.

Then one day, Pa finally came home from the war. On his first night home, he must have gotten out of bed to grab a glass of water when he heard Ava whimpering in her bedroom. He knocked on the door before letting himself in.

'What's the matter, Ava? Everything OK?' he had said.

Ava couldn't bring herself to tell her father that she was scared of the dark. But Pa seemed to know anyway. He always seemed to know these things. Especially things about darkness and fear.

'It's OK, darling. I used to be scared of the dark too. It's because you can't see what's ahead of you, right?' he continued, without waiting for a reply. 'Cos when you see things, you can understand them. In the dark, you can't do that.'

'But you can rationalise things. For example, you know that monsters don't exist, right? So, sometimes, you've just got to think logically and stop worrying. But let me tell you a little secret that's going to help you. It's going to blow your mind.'

He leaned closer and said in a whisper, 'If there *is* something in the dark, it can't see you either.'

He grinned, patted Ava on the head, and went to bed. That was the first time Ava could remember sleeping well as a child.

A few years later, Ava had gone away on the Duke of Edinburgh program. They had been to the Brecon Beacons National Park in Wales with some other school children. The instructor, a bespectacled gentleman, had only realised that Tim, the youngest in the group, was missing when they made it back to the campsite after nightfall.

He couldn't leave the rest of the children to go and search for Tim. He called the local police station and a search party had been organised, but they would take at least two hours to reach the remote location in the dead of the night.

Ava made a decision. She would go find poor Timmy herself. Besides, Timmy had borrowed Ava's model of the Ferrari 275, which Pa had given her, and it was probably still in his pocket. Ava couldn't lose that – it was the last gift Pa had given her before the incident that had taken him away. So, she crept away from the group and disappeared into the night, trying to retrace the route they had taken.

At first, the forest seemed cool, quiet and dangerous. She could smell the earth; it had just rained. The narrow walking path was very muddy, strewn with rocks and the roots of trees – she had to be careful about where she placed her foot.

Ava kept worrying about what lay outside of the circle of illumination from her torch – it was perturbing to limit her vision to a small circle of light. She started to regret her bravado. Then, the batteries in her torch died and she was left in complete darkness, in the middle of the forest.

Alone.

She could feel the terror rising from the core of her stomach and travelling up her throat. Then she remembered what her father had said: Take a deep breath, think logically, and stop worrying.

It took her a good ten minutes to accomplish this. She recalled something from David Attenborough's show on the radio: there was very little harmful wildlife in the United Kingdom. The most dangerous thing there could be is an adder. David had mentioned the venomous snake very rarely attacked humans, even when provoked. Besides, its bite, although painful, was not fatal. The only other animals to watch for were foxes. And Ava had seen plenty of those at night in London from her bedroom window. They were kind of cute, and they ran away whenever anyone went near them.

So, what was she scared of really? Ghosts did not exist; she had made that decision last year. Unpleasant humans living in the forest seemed too remote a possibility. And even if any of those existed in the forest, they simply wouldn't know she was there now that her torch was off. She pictured the forest as she had seen it a few hours ago: beautiful, elegant trees, colourful flowers and the cheerful cries of numerous birds in the fresh air.

It dawned on her that being in the middle of a remote Welsh forest, alone, at night, was probably one of the safest places on the planet.

Ava was no longer scared. Earlier, she had just been able to see what lay in the beam of her flashlight, but now, as her eyes adjusted to the dark, she could see a lot more in the moonlight filtering through the trees.

She noticed a discarded packet of crisps on the grass – she was still on track. She remembered something else she had read in a book: when one of your senses is impaired, another becomes sharper. Just as she thought this, she heard a whimper in the distance. It was the sort of whimper a person makes when they've shed all their tears in the dark and have no energy left to cry. Ava knew this sound well. She moved toward it.

Tim was sitting under a tree not far away, looking scared to death. Ava grinned and sat beside him as if she was taking a seat near a friend she had bumped into on the tube. She thought she better tell Timmy Pa's theory about the darkness.

By the time they emerged from the forest, they looked like they had only been for a stroll in Hyde Park. The instructor was angry with Ava for disappearing, but she could also recall the admiration in his eyes.

These days, the cover of night was a distinct advantage, thought Ava as she sat in the shrubbery. And she never used a torch either – the people she liked to watch were usually very easy to see.

This particular individual was the last one on Ava's list.

The wealthy heir of a coal magnate, he seemed to spend most of his time playing golf and entertaining a series of guests, mostly lissom young women. He was also known to be a dodgy character – there were at least six divisions of Scotland Yard that would have been pleased to make his acquaintance ranging from the tax evasion unit to the one for violent crime.

He was the sort of person who would never go to the authorities if he had been crossed – even if, for example, his car was stolen. Even if it was, say, an Aston Martin DB4GT Zagato, stolen from right under his nose.

The car in question was a real beauty, no doubt, and its owner was extremely lucky to have acquired one, regardless of his copious wealth.

This variant of the DB4GT was one of only 19 originals ever built in partnership with Zagato, the famous Italian coachbuilder. Lighter and faster than the original car, it was built to take on the Ferrari 250GT in the 1961 Le Mans.

With its beautiful curves and lightweight body, it had taken people's breath away when it was unveiled in 1960, and it had exactly the same effect on enthusiasts like Ava today. The last of its kind to be auctioned fetched ten million pounds.

Ava was a thief, true, but she had one principle. She never stole from those who had put their life savings into buying their dream car. She only stole from assholes. Particularly, assholes who were in trouble with the law. She was no Robin Hood, there were very practical reasons for her principles; when assholes were robbed, no one really gave a shit. It was amazing how many of them did not even report the crime.

Her principles had enabled her to stay out of trouble with the law but also had an added bonus: she slept easily at night.

Stealing a car like this was a decade-long investment that took research, planning, patience, creativity and workmanship. A car so rare would not be easy to sell on, of course, as it could easily be identified. It would have to sit in a secret underground vault for many years, carefully tended to by Ava.

When the heat had died down, she would completely remove any trait or mark distinguishing the car from any of its 18 other siblings, including the chassis and engine numbers, and then carefully forge new marks onto it, identifying it as one of the other 18 cars, perhaps the one known to have fallen off the radar in the eighties.

In time, she would partner with a dealer who would proclaim that he or she had 'found' the car in a barn or a vault or a collection somewhere. It would then find a new owner and Ava would get paid a significant amount of money.

But between the time she stole the car and the time she passed it on, Ava would make it a point to drive the Aston Martin a few times, whatever the risk. Not doing so would have been a far greater crime, in her opinion.

She played back today's challenge in her head. The car had to be stolen on the individual's property, further reducing the chances of him reporting the crime as this particular individual would not want the police anywhere near his home.

The car sat in an underground garage. The garage was accessed by a car lift, concealed within a small building that sat beside the manor house. The building could only be accessed with an electronic pin code.

All the usual security measures were present: the infrared cameras, the alarms.

The car itself would surely be fitted with an alarm and would possibly have extra wheel and steering locks on to boot. Perhaps it was even retrofitted with an engine immobiliser and a GPS tracker. With a car as valuable as that, one would take every precaution.

If this was a modern supercar, Ava would have to break the window and plug a device into the dashboard. This device was similar to the one used by car dealerships to re-program automobiles when the owner had lost the key, or when the car needed to be resold. The powerful computer inside the gadget would decrypt the car's security system, disable the alarm and reprogram a blank key fob with the car's unique electronic code so that the engine could be started.

With vintage cars, this was seldom the case, although Ava had come across one or two that had been fitted with ultramodern security measures.

On an older car, one had to take apart the steering column, detect the starter and power wires, connect the starter wires, and touch the power wires to start the ignition process of the engine. Any physical barriers like steering locks or wheel clamps needed to be disabled with a portable angle-grinder. Later, you could scan for, and disable any tracking devices that happened to be on the car, but this was still quite rare.

Ava had no intention of doing *any* of this today.

No, she would simply wait until the individual went to his car in the basement garage, unlocked it, rode up the car elevator, exited the building and drove down the road as he did every Friday.

One of his tyres would burst as he approached the main gate of the property. Ava had made sure of that by placing a specially modified and nearly invisible spike strip in a location which the car was bound to pass through. Her design was based on the original 'caltrop', a defensive weapon used by Darius III in ancient Persian battles. In those days, they littered the ground as a defence against horses, chariots, war elephants and camels. Made of two or more sharp nails, they would pierce the soles of attacking cavalry. In this instance, the tiny, black devices merged almost completely into the gravel driveway. In the dark, they would be impossible to spot, even if one were standing over them.

Once he realised his tyre was flat, the individual would curse hideously, exit the car and walk to the house to change out of his dinner jacket and get what he needed to fit the spare; Ava hoped.

However, between the time the individual left the car and the time he returned, the car would mysteriously vanish without a trace; nice and clean.

Ava had calculated the amount of time it would take the individual to exit the car, walk to the house and return with tools. The process would take approximately eight minutes at the very quickest. In that time, Ava would have to remove the old tyre, replace it with a spare, remove the spikes from the ground and drive away.

She had simulated the entire process in her garage, testing how far apart she needed to place the spikes to disable no more than one tyre, and how quickly she could change the tyre of a similar car. After several trials, she had it down to seven minutes and thirty seconds with special electronic tools. Close, but doable.

She had also driven the escape route twice in her old Jaguar E-Type, the closest car to the Aston that she could get her hands on. And no headlamps either, just moonlight – pushing her skills and the car to their very limit on the winding and narrow country lanes.

After all, if it was dark, they couldn't see you.

Ava looked at her watch. It was 8:47 p.m. She switched on the timer and set it to eight minutes. The start button would be ready to press once the target got out of his car. She checked her toolkit one last time. Ava knew her target was leaving for a long vacation to Switzerland the next day and, more than likely, would take the car with him. This would be her last chance.

Finally, she heard the unmistakable roar of a 3.7-litre straight-six engine starting up, followed by two brilliant ovals of light emerging from the darkness.

As one of its tyres burst, according to plan, Ava noticed something she hadn't anticipated – in a departure from the target's usual activity, there were two figures in the car instead of one: the owner, and a young blonde girl in a little black dress. A complication.

The man killed the engine and cursed. He got out of the car and walked towards the house at a brisk pace.

But the girl waited inside the car.

3. Uday

It was a hot day, and the Baghdad street-market was full of activity. The stalls were brimming with fruit, vegetables, baked goods, clothes, second-hand electronics and anything else one cared to buy.

Sellers cried out their wares, and furious bargaining could be heard from all directions.

Uday Hussein was in his purple Bentley, crawling slowly through the hordes of traffic. His security detail trailed behind him in black SUVs. He came here every Thursday at 3 p.m. if he had recovered sufficiently from the night before. It was around the time when the schools ended, including all the girls' schools and colleges.

For as long as he could remember, Uday Hussein had loved watching people.

At the age of five, when other children were watching Disney cartoons, his father had left instructions that he and his younger brother, Qusay, were to watch recorded sessions from the torture chamber, in an effort to toughen them up. 'A ruler must be unafraid to wield power in order to keep power,' he had always said to them.

Uday clearly remembered the day his father's assistant had come to their lounge with a stack of VHS tapes. 'Little Uday! Little Qusay! I have gifts for you!' he had said.

They had put the tapes into the player and sat on the opulent swan-shaped sofa opposite the huge screen. The maid, thinking that they were about to watch a film, had made some popcorn. She made the mistake of glancing at the screen when she came out of the kitchen. She saw a man being flayed alive on the screen and immediately dropped the bowl.

Qusay hadn't reacted well either. Two minutes in, he had started crying. Ten minutes later, he was sick all over the sofa.

Uday was indifferent. He watched the videos and felt slightly bored as his father's assistant explained who the man being tortured was, the crimes he had committed and why it was important to torture him. All that really didn't interest Uday.

He only started paying attention when he heard the man scream as they removed the skin from his body with a sharp knife. Uday quite enjoyed the screams.

When the video was over, he asked to see another.

The next 'gift' from his father came on the day he turned 13. His father came up to his room personally that morning, carrying a box. He sat on Uday's bed and opened it. Inside it was a small, gold-plated Glock semi-automatic with an ivory grip.

After thanking his father, they walked together across the palace grounds to a small building in the corner of the compound. Uday had never been inside that building. He had heard muffled screams coming from it when he played in the garden, so he had vaguely assumed that it was where the torture videos were made.

When they walked in, Uday knew he was right. What could only be explained as the smell of death hung in the air. Not wholly unpleasant, Uday remembered thinking.

He was surprised to see the building descend three stories underground. Used to immaculately maintained and ornately decorated palaces, he took in the anonymous brown splashes on the tiled walls and dirty concrete floors with amazement. The facility was a warren of narrow passages with sturdy doors that lined each side.

They went two levels down and his father's guards unlocked the door to a room. Inside, a man wearing a loincloth was cowering in a corner while mumbling incoherently.

Saddam opened the box once again and took out the gun. The man in the corner saw this and screamed. A guard hit him in the face and told him to be quiet.

'Now that you are no longer a child, you must learn that violence is a tool you can never be afraid to use. This man here is a traitor. We have to make an example of him,' said Saddam, giving his son the gun. Uday wasn't sure what his father meant, but he wanted to shoot the man, so he nodded along.

Uday lifted the gun and brought it up to the level of the man's head. Knowing the man was listening he said, 'OK I'm going to shoot the man now, Baba.' Then, instead of pulling the trigger, he screamed, 'Bang!' into the man's ear.

The man jumped in shock and lost control of his bowels. Then, realising he wasn't dead, he started crying, each sob racking his body with a violent shiver. Proud of his little joke, Uday started laughing just as hysterically.

He repeated this process twice until, just when the man thought he might not get shot, Uday fired the pistol. He remembered the flecks of blood, gore and bone that showered the wall behind the man. It was at that moment that Uday realised he could do anything and there would never be any consequences.

He was Saddam's firstborn son.

As Uday grew up, he started noticing girls. At first, he noticed that several girls were always being brought into and taken out of his father's section of the palace by one of his father's aides, Kamel.

One day he walked over to Kamel and asked him why.

'Aah little prince! You see, every king must satisfy his desires so that he may rule the land without any distractions. I have the honour of helping your esteemed father to do this.'

As time passed, Uday realised which 'desires' Kamel had been talking about. He also realised why his mother always wore a pained expression on her face when the girls were brought into the palace. He knew there was nothing she could do. This angered him and, in turn, he blamed Kamel for the discord between his father and mother.

But that did not stop him from finding women of his own.

The first unfortunate victim of his attention was a maid in his palace, although the experience hadn't quite unfolded as Uday would have liked.

She was a petite little thing, perhaps about 16 or 17. Kamel had found her in the streets and brought her to the palace to serve as part of the kitchen staff.

The others had warned her about Uday, and she usually made herself scarce when he was around. The full extent of his perversions had not yet emerged but, even at the age of 14, he was known to indiscriminately hit his staff with a riding crop – one he specifically carried for this purpose – if he judged them to have committed even a minor infraction.

One day, Uday noticed the delicate figure in the frilly European maid's outfit, which all female palace staff were obliged to wear. She seemed to be chopping some vegetables, absorbed in her task. She hadn't noticed him. He felt a pang of desire.

Uday had been brought up to take whatever he wanted. 'You, there!' he shouted in Arabic. The poor girl started trembling immediately. He noticed this and was inflamed even more.

'Clothes off. Now. And undress me, too.' he said, standing with his arms outstretched.

She whimpered in protest.

He walked over to her, raised his hand, and struck her face hard.

This time she did as she was told.

Uday was immediately excited at being naked in front of her. He remembered the magazines he had discovered in his father's study a few years before. Suddenly he knew what he wanted, what he needed.

'Massage me,' he said.

'Sir, please...' she stammered, so nervous she was barely able to speak.

'Silence! Do as I say. Now!' He brandished the riding crop. Not for one minute did he feel like he was doing anything wrong – after all she was just a maid, an object, a plaything like everything else in his world. He felt it was his birthright to do with her as he pleased. He was, after all, Saddam's firstborn son.

The poor girl got to work, working his shaft up and down with her hands.

Uday sighed with pleasure. Then, suddenly, he felt a tingling sensation. The tingling soon became an agonising, burning sensation.

'Aaaaaa! Stop! What did you do?'

She looked sideways towards the kitchen counter at the bowl of potent chillies she had been de-seeding by hand when he had interrupted her. Obviously, he hadn't cared to notice what she was doing when he attacked her.

Uday followed her eyes. Noticing the chillies, he realised what had happened and bellowed with rage. Now in unbearable pain, he ran out of the kitchen towards the nearest bathroom and the cold-water tap.

The maid had known that his vengeance would be terrible and had fled, never to return. In doing so, she was spared the worst of Uday's attention towards her. However, Uday had been left with a hatred towards women, tinged with an unmet desire for satisfaction. The next few days had not been pleasant for any member of staff at the palace – the riding crop could be heard whistling through the air far more than usual. Since that day, rape had become part of his lifestyle – something he did as nonchalantly as running a traffic light.

Uday's childhood memories were suddenly interrupted as he saw something he liked in the busy market.

She had just gotten out of a Mercedes and was walking down the street, her head buried in a book. Uday wondered why people bothered to read at all, much less why they did it while navigating a busy street. What was the point of reading when one could simply watch a movie? It was so much easier!

This one was ripe for the picking in his estimation: dark curly hair and dusky skin. A lovely figure, too. She looked young but was older than the girls he usually went for, he knew, perhaps 18 or 20.

What would he do with her afterwards? The dogs would already have been fed, he thought, glancing at his watch. He had not thrown anyone off the terrace recently, but his mother enjoyed the rose bed underneath it when she visited, and he did not wish to spoil it for her yet again. He could always play that game he liked, the one involving the rats that bred in the basement.

Then, Uday had a brainwave: his new toys from Mamello's farm in Africa had not yet tasted human blood, not that he knew of anyway. Today would be as good a day as any. He made a note to call Kasim to ensure the video camera had been charged.

He forced his attention back to the present. One must focus if one wants to achieve anything in life, he thought.

Uday was careful not to alert his victim to his presence. He wanted to study her from afar, to think of what it would be like to take her. For him, it made what was to follow far more enjoyable.

She lowered the book and paused in front of a shop window, seemingly oblivious to his presence. He slowed his Bentley to a crawl as he passed directly behind her, staring at her, drinking her in. Hookah pipes were displayed behind the highly polished glass window she was looking into. He thought she must have seen something she liked because she gave a little start before quickly entering the shop.

Uday stopped the car and waited for her to come out. His security detail stopped a respectful distance behind him. The activity in the market continued around them.

There were two things people enjoyed very much in the Middle East – food and poetry – and the market had both in spades. The food was everywhere. For the poetry, one had to look harder. But, with the right pair of eyes, one could see it in the colourful market stalls, hear it in the cries of the sellers, and smell it in the aroma of a thousand clay ovens.

Uday did not notice the food nor sense the poetry in the marketplace that day, or any other day. These things were lost on him. He was addicted to seeing fear – that was his food, that was his poetry.

He started to get bored waiting. His impatience coupled with his denied libido formed a potent cocktail. Perhaps he would take the girl to the back room of the shop itself. He knew his bodyguards were right behind him, trigger-happy and eager to please him.

What had she seen in the tobacco shop, he wondered. Upon reflection, she did not seem like a smoker. Enough is enough, he thought, getting out of the car and wandering over to the shop.

He kicked open the door.

4. Abdul

Excerpt from Whistler's Blog:

Cairo writes. Beirut prints. Baghdad reads. Or so the cliché goes. But why do we read in Baghdad? Is it because reading is a window with which to access the world, which is otherwise so inaccessible to the common Iraqi in this day and age?

Or is it because books can also prove to be windows that one can climb through to escape the world?

The latter, I think, has always been a necessary skill to develop as a Baghdadi.

Opening a good book is like a potent drug, enabling time travel, inducing visions and leading you firmly away from your present reality of food rations, economic sanctions, war, suicide bombs and whatever other misfortunes happen to befall you.

Whatever the reason, the biggest public library in the world – the House of Wisdom – was said to have been established during the Abbasid era in Iraq. Perhaps the caliph had a premonition of the unrest that was to follow – almost constantly up to the present day – and the coming need for distraction.

But alas, it was not meant to be. Even the library was destroyed by people who wanted to seize control of the city. However, at the time, a book traders' market was established near the old quarter of the city, what is now Mutanabbi Street.

Even today, hundreds of years later, the street is lined by booksellers of every description. Some are in air-conditioned shops, while others have books spread on rugs over the pavement.

If you ever want to know who's in power or gauge the political temperature of Iraq, you only have to walk down this road. My parents told me they saw Marxist texts be replaced by nationalist pan-Arabian works. In my lifetime these sellers have primarily stocked odes to the glory of our current president. But of late, I'm seeing fewer and fewer of them.

However, as every book lover in Baghdad knows, one only has to wink at the seller and move aside the row of books displayed at the front, to get at the good stuff underneath.

Literature that is considered taboo or pornographic appears as if by magic, often alongside actual pornography. Fiction, nonfiction and academic texts of every flavour. The human propensity for curiosity and exploration cannot be curbed by a police state. In fact, I would argue, the best way to make a book famous anywhere, is simply to ban it.

As the great war machine draws closer and closer, I'm noticing an increased amount of sci-fi and horror fiction on the streets. I even noticed my old favourite, ***The Stand*** by Stephen King.

Anyway, speaking of horror, there are plans being made in Washington for Iraq, after our current administration is wiped out. Plans to establish a true democracy. Plans that no common man on the streets of Baghdad has any idea are being drawn up, or any control over.

The idea is for Washington to create an Iraqi opposition force to take the place of the current administration, but one that is created and controlled entirely by the United States, providing the actions of the coalition forces with legitimacy. What a farce.

Everyone who reads this blog knows that I am no fan of the current administration. It is the actions of our despotic leader that have led to years of sanctions, poverty, war and hunger. But is this the way we should be rid of him? By letting another country do it for us? By being stupid enough to believe that they wish to do it purely from the kindness of their hearts, to give us 'freedom'?

I think it is about time we Baghdadis stop limiting ourselves to reading about the glories of the past or letting others control our future, be it despotic leaders or foreign powers.

I think it's about time we start thinking of how we are going to write our own future.

***

Abdul pressed enter to publish the blog.

Once again, he wondered how he hadn't been caught yet. He knew of people who had been dragged away by the secret police for much smaller transgressions than writing a seditious blog. But his luck, so far, had held, and he had been able to continue his dual life: automobile mechanic by day, subversive blogger by night.

Rumours about his identity were everywhere: some thought he was a secret police officer pretending to be a student to trap dissidents, while others said he was a US government agent, spreading propaganda about the Saddam regime.

Of course, in times like these, it was even more important to continue his writing – the world must know the reality on the ground in Baghdad, not the far-removed picture being painted by most Western media outlets.

But, today, he wanted to forget about Saddam and Uday Hussein, about America and the impending war.

Today, he was just a boy who was thinking about a girl. A girl whose name or contact details he did not know. The one thing he did know about her, was that she read his blog. And, during their exchange at his garage, he had told her his favourite book was *The Stand* by Stephen King.

So, he had done the only thing he could think to do. He mentioned a rare personal detail – that his, or rather Whistler's, favourite book was *The Stand*.

Would she put it together? Would she realise it was a message to her?

The blog website he used had a feature that allowed visitors to leave comments, however, each comment had to be approved by him before it appeared publicly, and his readers knew this.

It had been scarcely fifteen minutes when he received a comment. It simply said:

'The same book being mentioned twice in the space of two days? This can't be a coincidence. I think we need to take a stand and write our own future too. Your secret is safe with me, but I would love to speak with you again at some point, if I may.'

Abdul was excited and terrified at the same time: excited because she had replied, but terrified because it was hard to know who to trust when you were a wanted man. Had he made a grievous error of judgement? He had a horrible thought.

How could he be certain the words had been posted by the girl in question? And if they had been, who was to say that she wasn't part of an operation to ensnare him? To confirm Whistler's true identity? He already knew her father was a Baathist party official.

Even if she was genuine, he shouldn't be getting close to anyone lest he endanger them. Entire families regularly disappeared because one person was suspected to be a traitor. He did not want to endanger anyone he liked. At least no more than necessary.

Abdul decided he needed a second opinion, and there was only one person he could trust. He put on his jacket and left his small apartment atop the garage.

The evening prayers had just concluded and people in the area were walking towards their homes as Abdul set off in the opposite direction towards Mansur, the wealthy suburb.

Abdul remembered the first time he met Rafan. They were in school when their country was at war with Iran.

Poverty in Iraq was at an all-time high and Abdul's mother was grateful for the extra income that Abdul's work at the garage after school brought in. Abdul's father had been conscripted into the army and had not been seen or heard from in months. Nor had his paycheque. None of the families of those men who had been sped through basic training and dispatched to war had received a penny. There were rumours that the country was heading towards bankruptcy, but those rumours had been as much of a constant in Iraqi life as had been the wars.

But however bad things had gotten, Abdul's mother insisted he go to school rather than drop out and work full-time at the garage. New books, both permitted and banned, appeared regularly on the family bookshelf – fiction, poetry and history featured prominently. He was encouraged to read as much as he could.

Even though his mechanical talent was being nurtured, Abdul's mother wanted to make sure he turned out a well-rounded individual. She would wait up for Abdul until he returned from the garage, and then engage him in a conversation about her own passions like politics or history. At first, Abdul was resistant, but this mother knew her son. 'So, you see Abdul, just like the spark plug ignites the air-fuel mixture in the engine, causing a chain of events that eventually drives the car forward, so too can a small event in history spark a revolution that drives forward a tide of change.'

One thing she could not change easily was Abdul's shyness. He seemed perfectly content to work on a car or read a book by himself as other children played in the street outside. She worried he would be lonely after she was gone, a destiny she knew she was creeping towards, slowly but surely.

The sanctions and rationing, combined with low levels of income, had affected some of the proud Baghdadis worse than others. In particular, there was one little boy at Abdul and Rafan's school who would bring in an empty lunchbox every day, retire to the corner of the playground, and pretend to eat to spare himself the shame of poverty.

Rafan's family, still relatively well off, always packed him a big school lunch, so that he could share it with his less fortunate friends. Most days, Rafan would walk over to the little boy in the corner of the playground and begin the charade. Sometimes, he would claim to be too full, asking the boy if he wanted some of his food. At other times, he would tell the boy his mother had tried a new recipe and insisted on his opinion.

One of the older boys had noticed this happening after he had been jealously eyeing Rafan's lunch. He walked over and threatened violence unless the entire box was handed over.

Even though Abdul did not know Rafan then, he was always touched by the boy's generosity. There were times he could have sworn that Rafan hadn't eaten a morsel himself, just so the little boy could have at least one square meal. He did not deserve to have his entire lunch box taken away by force, just because the older boy was bigger and stronger.

Rafan put the lunch box down and stood up, facing the big boy in the schoolyard.

Abdul was not a big child, but a few years of handling wrenches, spanners and jacks had given his muscles a definition beyond that normally found in an eleven-year-old.

He picked up a large stick lying on the ground and walked to the two boys. Wordlessly, he stood behind Rafan and glared at the bigger boy. There was no mistaking the message in that glare: go away, or I will get involved.

Eventually, the bully backed off and after that day Rafan and Abdul became inseparable.

As they grew up, Abdul's passion for mechanics proved to be infectious. At first, Rafan showed little interest in cars, but within mere months, classes were spent with the two of them huddled over their notebooks, collaborating on designs for imagined sportscars while their teachers looked on admiring their apparent studiousness.

The boys dreamt of starting an automotive garage together. Abdul was good with his hands and seemed to be able to take apart anything mechanical and put it back together. Rafan, however, was more interested in aerodynamics, fuel efficiency and electronics. He was not as gifted or as knowledgeable as Abdul, but he swore to get better, even insisting he would study engineering when he was old enough. Abdul's education, meanwhile, continued at the garage but, by this point, he was already reputed to be the best mechanic east of the Tigris. When Rafan could match his ability, and they could find the money, their garage would become famous.

Their dreams, however, were shattered when Rafan's parents insisted that he take over the profitable family business of plastic goods production. Abdul was sorry Rafan couldn't join him, but worked hard to realise his dream and opened the garage anyway.

They didn't see each other on a daily basis anymore but made it a point to share a couple of beers whenever they got the chance.

Recently, due to the political tension, most of Rafan's family had flown to the West for an extended holiday. Rafan had not gone. He did not wish to leave his beloved city and, so, stayed on to manage the family business. It wasn't the most challenging work. For the most part, it ran itself, the managers Rafan's family had employed taking care of each of their individual divisions. Rafan turned up at the factory a couple of times a week and looked at the accounts but, other than that, he lived a life of leisure. This allowed him plenty of time to nap.

Abdul woke Rafan when he arrived at his home. Despite looking bleary-eyed, Rafan seemed pleased to see him. Bottles of beer were produced. They started chatting and, before they knew it, the topic of conversation moved towards the latest antics of the Hussein family, as it invariably did after the usual subject of impending Western invasion and the latest political developments had been exhausted, or purposefully pushed aside.

'Did you hear that Uday bought a Ferrari Testarossa?' said Rafan.

'So what?' asked Abdul. He was used to hearing about Uday's cars. It pained him to hear that another marvel of engineering had been purchased by a man who had no appreciation for it.

'Well, first off, he's painted it bright pink,' said Rafan, 'and secondly, he's modified the back of it and replaced the standard spoiler with one that has fins!'

That made Abdul take notice. Not only had the undeserving Uday bought another Ferrari, but he had also ruined it completely to make it look more flamboyant. Abdul knew that Uday had a full-time 'procurement officer' who would trawl the internet looking for flashy cars. Another would do the same but for clothes; the brighter, the weirder and the more expensive the better. He purchased both clothes and cars in vast quantities, along with Rolex watches, gold-plated AK-47s and whatever else he desired. It was said that he now had over 1,000 cars, parked in various underground parking lots around Baghdad. Uday had even placed a ban on the import of Ferraris to Iraq to ensure he could be the only one to own them in the city. His 'love' of cars and clothes met behind his mansion. Back there, he had his own private car painting facility. Each day, he would have his car painted to match the colour of his suit. As car enthusiasts, Abdul and Rafan thought this was absolute sacrilege.

'He's done worse before,' said Abdul. 'Remember the vintage Merc, the 300SL? The fucker removed the 1950s engine and had one put in from a new Porsche 911.'

'What a way to destroy the soul of the car. I wonder what he did with the engine from the gull-wing. Probably threw it away. Imagine if he did the same with the other old Mercs in the family; the 540k and the 770 they roll out every time they have a parade on TV?'

'Haha. Those are probably too valuable even for Uday to fuck with,' said Abdul. 'Besides, they are as much his dad's as they are his. Saddam would have a fit. Tell you what, I'd love to get my hands on those, open them up, and see what makes them tick. I've read that the 540k is still considered an engineering marvel.'

'Imagine what it must be worth.'

'If it's in running condition, which we know it is, from the parades, it has to be over ten million dollars, easily. That's if you don't consider the fact that it's previously been owned by two kings and now a dictator. That probably doubles the price.'

They both sighed in unison and, not for the first time, thought of how wasted all those cars were on the Hussein family, particularly Uday.

'Anyway, I don't care about what he's doing to the cars,' Abdul lied. 'I'm more concerned about the women of Baghdad. I hear he's modifying those too.'

Several people of Baghdad had tried to do something about it, even though they knew they were risking their lives. The father of one of the girls Uday had raped had even gone to petition Saddam about his son's indiscretions. He was foolish enough to believe that Saddam was an honourable ruler, as he had been told over and over by the newspapers and the radio. But Saddam wouldn't hear from him. After many months of petitioning for a hearing and being refused, he became more and more vocal about what Uday had done to his daughter. Lo and behold, he was granted a meeting. He went to the palace and, to absolutely no one's surprise, he never came back.

Since then, many suggestions on how to solve the problem of Uday had been raised by the good people of Baghdad. Assassination had been tried twice, even though it was a suicide mission. The first time it had failed miserably, but the second time it had come close. Uday had been shot seven times, but he recovered after months of surgery. In fact, it had made him even more unhinged than before. Except, now, he had learnt his lesson and was too well protected by his fleet of bodyguards.

Knowing the Hussein family's keen interest in exotic methods of torture, no one wanted to contemplate what would happen to them if they were caught hatching a plan to kill Uday. Recently, there had been rumours that Uday had expanded his torture arsenal to include lions from Africa. The rumours had been so outlandish, even for Uday, that many hadn't believed them until he had appeared for the Iraq vs. Qatar football match with the two beasts chained by his side. Observers noticed that the lions, even though heavily sedated, seemed to get more and more agitated every time there was an attempt to score a goal due to the noise from the crowd. After Qatar's second goal, there was a roar from the presidential box. No one could see exactly what had happened but, almost immediately, an ambulance had rushed a member of Uday's security detail to the hospital. The stadium cleaning crew said they had never seen so much blood in their lives.

However hard he tried, Abdul could not think of a solution. It was time to change the subject and ask Rafan for his opinion on the subject of his infatuation.

Abdul spent the next half an hour filling him in while Rafan, ever the romantic, listened attentively. Abdul concluded by presenting the dilemma around whether he should trust the girl and risk exploring the relationship.

'Listen,' said Rafan, 'the truth is, we should have been having this conversation *before* you revealed yourself to her on the blog. If she was reporting to the Mukhabarat, then your garage and apartment would have been raided the moment she read your message, and you would be sitting chained up in an interrogation room. So, you're *probably* fine. Besides, it has been a year since your last girlfriend.'

And so, it went on, Rafan firmly defending his opinion that Abdul would likely be fine, and Abdul playing devil's advocate, listing all the risks involved.

After a while, Abdul left Rafan's house. They had a good time, but all that talk of the deranged Uday Hussein and potential raids on his apartment had left him feeling on edge. He stepped out into the cool night air and made his way home on foot, through narrow streets, alleys and deserted markets.

Those who had visited Iraq a decade ago had commented on how it looked like a futuristic city. Back then, oil revenues had been at their highest, and Saddam had initiated an ambitious program to build a set of super-highways that crisscrossed the metropolis with overpasses, rotaries and cloverleaf intersections. Many Iraqis had purchased cars for the first time; the economy was booming, and skyscrapers had emerged from between the overpasses, reaching upwards towards the sky.

All that had come to a crushing halt when the UN placed sanctions on Iraq following the Gulf War. Overnight, the super-highway program was discarded – there weren't enough funds to maintain the existing highways, let alone complete the new ones.

Over time, the half-built super-highways took on an increasingly dystopian and faded look – a stark reminder of better times that Iraqis eventually learned to ignore.

As he walked home, the dusty roads and the chill in the air reminded Abdul of the desert that lay just outside the city. Towering statues of Saddam littered the streets and poked between office blocks and residential buildings. Somehow, there had always seemed to be enough funds available to finish those.

The statues appeared dark and menacing, silhouetted against the last remnants of daylight. The military checkpoints that had popped up across the city due to the recent tensions with the West, along with the sandbags sheltering every government building, didn't make the city any more appealing. By the time he reached his street, the sun had set completely on Baghdad, and everything was shrouded in darkness. Everyone was indoors, dining with their family.

Abdul often thought of what that would be like. One day, he hoped he would have a family of his own to dine with. Even though his children would never know their grandparents, he would tell them the stories.

The story of how his mother and father had met at Baghdad University. The story of how they competed for the physics award and wound up winning each other instead. How he would watch his father fix the old Morris. And yes, the story of how his father had been forced to leave with the army when the wars started. How his mother had given him all her rations, and never told him that she was sick.

How, on a cold evening, when she was close to the end, she had wondered aloud if things would have been different if the world knew what it was like in Iraq. Would they make their governments lift the sanctions? Would they make Saddam stop the wars?

Lost in thought, Abdul eventually found himself two buildings away from his apartment, when he looked up and saw something that made his blood run cold. The light in his apartment was on.

He was certain he had switched it off when he had left for Rafan's house.

5. Ava

Ava looked out from her perch inside the bush.

The owner of the vintage Aston Martin was halfway to the manor house, but the girl was still sitting inside the car. Every second that passed reduced her chances of successfully getting away with the theft. She now had seven minutes until the owner returned with the tools to replace the tyre. But what could she do? How could she make the girl get out of the car without raising the alarm? Even if she forced her out, the girl would see her, and it wouldn't be a clean getaway. Besides, the use of force just wasn't her style.

She heard a croaking sound from a few inches to her right and looked at the toad that had been keeping her company for the last couple of hours. 'Got any ideas fella?' That was when a brainwave struck her. She carefully picked up the toad and crept out of the bush into the dark road, the only source of light coming from inside the car. She could see the girl through the open window, reading something on her mobile phone.

Ava crept up to the passenger side of the car, quiet as a mouse. For a moment, she sat on the ground in the darkness with her back to the car, listening to the radio inside, tuned in to a pop station.

Ava took a deep breath and threw the toad into the open window, toward the plunging neckline of the girl's black dress before quickly rolling underneath the car.

This, luckily, had the desired reaction: shrill screams, scrambling at the door handles, and a pair of heels clicking along the ground only inches from her face.

After a few moments, the girl turned back towards the car and craned her neck, attempting to peer through the window without being too close to it. Ava knew what would happen. The girl wouldn't be able to see the toad, having brushed him off her skin and onto the floor. But Ava was betting she wouldn't want to get back into the car with the possibility of being shut inside with the slimy amphibian.

Ava was right.

The girl walked off towards the mansion at a brisk, if unsteady trot in her high heels. Ava got to work on removing the hubcap with her electronic spanner before the girl was even out of sight. Her heart was thumping in her chest, and she loved every second of it. In no time, she had the hubcap and shredded tyre off the car. She glanced at her watch: four minutes of the eight-minute time limit had elapsed. She rushed to the boot and opened it, undoing the leather straps that held the spare tyre in place. Then she quicky hauled the tyre out and brought it out towards the jacked up side of the car.

Ava could hear faint but brisk footsteps on the gravel in the distance. As they seemed to get louder, she realised that a man was walking towards her. Had she been seen? Thank goodness she had put on the black turtleneck after all.

Still, she did not have far to go, and she forced herself to focus. Ava placed the spare on the hub and screwed the first two of the four lug nuts back on, opposite to each other.

The footfalls on the gravel got louder, and they were no longer a brisk stride. They were a run, now possibly only yards away.

Then suddenly, a loud bang and a flash of light – the gravel a few inches from her feet exploded into a thousand fragments, showering her with debris. Ava had been holding it together so far but was now at her limit. It was time to call it quits. Two out of four bolts would have to do.

Leaving the burst tyre, car jack and the two remaining lug nuts on the drive, she dashed into the car.

It was nowhere near as clean a getaway as she would have liked, but at least they wouldn't see her face. She jumped into the car and shut the door, feeling for the key near the ignition. It wasn't there. The girl had taken it as she had left.

Before she could think of what to do, the man was next to the car. He had the gun raised and pointed at Ava through the window, but he hesitated before shooting. Perhaps, in his arrogance, he thought this would be enough to threaten the intruder out of his car. Perhaps he didn't want to make a mess of the beautiful interior or leave the authorities anything to find inside.

The moment of hesitation was enough for Ava. With a swift motion, she opened the door, bashing it into the gun hand of the owner, while ducking below the dashboard. The gun went off, shooting a bullet harmlessly into the night sky. Ava got out and swung for the man's head with her fist. It was a well-timed blow, honed through countless boxing classes at the gym. She connected with the man's temple, knocking him to the ground. Quickly, she reached into the man's pocket and found the key.

The next minute, she had pulled away, into the night.

This was the part Ava usually enjoyed the most, but this time the exhilaration had turned into nervousness. Her wrist hurt, as well as her knuckles, where they had connected with the man's temple. She knew there was probably a fracture somewhere. It was the first time she had ever driven an Aston Martin DB4GT Zagato - and she knew she would have to push the car to its limits. And she knew she'd have to do it in the dark.

She passed 60mph a few seconds after she exited the main gate and accelerated to 147 mph on the 40-year-old car only a minute later. The leather bucket seats, also designed by Zagato, held her firmly in position even though she hadn't had the time to do up her seatbelt.

As the car got faster, she became totally focused on the road; all thoughts of the narrow escape and her injured hand left her mind. She needed every ounce of concentration to avoid an accident.

She had to admit, the owner (was it safe to say previous owner?) had taken good care of the car.

An hour later, she reached the large transporter van she had parked on a deserted countryside lane. It was close to midnight. She jumped out of the car and almost fell to the ground thanks to her shaky feet, but she powered through and climbed into the cab of the van. A few seconds later, a ramp slid out of the back, and she drove the Aston into it.

It seemed like she had pulled off the heist, so far. Not her cleanest ever, but still.

She followed the usual routine. The large van took a convoluted route back to the workshop, confounding anyone who might try to find the car via street cameras. She then burned every shred of clothing that she had worn during that evening, including the turtleneck, the black gloves, the shoes and even the socks. She removed the blue contact lenses and threw them away, along with the pads from within her cheeks that she used in order to make her face appear structurally different. She washed the temporary blonde dye from her hair.

Then she sat down in the plush armchair she had in the workshop, lit a joint and smoked it end to end without taking her eyes off the car.

Finally, she got up, turned out the lights, and left the workshop in her nondescript BMW.

Everyone had the impression that she worked on and developed some sort of top-secret automobile components for an American car company (which was true) and that her workshop was in a remote industrial location (which, to be fair, was also true). Of course, no one knew about the second workshop, in the hidden vault under the first. The work she did for the American automotive startup paid well, but it also served as a legitimate front for her primary occupation of high-end automobile theft.

Of course, being a petite young lady helped tremendously in this line of work. Most people, and almost all men, could hardly believe she was in the automobile industry, let alone a car thief. Throughout her life, she had been constantly underestimated and undermined by men. At first, it had irked her. Now, she was very happy to indulge this attitude while she counted the money piling up in her Swiss bank account.

Of course, her father had been an exception to this rule – he had seemed instinctively aware of what she was capable of. As such, she would always look forward to Sundays when he was home. They would wake up early and jump into the dark green Jaguar E-Type, her father's pride and joy. They would make their way through the Chiltern Hills as dawn broke, her father expertly taking the apex of each corner at speed.

As they drove, he would tell her stories – of famous automotive races, daring race car drivers, genius automotive designers and, most of all, about the cars he had known and loved.

At age 12, on one of those drives, she had half-jokingly asked her father if she could drive the car. It almost seemed like he had been waiting for the question. Wordlessly, he slowed down and patted his lap. She climbed on and took the wheel.

Ava often wondered if it was nature or nurture that made her who she was, but by age 16 she had won every youth go-carting trophy there was to win in the country and beyond, putting all the boys (and the small handful of other girls) to shame. It was during this period that she realised she had a ruthless streak within her; she was willing to do whatever it took to win. On some tracks, when there was only room for one car to corner at a time, she would pull up next to the driver in pole position as the corner approached and floor the accelerator, forcing the other driver to give up their spot lest they both smash into the wall or each other.

Before every race, some of the boys would dismiss her entirely, some would look at her with smug condescension, and the ones who found her attractive would try to give her advice on what to do during the race. Every time she would play along innocently, enjoying the stunned looks on their face when she took the podium.

She pushed hard. And, in time, she realised she loved the adrenaline rush that came with pushing herself and a machine like that.

When the incident with Pa had taken place, everything had been taken away from them: their house, their possessions, their lives. Everything except her dad's old Jaguar E-Type. She had hidden it away before they found it and it remained one of her most prized possessions.

If she had been independent with a ruthless streak before everything happened with her father, now she was doubly so. She had been left with a sense that she had to look out for herself; her determination and her firm grip on the steering wheel would get her where she wanted to go, even though it didn't win her any friends along the way. On longer cross-country races, where it was customary to have a navigator, she would, as in life, eschew company, preferring to drive alone.

Then, overnight, all the racing stopped in favour of other occupations. Ava started a car dealership in partnership with some others she knew from the racing circuit. It had done quite well, but she didn't particularly enjoy working with the others. And, more importantly, she missed the adrenaline of the racetrack.

One day she met Monty, a local gangster, who had come to buy a car from the dealership. Loud and belligerent, Monty demanded the latest models and always paid cash. He liked his cars, or rather he liked to brag about them, just like he liked to brag about the women he called his. He made the mistake of looking at Ava in the same way he looked at the cars: hungrily.

A week later he didn't have any cars. And Ava had suddenly become a lot wealthier. She had found her true calling.

That was eight years ago. Since then, she had stolen 27 cars, none valued at less than two hundred thousand pounds on the black market.

Recently, she had become even more selective, choosing her targets very carefully. She had been focussing on vintage sportscars from the 1940s to the 1980s. Sure, they were worth far more, but the driving factor behind the decision was not a practical one – Ava simply wanted to own them, even if for a short period.

When she got home, Ava showered, dressed, and then made a full English breakfast and a pot of Jamaican Blue

Mountain Coffee, part of the reward to herself for a job well done.

Then she booted up her computer, read the news, checked her email and started researching her next job. She looked at her spreadsheet of possible targets and locations, a document she kept updated. But, as she worked her way down the list, the timing or circumstances weren't quite right for any of them. She trawled through vintage automobile message boards and chat rooms, as well as auction house catalogues looking for new targets that she had previously been unaware of. It was becoming harder and harder to find targets in the UK, in part, because she'd saturated the market.

Getting restless, she walked across the study and looked out of the large bay window. The leafy and affluent London suburb of Highgate lay spread before her. She poured herself another cup of the exclusive coffee. Taking a sip, she picked up the newspaper from her desk and snorted with disgust. Tony Blair, the prime minister, seemed hell-bent on supporting America in their war on Iraq. Why couldn't people just mind their own business and get along? It wasn't that hard, she thought.

There it was again, she thought to herself. Every time she wasn't working on a job she got agitated. The fact was, she got bored easily. She needed a challenge, something worthy of her skills. But she didn't know what to do. Sure, there were plenty of sports cars around, but none of them were vintage and that made them less valuable, and their owners didn't fit the criteria for suitable victims. She would have to keep looking.

Suddenly, she was roused out of her thoughts by a loud beeping.

She turned towards the monitor that displayed the output from several cameras she had dotted around the house and its grounds. Her jaw dropped. There were several uniformed policemen *inside* her garden, arms drawn.

Ava had often played this moment out in her head. She had long ago established a plan of action for a moment like this, but it still took a few seconds to recollect what she needed to do.

With shaking hands, she triggered a complete overwrite of her computer hard disc. The process would not only wipe her computer but also back up her records on a server in China, which she could access later with a password.

She heard a loud crash, immediately realising they had broken into her patio doors. She glanced at the monitor quickly - the uniformed men were inside the house, moving in the direction of her study.

Racked with tension, she tried to send a text message to the person who worked with her. It merely said 'Uhlenhaut'. This was code to secure all the cars and brick up the secret entrance to the workshop.

A split second later, the door of her study opened, and a burly officer entered cautiously, his gun drawn. He looked at Ava who was clearly unarmed. Looking pleased, he holstered his gun, bunched his fingers into a gigantic fist and smashed it into Ava's head.

As the lights went out around her, Ava realised she still had the keys to the freshly stolen Aston Martin in her jacket pocket.

6. Uday

It had been at least half an hour since he had snorted his last line of cocaine, and Uday was getting skittish. He fiddled with the large gold ring on his finger.

He had known it was going to be a long meeting. He couldn't remember the last time he had been able to face his father without a bit of powdered courage.

He looked around – the entire Security Council of Iraq was present. Maps of Iraq lay strewn all over the large table. Borders, trenches, points of attack, fallback positions, strengths and weaknesses were marked in shades of red, green, blue and black. Long debates had been held over the merits and weaknesses of each plan to which Uday had very little to contribute. He was very bored.

His mind wandered back to the girl he had been stalking in the marketplace the day before. Uday had kicked open the door of the shop the girl had entered and barged in. Inside, he had seen an old man with a large moustache reading a newspaper behind the till. A thousand different boxes of tobacco lined the walls. But the girl was nowhere to be seen.

'Where is she?' he had asked without preamble.

Uday remembered seeing the alarm register in the old man's eyes as he looked first at Uday's face, and then, further down at the bulge in his trousers. 'Umm… She… She was here a second ago. She must have gone out from there,' he said, pointing at a back door.

Uday had rushed to it, shoulder first, and burst into the sunshine outside. All he could see was a dirty pool of stagnant water in the gutters that lined the back alley.

And no girl.

Uday was enraged. It would take the old man days to re-shelf all the boxes of tobacco that he flung to the floor in anger.

He realised she must have seen him in the reflection of the tobacco shop window and decided to escape through the back door. It was truly infuriating. His father had taught him at a young age that a man who 'lost' was not a man who 'led'. Losing was a weakness. It did not matter if it was business, politics, sports, love or war; one must do whatever it takes to win. To hell with fair play.

Uday ordered his guards to fan out from the shop and look for the girl. But after two hours, there was still no sign of her. It seemed that she had escaped into the crowded market.

Eager to please, the head of Uday's security detail offered to find another girl for his evening's entertainment. He would phone Uday's usual pimp to ask if any new girls had been flown in for his pleasure.

Uday sighed. There were some things that money just could not buy – he knew this because he had tried. Even the young girls in the darker corners of the world, those who were hired out to be beaten and violated, did not have the same fear in their eyes as the innocent girls he picked off the streets.

And so, on his journey back, he had pointed out several girls to his security detail, and his guards had been kept busy carrying out his orders. Two had been schoolgirls. One had been covered from head to toe in conservative black robes and a veil. Uday called this a, 'Lucky draw.'

But nothing had gone his way that day.

The figure in the burkha turned out to be a woman in her forties. He had her thrown to the lions without even touching her. The schoolgirls had been infuriating too.

Recently, he had imported extremely rare medieval leg and neck irons from Germany; authentic 13th-century stuff, found inside a ruined castle by explorers decades ago. He intended to use the exceedingly expensive and barbaric restraints on his victims while he exploited them in some horrific way.

But even the smallest restraints were designed for a much larger prisoner than a twelve-year-old Middle Eastern girl, who could easily wriggle out. He asked for the girls to be thrown into the dungeons. But before they could be moved, his mechanic and secretary, Kasim, had tried to convince him to let the two girls go. He argued that they hadn't been used yet so there was no need to keep them locked up. There was nothing they could say.

'Why waste?' Uday had responded. 'Keep them for a rainy day, Kasim. Wise men always have a backup.' He knew full well that in two days he would forget all about their existence, just like he had with several other prisoners he had stored away over the years. He had no idea what eventually happened to any of them.

Finally, he had written to the head of the Fedayeen Saddam, describing the time and place where he had seen the girl in the market. He described her appearance, including the Baghdad Girls College uniform. He did not mention what he needed; the head of the paramilitary force had been through the same routine several times with different women. This was to be their first priority, even before the tracking down of that Whistler fellow from the internet, the one his father had wanted him to focus his network on. His father and brother had enough resources to deal with a man hiding behind his computer. He would focus on more important things.

The truth was, he had been sidelined from doing anything important, and he resented it.

As Saddam's first-born son, he was given every leeway to do whatever he wanted by the army of nannies and aides who had been hired to take care of him when he was growing up. Everyone had treated him with deference, fearful that he would utter a harsh word against them to his father.

Uday felt like he could say and do anything without consequence, and he would automatically receive the full support of his father's vast resources. His younger brother, Qusay, on the other hand, was always conscious that he would have to work doubly hard to gain his father's respect. As they grew up, Uday did not even notice the point at which his antics made him fall out of favour with his father. Nor the day when his father had first handed more responsibility, and with it, power, to Qusay.

The voice of Muhammad Saeed al-Sahhaf, the information minister, summoned his mind back to the Security Council meeting. He was currently gesturing with his hands and telling the room how he would conduct his daily press briefings, should the coalition forces invade.

'We will describe how the noble and holy forces of Iraq are massacring the infidels. In doing so, the world will know that Iraq is not to be interfered with, and their soldiers will be scared to advance on our troops!', he said in Arabic.

At one time the minister had wanted to become an English teacher, and Uday thought he should have followed through with that ambition. The man was as boring as a schoolteacher. Uday looked around the room looking for a distraction. His eyes settled on one of the younger female members of staff, standing with a tea tray. He wondered what she would look like naked while restlessly shifting in his seat and scratching his nether regions under the table. That reminded him of the girl in the market yet again, and he felt a surge of frustration. Uday glanced again at the ring on his finger. It contained a secret compartment holding his emergency ration of cocaine. It wasn't much, but it would get him through the meeting. The problem was, Saddam had said no one would be allowed to leave the table until they had finished talking.

Everyone was totally absorbed in the discussion at the other end of the long boardroom table. Perhaps, he thought, he could get away with it. One flick of the finger to open the hidden compartment, a quick sniff, and that would be that. God knew he needed it before his turn to report to his father arrived.

Qusay was questioning the information minister about various preparations, and Saddam was nodding approvingly at Qusay's questions.

That pretentious bastard, Uday thought. His father always favoured Qusay, even though he was the younger son. He stared at Qusay with loathing, even though he had no idea what the discussion was about. Uday had switched off long ago. All he could think about now was the cocaine on his finger.

'What preparations have been made for Western journalists who wish to come to Iraq to report back to the West?' asked Saddam. 'We have to show the people of the world that Iraq has nothing to hide!'

'Yes sir, we have built a facility for them to work from, in the Information Ministry,' replied Muhammad. 'It is a large room with many desks. We have planted listening devices in each desk so we know what they are doing, just as we have in the Rashid Hotel.'

Now or never, thought Uday, glancing at his ring. All of them are distracted by this conversation.

'But of course, we will have to monitor them carefully,' chimed Qusay. 'There are many traitors in the country who wish to speak ill of my father, and we will have to ensure none of the journalists come in contact with these treacherous elements.'

Uday raised his ring finger closer to his face. He held his chin with his thumb and forefinger as if he were in deep thought about the ongoing discussion. The hidden compartment was now directly below his nose.

'Yes,' replied the minister. 'We have also assigned each journalist a guide and translator. These are all trusted men who will ensure that none of these infidel journalists speak to the wrong person. They have been ordered never to leave the side of their assigned charge.'

'Of course, if the invasion happens, then the role of these journalists will become even more important – to document the cowardly acts of the American soldiers. If they take pictures of civilian casualties, the world will side with Iraq, the righteous.'

Uday flicked open the hidden compartment with his thumb. The little heap of cocaine looked snowy white against the dull gold.

'Good, that is good,' said Qusay, 'but not enough. We also need to ensure that the local dissidents themselves are quelled so they do not seek out the journalists in some way.'

Uday was now trembling with anticipation. Even though he was looking in the direction of the conversation, his mind was far, far away. He slowly inched his finger closer and closer to his nose. Now all he had to do was…

'Uday!' Qusay shouted, turning towards him, 'have you made progress with the project to quell the dissidents yet?'

Uday froze. Eight heads turned and looked at him from around the table. His finger was inches away from his nostril. What excuse could he have for doing such a thing? Suddenly, he had an idea. There was only one thing he could do.

He rubbed his nose with his knuckles and then inserted a finger casually into his nose as if he were digging it.

A flicker of disgust could be seen on the faces turned towards him, including Saddam. Hell, it was better than being caught snorting cocaine, thought Uday. He was sure that his bastard of a brother, Qusay, must have called him out on purpose.

Disaster averted, he tried to collect himself and replied, 'Yes, brother. Our plans are well underway to catch these traitorous snakes and chop off their heads.'

'Yes, yes, but what progress have you made? How many have you caught?'

'At least seven of them are currently in my dungeons at this time, with more on the way.'

'It is very curious,' said Qusay, 'that records show all the dissidents you have caught are female.'

'Women are very two-faced, brother,' replied Uday. 'You would know if you spent more time with them.'

Qusay shrugged off the insult. 'And what about the internet traitor, Whistler?'

'We are, as we speak, tightening the net around him. Soon he will be in our clutches and we can do with him as we please. I am also looking at ways of eliminating his website.'

'No, my boy,' Saddam interjected. 'Once we have caught him, we can use this website of his for our own propaganda.

So, make sure you catch him alive and do not take down his website. Muhammad tells me there are many who heed his writings outside of Iraq. We can continue his narrative but in our favour! Surely you can accomplish this? After all, you have the entire Fedayeen Saddam under your command! Now, tell me, are you capable of doing this one thing? For your father? For Iraq?'

There was only one way in which anyone could reply to such a request from Saddam. So, trying to look as confident as he possibly could, he replied, 'It will be done within the week Father.'

'Good,' said Saddam, adjourning the meeting.

7. Abdul

Excerpt from Whistler's Blog:

Last night the BBC World Service described the people of Iraq as poor and illiterate.

I'll have you know, Iraq was known as the 'cradle of civilisation' in the 6th and 7th centuries. Baghdad was home to the famous House of Wisdom, where scholars from all four corners of the globe congregated to share and advance the collective knowledge of the world. We were building extremely complex ports, highways and irrigation systems when the West had barely even discovered how to grow their own food.

But in Iraq, all good things always come to an end. The country changed hands from the Abbasids to the Mongols, then to the British and finally, in more recent times, to an ambitious dictator. You will excuse me if I don't use his name – I don't want my blog to be the first thing he sees when he puts his name into Google.

But hell, even he wasn't all bad.

In fact, one of the few good things he did after seizing power in 1979 was to order that school was to be free and compulsory. And, of course, whatever he ordered, you always did – unless you wanted to lose your head.

So, children went to school. They learned how to be patriotic and proud and loyal to the regime. But thankfully, somewhere along the line, they also learnt how to read. In fact, this particular dictator picked up a UNESCO award for dramatically increasing literacy in the Middle East.

A fucking award from the United Nations. Can you believe it?

Those were the days when the UK was willing to sell our friendly neighbourhood dictator arms-related equipment on favourable credit terms. Those were the days when the CIA ensured he had enough weapons and ammunition to avoid losing the Iran-Iraq war.

And now we find ourselves on the brink of war with the very countries who supported our foolish battles.

To all those reading this blog abroad, please be aware, that the real reason for this current war isn't clear to anyone in Baghdad. In fact, most are thoroughly confused.

At first, Bush claimed it was because Iraq supported the terrorism that had led to the infamous attack on the World Trade Centre. When that was disproven, it was because Iraq had weapons of mass destruction. Now that none of those can be found, it seems that America has suddenly become very altruistic and wishes to liberate the Iraqi people from the tyranny of said dictator, after supporting his many crimes in the past.

I am almost reminded of my petulant eight-year-old cousin who wanted fancy new sports shoes. At first, he said he had outgrown his old ones. When his mother, who was struggling to make ends meet, checked the shoes, they seemed to fit just fine. Next, he claimed they hurt his feet, which was also dismissed – his feet showed no signs of distress after a vigorous game of football. Finally, when he thought no one was looking, he tore one of his shoes, taking it to his mother and saying, 'See! They are so old they tore! We HAVE to go to the shoe shop now.' The truth is, he just wanted new shoes.

The real reason for the war, some say, is because our dictator once, many years ago, made a failed attempt on Bush Senior's life. This could just be a simple personal vendetta between two leaders.

In the meantime, Iraq still hasn't recovered economically from the CIA-supported Iran war. Sure, we didn't lose, but we sure as hell did not win either. Our country is so bankrupt that my aforementioned cousin's parents STILL don't have enough money to buy him new shoes. The poor little fucker plays football with a toe sticking out. All this happens while the dictator who took this country to war swims in his Olympic-size personal swimming pool then sits down to a six-course meal with his second wife while a team of valets polish his fleet of vintage Mercedes cars and a team of hookers polish his deranged son's… well, you get the picture.

As one of my favourite authors once wrote:

The common people pray for rain, healthy children, and a summer that never ends (and perhaps new shoes?) It is no matter to them if the high lords play their game of thrones, so long as they are left in peace. They never are.

Have truer words ever been written?

***

Abdul surprised himself when he saw the light in his apartment window, as he walked back home from Rafan's house. He surprised himself because the first thought that crossed his mind was not one of fear. It was disappointment. Disappointment that the girl had given him up. Disappointment that someone who seemed so gentle and kind had stabbed him in the back. Disappointment that, in all likelihood, they would never discuss their favourite authors again.

So be it, he thought. At least he hadn't been at home when they raided his apartment. He would have to disappear, never to return to his precious garage or his computer.

But he couldn't turn away. Standing transfixed, he stared at the window. Why weren't there any armed men on the street below? Or any government vehicles? This didn't really seem like the style of the Mukhabarat, who generally made a big show of every arrest. Stealth was not their usual weapon of choice, despite being the 'secret' police.

As he watched, he noticed the silhouette behind the window. He could only see the outline of one single person, who seemed to be sitting on his bed. And unless he was much mistaken, it seemed like a person with long hair and a curvy body; not the typical Mukhabarat operative. But he had no idea who it could possibly be. No one had the keys to his apartment besides his neighbour, an old man whom Abdul trusted with them in case of emergencies. In the few years that Abdul lived there, the grouchy but loyal old man had never once given the keys to anyone.

He decided to cautiously approach his neighbour's house.

Before he could knock, the old man opened his door, speaking in Arabic at the same time. 'There you are! You never mentioned you had a sister, Abdul. The poor thing travelled all the way from Fallujah by bus, and you weren't even home to receive her! I let her in and made her a cup of tea.'

Abdul was speechless. He did not have a sister. In fact, he did not have any surviving family.

Just then, he heard the patter of footsteps coming down the stairs to his apartment. His jaw dropped when he saw the girl from the Mercedes poke her head around the wall.

'There you are! Dear brother, it's bad enough that you don't visit me, but you could, at least, be home when I tell you I'm coming! Why are you so surprised? You forgot, didn't you?'

Her eyes sparkled with the same intensity he had seen in the car.

'Eh… yes. I guess it must have slipped my mind.'

'Well, come on upstairs,' she said, taking his arm. Turning around she flashed a smile at the old neighbour. 'Thank you, sir, for coming to my rescue! I would have hated to wait for this idiot in the cold, outside.' The neighbour smiled, nodded and disappeared into his apartment.

It turned out her name was Sofia.

'I'm really sorry to have barged in on you like this,' she said, switching to the blend of English and Arabic commonly spoken by the youth. 'But it's not often that I get the chance to escape unaccompanied, so I took the opportunity to come and say hello. You realise I nearly fainted when I read your blog?'

'Well, I nearly fainted when I got your comment.'

'You're crazy to have taken the risk. But I'm glad you did,' she smiled. 'My parents think I'm having dinner with my cousin, who thinks I've ditched her to see a boy. Which, I suppose, is true, even if it is just to discuss literature.'

She flashed him a smile and continued to breathe heavily from all the excitement, clearly enjoying herself. But still, he was surprised by how self-assured and in control of the entire situation she was.

He found her even more irresistible.

'You're a good actress. Old Ali downstairs is entirely convinced you are my sister.'

'Well, I have lots of experience. Without lies, I wouldn't be able to do anything or go anywhere. I do not like being cooped up at home. Even with a Stephen King book to keep me company.'

They sat down on the sofa in Abdul's studio apartment.

'I feel like I know you so well, having read your blog for months. I always wondered what you looked like. In my head, you were a little bit taller. But your smile – that is exactly how I imagined it.'

Abdul didn't know quite what to make of that, but perhaps it was why she seemed so comfortable around him. She knew how he thought and felt because of his writing – which he had always taken pains to make as honest and vulnerable as possible. Easy to do when you're anonymous, much harder when you're not, he thought and said as much.

'Well, let me try to even the scales just a little bit then,' she said. She told him all about herself.

Her conservative father was in Saddam's inner circle. Even though she didn't agree with his politics, she loved her father dearly. In return, she was paranoid about her safety. This was unsurprising, as kidnapping and crimes against women had become increasingly common as the poverty levels in Iraq had increased. This fear was particularly compounded by her father's politically sensitive position. Tonight, sneaking into Abdul's apartment, was an extremely uncommon instance in which she was unchaperoned; her driver had one of his rare evenings off, and her cousin had sworn to keep an eye on her.

Abdul nodded – even though his parents hadn't been conservative, he knew how much they worried about him when he was out and about in the war-torn and poverty-stricken country. Bad things tended to happen.

He had a faint sense of the fact that she may not have come just to say hello. All this time she had been talking about herself, it seemed like she was putting off telling him something. He was sure it couldn't have been anything personal though; she certainly wasn't shy.

He smiled at her in an attempt to put her at ease. 'Would you like another cup of tea?'

'Do you have anything stronger?' she smiled back.

For some reason, Abdul wasn't surprised. He reached for the whisky he kept hidden under a bundle of old clothes in the closet and poured two measures, handing her one.

They clinked glasses and each took a sip.

'To the people of Baghdad. May our ship sail through the impending storm,' Abdul toasted.

She looked at him intently for a few moments, not speaking or drinking. Abdul waited silently. He liked that she looked directly into his eyes, unapologetically. He surprised himself by noticing he did not feel the uneasiness that would usually have come from being looked at in this manner. Then, as if she had come to a decision, she nodded her head once. 'Does that CD player work? And is that Massive Attack I see on the shelf?'

'Yes,' said Abdul, immediately realising what she was doing. He walked over and turned on the music. Then he walked back to the armchair, pulled it closer to Sofia and waited.

'Listen,' she said, 'the truth is, I haven't come just to see you. There's something you should know. Something vitally important.' She leaned in closer, gesturing for him to do the same. This was standard operating procedure if one wished to talk politics in Baghdad. One never knew who was listening, either physically behind the door or electronically many miles away. Still, as he leaned closer, he could not help but feel a small thrill to be a few inches away from her face. Despite his curiosity about what she was going to say, he registered the smell of her shampoo when she leaned in. Apricots. He felt glad that he had chewed some gum on the way home from Rafan's house. He wondered if she had similar thoughts.

She lowered her voice to a whisper. 'The other day I was in Baba's study looking for some ink for my fountain pen,' she said. 'I came across a report from the head of a Baathist think tank, hidden in his desk amidst his files. They think American military intervention in Iraq is now unavoidable.'

This is something Abdul already suspected, as did many in the country.

'The report stated that the Americans are planning to begin the invasion with an overwhelming show of force with the use of over 500 cruise missiles against Baghdad before ground forces even approach the city.'

Abdul was alarmed. This would result in devastating civilian casualties.

'Unfortunately, that's not the bad news I have come to tell you.'

Abdul's eyes widened, 'There's more?'

'Yes. The report goes on to say that the Americans are planning to avoid the bombing of civilian infrastructure like water treatment plants, the refinery, schools and hospitals, in order to claim the moral high ground and garner a modicum of support from the civilian population. This way, they are able to say their quarrel is not with the Iraqi people but with our leaders.'

'Well, I don't see how they can avoid civilian casualties with over 500 cruise missiles being fired into one city. But, I suppose that's relatively good news, right?'

'It might have been, if Saddam hadn't known of this in advance. The report suggests that he's planning to turn the people of Iraq against the coalition forces by placing a large number of civilians, and perhaps even the remaining Westerners, in government buildings that are sure to be on the hit list of the initial missile attack. He wants to make them into unwitting martyrs to motivate every man, woman and child in Iraq to mobilise against the invading forces.'

Abdul nodded sadly. Having been a Saddam watcher his entire life, this fit perfectly with the way the dictator would think. For a moment, he forgot their knees were almost touching.

'There might be a way out though,' Sofia continued. 'You, or rather, Whistler, must make the story public. I know your blog is read in the West. The American intelligence agencies are sure to be keeping an eye on it. Tell them Saddam knows about the cruise missile attack. And reveal Saddam's hand before he plays it so that the Americans re-think their plan of attack. We may be able to prevent loss of life yet, and who knows, perhaps the Iraqi people will hear this and rise up against Saddam themselves, taking away the Americans' key rationalisation for the war. There's only one problem.'

'Just one, eh?'

Sofia pursed her lips and instantly looked far more mature than her age would suggest.

'Well, one of the many problems, I should say, is that we do not know which government building Saddam is planning to hide the civilians in. My guess is that it will be selected at random at the last possible minute, to prevent the information from leaking out. May I have another drink?'

Abdul retrieved the bottle and poured two larger measures of the amber liquid. Handing one to Sofia, he gazed into his glass, lost in thought.

'Of course I'll do it. I'll try to make it my best piece of writing yet. I'm sure it will be picked up by all the underground publications in Baghdad, and I'm sure it will also be read by the Americans. I'm not sure that will be enough to stop the entire bombing campaign, but we will sure as hell try. At the very least, it may stop Saddam from sacrificing innocent civilians. If we make his plans public, proceeding with this scheme, knowing that all of Baghdad is aware of what he is doing, would be madness. He would lose what little support he has left from the people. We'll have to go into hiding, of course. Once this comes out, Saddam will double down on trying to find me and my sources. I will no longer be a minor irritant to the government; I will be a full-blown liability.'

She looked at him sadly, realising he was right. 'Unfortunately, I'm already on Uday's radar. The dirty bastard was following me in the marketplace the other day. He's so full of himself, he thought I didn't know. Thankfully I gave him the slip. I don't think he knows who I am, who my father is, I mean. But I wouldn't care to think about what he would have done if he had caught me.'

Abdul felt something twist in the depths of his stomach. 'So, that settles it,' said Abdul, his brow furrowed. 'It's probably best if we leave the city as soon as possible before we publish the blog. If you have caught Uday's attention, he will stop at nothing until he has found you. Even more so because you escaped him – his ego will not withstand that.'

'I've never been away from home for more than three days', replied Sofia, but her eyes shined as she said it. 'Escaping Saddam is going to be easy compared to escaping from my father'. She smiled.

She smiled, amused at the ridiculousness of her domestic but nonetheless pertinent issue, in comparison to the gravity of the events they had been discussing. Then a determined look overcame her. 'No one, including my father, must know the real reason I've run away either. I must make it look like I have run away for some reason other than sedition, in case they suspect the leak came from our house. I couldn't bear it they were blamed for it. And we must succeed in telling the world of Saddam's plan. No doubt, there will be many lives lost in the coming days, but if we can save a few innocent lives, we must.'

For the first time, he noticed the worry lurking behind her determined face.

He put his hand on top of hers and looked into her eyes, wordlessly signalling his full support. He noticed a cocktail of relief and gratitude in her eyes, but there was something else too, a warmth that hinted at affection.

'Don't worry. We'll think of something,' he said, draining his glass, stifling the fear that arose in his throat. So far, all he had done was blog and hide behind a screen. Who was he really if all he could do was hide behind the screen of a computer and pass judgment on all and sundry? Now, for the first time, he was committing to doing something that extended beyond cyberspace, something that had immediate and tangible repercussions in the real world.

This, he thought, was the moment he had been waiting for his whole life.

They had another drink before Sofia left to prevent arousing suspicion with her family.

***

It was Rafan who eventually came up with the solution.

In his younger days, Rafan's parents had been equally overprotective of him, and over the years he had become a master of deception in order to bypass their restrictions on his social life. His considerable intelligence had been applied to the problems of staying out late, going to parties his parents did not approve of, and meeting girls whose parents did not approve of him. He had perfected it to a fine art.

'Listen,' he said with the authority of a wise teacher educating an eager pupil. 'Sad as I will be to lose you, there's no other choice – you and Sofia must pretend to elope and run away together before you publish your blog. Here's what you have to do.

'She goes to that posh school, right? Baghdad College for Girls? Good. Every evening when school finishes, all the pupils are collected by their drivers or parents in their cars. Because it's a posh school, and because all of Iraq's high society send their 'delicate darlings' to that school, security is very tight. Even though they are technically adults, the girls aren't allowed to enter their cars until the registration number and description of the car are checked against the one in the watchman's logbook. So, you can't just pick her up after school in your own car, pretending to be her driver or her father.'

Rafan had the flair of a good orator. He paused for a sip of beer to build up suspense. Abdul wondered where he was going with this line of thought.

'All you have to do,' he continued, 'is get her to disconnect the valves in her Mercedes, at home, when no one is looking. Where will her driver bring the car for repair? To you of course. You've done a good job once, and he has no reason not to trust you with the car again. You tell him there is a problem and you need to keep the car in the garage for a couple of days.

'Then, the next day, when Sofia's driver is collecting her from school in one of the family's other cars, he will be delayed due to an unfortunate but minor accident with a bicycle which suddenly appears in his path – you know how rashly these cyclists ride.' He glanced sideways at an old and rusty bicycle leaning against his wall. 'The cyclist will kick up a fuss and insist on being taken to the hospital, then maybe the police station, delaying his collection of Sofia even further.

'But never fear! Sofia will not be stranded at school without transport. Why, her regular Mercedes will appear at the school gates, promptly at closing time. The licence plate number checks out fine. Her regular driver will be missing, sure, but there will be a new one in his place. In fact, he will look suspiciously like you!' Rafan ended his description of the cunning plan with an exaggerated wink and a bow. 'Then, you simply drive to the border and escape into Jordan. A minor scandal will ensue. I can only imagine the gossip that will be stirred up by the story of a lowly mechanic seducing the daughter of a minister. But no one dies. And who knows, perhaps, in time, the seduction bit might even come true, eh?'

Abdul scratched his goatee. 'Maybe we could also leave word that she is running away with the boy she loves to escape from Uday. It'd be an even more credible excuse.'

It was so outrageous it might work, Abdul thought. With the right preparation and precision-perfect timing, it might just go according to plan. Besides, he was preoccupied with the task of writing the blog and he couldn't think of anything better. 'I'm in,' he said.

8. Ava

Ava had always loved a good challenge.

She enjoyed putting her mind to a problem, listing out all the variables, making plans and thinking of contingencies. Planning, she realised, was meditative. It was a way of carefully thinking about the future by drawing on the experiences of the past.

Putting those plans into action, on the other hand, was about being entirely 'in the moment'. It was about split-second responses and instinct. There was nothing like the possibility of going to prison for a long time to motivate a person to remain entirely focused on the job at hand. Planning and action excited her in equal measure.

But now she *was* in prison.

The police had found the keys to the stolen car in her pocket in seconds, almost as if that was exactly what they had been looking for. That triggered a horrible string of events. Eventually, the evidence had led back to her official garage, and then, sadly, to the hidden one underneath. Seven stolen cars and two years' worth of work had been wasted.

She had even made the news. 'Haul of vintage sportscars found, suspect apprehended,' proclaimed the headlines.

Ava had no idea where she had gone wrong. But it couldn't possibly be a coincidence that the raid happened the morning after she had stolen the vintage Aston.

She stared up at the small window, high up in the corner of the cell she occupied, at Her Majesty's pleasure, in Holloway Prison. It let in a narrow ray of sunlight, but it was too high to look out of.

She thought back on all the plans she had made over the last eight years and the actions she had taken to bring them to life. She wasn't angry with herself, and she had no regrets, that much was certain – but she was curious to find out where she had made a mistake.

'Oye! Ava, you have a visitor,' shouted the guard through the intercom. Ava could hear brisk, confident footsteps that got louder until they stopped in front of her cell door. The door opened, accompanied by an electronic buzzing sound, and a uniformed man walked in, before the door slammed shut again.

The man was about 60. He had short-cropped white hair and a khaki uniform. He carried an air of authority and discipline. He walked into the room and looked straight into Ava's eyes. 'You're Ava Wright,' he declared, by way of introduction.

Ava said that she was.

'The name's Bingley. Commander Bingley. I knew your pa – we fought side by side. A good man – he spoke about you a lot you know, his precious Ava.'

'Bingley. Yes, I remember your name sir. He mentioned it a couple of times at home,' Ava lied.

'Yes, we fought together in Yemen in the sixties. The people were nice enough, but the place was ghastly. Could scarcely get a decent drink there. Don't know why we even wanted the damn place. Well, anyway young Ava, what have you gotten yourself into here?', he said, while taking a seat on the only chair in the spartan cell.

Ava sat on side of metal cot and faced her father's friend. 'I have no idea why they brought me here. They said I'd stolen some cars. But they have the wrong person, sir.'

'Bollocks. They got the right person. Don't get smart with me, lass. I served with your father for 20 years, and if the two of you think alike as much as you look alike, I'll wager you did it. Knew it the moment I saw you.'

Ava didn't say anything. Somehow, she knew that it would not be in her best interests to lie to this man.

'But I have more than just intuition on my side,' he continued, smiling. 'I was hoping to visit your pa a few months ago. I didn't know he had passed on. So, I looked him up – it's easy for me to look things up, you see, I'm the Police-Army liaison and the lads at the Yard are always happy to do me favours. I found your pa's file. But, more surprisingly, I found a file on you too. Suspected automobile theft. So, I dug deeper and found out what you had been up to. I won't go into details now, but let's just say I was impressed. Some of the cars they say you took had never been stolen before because of all the new-fangled technology on them. And you never got caught selling the cars, either. They suspected you done it, but never had any evidence. So, I know you're quite smart and disciplined, just like your old man was.'

Commander Bingley paused for a moment and looked at Ava, smiling far more warmly than a man of the law ought to smile at a thief.

He continued, 'Then I looked at all the jobs the Yard thought you'd done. All the people you had stolen from – it read like a *Who's Who* of all the bastards in the country. That's when I knew they had the right girl for certain. I still remember the time your pa stole that bottle of whisky from that pompous arse, Commander Dawson. And the time he stole the motorcycle Rawlings had confiscated from a young Yemini lad for looking at him the wrong way. Strange thing is, I could have sworn I saw the lad riding his motorcycle again after your pa had stolen it.' He smiled distantly at the thought of days gone past.

'So, you see Ava, the apple doesn't fall far from the tree. But that brings us to our current predicament here. Now the last chap you stole from, he's a right prick, it's true, and the biggest tax evader in the United Kingdom. But he's got power, see, and he's got lots of people at the Yard in his pocket. If you're locked up Ava, you're going to be locked up for a long, long time.'

Ava knew when someone had finished talking, and this wasn't it. There was more. The old man struck her as a man of action, someone who took responsibility. A problem solver, like her. She was right.

'So, I've pulled some strings, and I've scratched some backs and the like. Turns out, there might be a deal we can do here. You don't have to go to prison. But they won't let you stay in the country for a while, either. So, what do we do? I could use a lady like you, a lady with your technical skills, in the Army. We can use a person of your skills in Iraq. Someone who will fly under the radar. In a nutshell, we can clear your record, all of it, if you give me your word that you will join the Army for a three-year contract.'

Commander Bingley leaned back. Ava could see that the man was now done; the offer was on the table.

'Sir. I appreciate your efforts, but let me just say at the outset, that I'm a pacifist. I hate war and I hate guns, and I really don't think any one of us in this country should be in Iraq, let alone myself.'

Bingley smiled. 'Just like your pa. Heck of a soldier, but every shot he fired ate away at him from the inside. I could tell.

'But tell me, young Ava, do you like prison more than you like war? You're a girl who won't like being locked up – that much is clear. Besides, it's not the sort of army you're thinking of. I promise you won't have to fire any guns, and we will massage those creative brain cells of yours. We'll massage the fuck out of them. You won't be bored, trust me.'

Ava looked at the old man in front of him. Another question occurred to her. 'Why me? Why not someone better suited to this sort of thing? I'm sure you have a bunch of people trained to do this.'

The old man looked pleased at this question. 'Astute as ever, Ava. It makes me even more confident in your abilities! Well, the reason is simple. Despite being an inefficient regime, Iraq's secret service isn't half bad. I can't say much, but I can tell you that recently we have suspected someone on our end is leaking them information. We can't be sure how much they know – it's possible that the identities of our agents, even those in training, have been compromised. So, we need someone entirely unknown, but someone used to conducting clandestine activities. And if this person is good with technology, calm under pressure and doesn't fit the mould of an average agent… well, so much the better!'

Ava made a pretence of thinking about it. But she was sure the old man already knew her answer.

***

The two months that followed had been a blur.

After she had agreed to Commander Bingley's deal to join the Army in exchange for her eventual freedom, things moved very quickly. She had been taken to an unmarked building at ITC Catterick, the Army's basic training facility.

There she had been subjected to a battery of physical and mental tests. She enjoyed the basic Arabic course, impressed the instructor of her self-defence classes, soaked up the first-aid lessons, and put some effort into what they called 'field craft'.

Her mission had been outlined to her. She was to be sent to Iraq as soon as possible, under the guise of being a freelance reporter for a small-time British newspaper. Once there, she would gather intelligence and pass it back to Bingley with a focus on finding out if Iraq was preparing for war with the West, and if so, how prepared it was.

There were others like her, she knew, each of them with a particular remit. Ava's area of focus would be to gather intelligence on Saddam's notorious eldest son, Uday Hussein.

As part of her preparation for the upcoming task, Ava had been given several dossiers of information on the person she was to spy on. What she read had shocked her.

While Uday's brother, Qussay, seemed like a perfectly ordinary maniacal mass murderer, Uday Hussein was just a completely different kettle of fish. Depraved and savage, he seemed to epitomise the term 'loose cannon'. He had even lost the favour of his father due to his antics, which were now out of control by any account and extended to paedophilia, torture, smuggling, murder and rape.

Over the last few years, Uday had been moved from position to position within his father's government. Whatever he had been put in charge of had failed. At first, it had been the cybercrimes division of the feared Mukhabarat. He had proved himself to be largely ineffective – primarily because his knowledge of information technology only extended to extreme online pornography.

Then he had been put in charge of several newspapers as Mass Media Minister. Again, he treated this position, quite literally, as a joke. One of his papers, Babel, published a story about how the state was about to double food rations and include bananas, chocolate and Pepsi at a time when the country was under heavy economic sanctions. The starving masses' jubilation was short-lived when they opened the same newspaper on the 1st of April – where Uday declared the entire article an April fool's day joke.

Funny guy.

These days, Uday oversaw the country's Olympic Committee with a focus on improving the soccer team. The dossier was full of unconfirmed stories about how he tortured underperforming players in hideous (albeit rather creative) ways. Aside from his role as the head of the Olympic Committee, there were rumours that Uday was vying to regain control of the Fedayeen Saddam, a position he had previously been fired from by his father, who finally realised that his son was using the paramilitary force not for the security of the first family, but to meet his own ends, including kidnapping, extortion and theft.

But by far the most interesting thing Ava had read was about Uday's fascination with cars, something they apparently had in common. What she had read filled her with derision and excitement in equal measures. If the reports were true, it meant that with over 1,300 vehicles in his possession, Uday Hussein was the owner of one of the largest collections of high-value cars worldwide. These were stored in various highly guarded and secret underground storage facilities dotted around Baghdad.

Ava's research on Uday's political and military ambitions quickly turned into research on his sports car collection.

When Kuwait had been ransacked by Saddam's Iraqi forces during the Gulf War, they had conducted a systematic campaign of pilfering and theft. Saddam had put together three teams – one in charge of stealing electronic items, one in charge of stealing art and jewellery, and the final team, run by Uday, was in charge of stealing every valuable car in the oil-rich city. It was clear that Uday had kept the choicest automobiles for himself before handing over the rest to his father to profitably dispose of.

Since then, his collection had grown through a mixture of purchase, theft and trade and included some of the rarest and most exquisite cars in the world. He had a team of 15 mechanics working to maintain his collection. Their jobs involved more than maintenance and modification, they also involved procurement (i.e.: stealing or coercion) of new vehicles from inside and outside Iraq.

His chief mechanic, a man known simply as Kasim, had studied Cadillacs in Toronto, Rolls-Royces in Birmingham, Mercedes-Benzes in Germany and Lamborghinis in a small town near Bologna, Italy. Ava knew this because there were records in her dossier of agents that had tried to intercept Kasim in the past and milk him for information on the regime. They had all failed – apparently, the Hussein family were well known for their vengeance on the families of those who informed on them.

Ava noted that Uday's collection included the usual suspects: Bugattis, Lamborghinis, Ferraris, Porsches, McLarens and other performance supercars. There were also luxury saloons from Bentley, Rolls Royce, Cadillac and

Mercedes-Benz. Besides those, Uday also seemed to be quite keen on less-known flamboyant vintage exotics from the likes of Excalibur, Zimmer, Plymouth and Stutz.

Then Ava read something in the dossier that made her jaw drop. She read the passage several times. When she finally pulled herself together, her first action was to pick up the telephone and call her friend, a leading automotive historian.

When she put down the phone, she poured herself a stiff drink and sat down to think. This was a turn of events she had not anticipated.

Apparently, amidst the modern supercars, the vintage exotics and custom-made saloons, there was something so rare and special that it made her want to laugh and cry at the same time.

The object of her amazement was an extremely rare pre-war Mercedes-Benz 540k roadster with bodywork by coach-makers Erdmann & Rossi, one of only two that had ever been made.

A specialist in post-war sportscars, Ava only had a basic knowledge of vintage pre-war classics. But her friend had given her all the information she could want.

The Mercedes-Benz company, as it's known today, had been a key supplier for the German war effort – both in terms of cars and aeroplane engines.

At the time, a major drawback in aero-engine design was the loss of power at high altitudes, resulting in unstable performance. Mercedes invented mechanical air compressors which supercharged the engine and compensated for the loss of power – revolutionising aeroplane engine design.

However, when they applied the same technology to their automobile engines, they realised they could reach speeds at sea level that had never been reached before. The technology culminated in the production of the 540k Roadster in 1935, a car that many considered the very pinnacle of pre-war automotive design.

Ava pulled up a picture of the car on her laptop. The regular version of the 540k looked impressive enough, but the version with coach-work by Erdmann & Rossi had a massive grille, sweeping fenders, integrated twin spotlights, an arrogantly long hood, low-slung windscreen and a majestic tail. Ava read that the car had stolen the imagination of millions when it was first released at the Berlin Automotive Show in 1935. However, nowhere near as many people would ever own it. Ava had read the official price was 'auf Anfrage' or available upon request to pre-vetted owners upon enquiry. Even then, there were a range of different configurations available.

One thing is certain, the original price was sure to be in proportion to the size of the car – and at 5 metres long and 1.8 metres wide, that was something to think about.

In one writers' words, the car had, 'a harmony and balance of line and mass which very simply defies any conceivable improvement. They are sculptural perfection. For many people of taste, more beautiful cars will never be designed and built.'

But it wasn't all about beauty. The 5.4-litre engine made it one of the few cars that could exceed 100 miles per hour, having been designed for Germany's autobahns which were being built by Hitler at the time.

Ava was surprised to learn the car also featured safety glass, hydraulic brakes and electric windshield wipers and door locks. She had no idea such advanced systems existed in the 1930s.

Ava pulled up a report from *Autocar* magazine's archives, written in May 1938. The driver's report read:

One's foot goes hard down, and an almost demoniacal howl comes in. The rev counter and speedometer needles leap round their dials: there is perhaps no other car noise in the world so distinctive as that produced by the Mercedes supercharger.

Ava had known for a very long time that a similar 540k Roadster had fetched the record price of $11,770,000 in a recent auction – and that one did not even have the distinctive bodywork, nor had it been owned by anyone famous.

The cost of a car is often evaluated based on its history and previous owners, and, apparently, the one owned by Saddam's family had quite an illustrious past as well.

Part myth, part legend, many had doubted this particular car ever existed. But a few previously, the former design chief of the famed Erdmann & Rossi finally spoke up about his firm's historic creation.

He confirmed that the 540k in question had indeed been made for and sold to King Ghazi of Iraq after the young royal saw a similar car at the Barcelona Car Exhibition in 1935. Unfortunately, the king died shortly after its purchase, ironically in an automotive accident. A few years later, it fell into Saddam Hussein's hands when he took over the country following a bloody coup. Erdmann & Rossi did not know much more about the fate of the car after Saddam acquired it, but a fanatical group of automotive historians had picked up the scent once again.

They claimed that Saddam had then swapped it for another extremely rare Mercedes, a 770k Tourenwagon, with the King of Jordan. The King of Jordan was a well-known car fanatic, who stripped the 540k of its paint and sent it to Germany for a full restoration. Unknown to anyone except his nearest and dearest, he also secretly commissioned an exact replica of the car to be made while it was in Germany – down to the same bodywork by Erdmann & Rossi.

Many years later, for reasons unknown, the King of Jordan sent the 540k Special Roadster back to Saddam, presumably the original, and even let him keep the 770k Tourenwagon for which it had been swapped a few years ago.

The Mercedes-Benz 770k Tourenwagon was an immensely special car in its own right. One of only 88 built, it was also one of the most expensive cars of its time – they had mainly been used by high-ranking Nazi officials, including the Fuhrer. In fact, one of them was used as Hitler's official parade car. Ava wondered if Saddam was inspired by Hitler in more ways than his choice of automobile.

Ava noted there were very few surviving 770K and the last known sale was by an unknown Russian billionaire for several millions.

Together, Ava estimated that the 540k and 770k were worth about 32 million dollars, depending on their condition – a fantastic last job for any car thief.

To her, it seemed, her mission in Baghdad had changed slightly.

9. Uday

Uday had exited Saddam's inner circle meeting deep in thought. Having grown up in the lap of luxury, he had never really had any sort of formal training in anything, much less in how to run a paramilitary organisation or a government department. It was a constant source of irritation to him that people just expected him to know these things because he was Saddam's son.

At school, he had considered everyone else beneath him. After the seventh or eighth year, when he realised he could do whatever he wanted, he completely ignored any of the school's rules – that is, if he attended at all. Dressed in jeans, a t-shirt, and metallic Ray-Ban sunglasses, Uday had no consideration for the uniform. What's more, he often turned up accompanied by much older 'girlfriends' with badly dyed hair, bright lipstick, high heels and short skirts – who he would insist on bringing into the class to sit with him while he puffed contentedly on a Havana cigar, completely oblivious to the teacher and the lecture.

Once a teacher had made the mistake of telling Uday not to bring his 'girlfriends' to class. At first, Uday couldn't believe someone had challenged him. Then, when he recovered, he looked the teacher in the eyes, then slowly and menacingly said, 'fuck off,' before returning his attention to the peroxide blonde by his side. When the teacher interrupted again, Uday stormed out of the class, angrily talking to the head of his security detail, which always waited outside the classroom doors. That was the last time the teacher lectured. He was never seen or heard of again. A few days after the incident, an unrecognisably mutilated body was found in the gutters outside Baghdad.

To compound the issue, his little brother, Qusay, *had* studied. His bookshelf bore titles like *Espionage in the 20th Century* and *The Police State – An Analysis*. Furthermore, he had sought out mentorship amidst some of his father's inner circle, who had only been too pleased to oblige. Last but not least, he had initiated and been on many educational trips to friendly countries, chief among them Jordan, to learn about their security apparatus. It had never even crossed Uday's mind to even consider such things.

More recently, Uday had been asked by his father, mother and some of Iraq's most senior ministers, 'Why don't you do X, Y or Z, like your brother?'

He could just about stop himself from grabbing the nearest heavy item and smashing it into the offending party's face.

This time, he was determined to show his father he could succeed. Not only would he catch Whistler, but he would devise a plan to leverage the website for propaganda purposes. Or, rather, he would get others to do so and then claim the credit.

But how does one go about catching a cybercriminal? Uday knew little about the internet, aside from the basics. He had briefed the information minister on the task a few months ago, and then let him get on with it. Save for sporadic and meaningless progress updates by text message, his preferred mode of communication for updates, he had not heard of any concrete advancement. What he needed, he realised, was a motivational technique. He slid into his father's library, one of the largest in Iraq, and picked out a volume called *Management Techniques*. After flipping through a few pages, he reached a chapter called 'Carrot and Stick Method.' It read:

Employees can be motivated to do well at work in a number of different ways. An effective example of this is the carrot and stick approach. This policy usually involves a reward for a job well done, but also repercussions if the desired outcome is not reached. Usually quick and simple to implement, it can be modified for your employee needs and company culture.

Uday carefully underlined the entire paragraph and took the book home to study it.

The next day, he turned up at the Ministry of Information & Technology unannounced and slammed a bottle of scotch on the table, along with a large bag of cocaine. Then he took out his revolver and placed it next to the two other objects. He looked up at the room full of people in his employ, perhaps 30 faces nervously peeping at him from behind their computer screens.

'The first one to obtain information on the identity of Whistler gets this bottle of whisky, along with my and Baba's personal thanks,' he said, 'but if no one comes up with any information, I will shoot you, one by one, every hour, until either all of you are dead, or until someone finds something. Your future is in your hands. You can do whatever it takes. You have three hours until I come back to this room with my gun.'

Then, remembering the bag of cocaine, he said, 'Oh, and I also brought something to keep you all going. This is for you all. Who says that I am unreasonable?' He smiled benevolently. The staff looked at him wide-eyed and terrified; most of them had never seen recreational drugs in their lives and couldn't even begin to guess what the bag contained.

With that, Uday left, thinking there was nothing else he could possibly do. However, as he was leaving the room, his cell phone buzzed. He glanced down at it, noticing he had received a text from the head of the Fedayeen. What he read made him forget all about Whistler:

Whore from market found. She is in class at Baghdad Girls College. Waiting outside with team to grab her as soon as she leaves. Will bring back to your palace tonight.

10. Abdul

Excerpt from Whistler's Blog:

I have been honoured and humbled by all the attention this blog has been getting over the last few years. Some of your comments have touched me deeply, and I would like to thank everyone, from all over the world, for reading my words. Sometimes, amidst all the chaos I see unfolding on the news, it's good to know that there are still reasonable people everywhere, working towards peace. The last few months have been interesting. We have seen the inability to prove that WMDs exist in Iraq. We have seen the largest anti-war protest in the history of the world. We have seen impassioned pleas made by several heads of state. But alas, I do not think that anything can derail the coalition war train, which is now set on a collision course with Iraq.

However, I want you to know that none of my blog posts have ever been as important as this one. It has come to my attention that the United States of America is planning an operation in which over five hundred cruise missiles will be launched into the heart of Baghdad, in an overwhelming display of force. This assault will soon be announced. The Americans will state that their quarrel is not with the people of Baghdad, but with its leadership, who will be the targets of these attacks.

This, in itself, is a futile act. None of the leadership will remain in the buildings they are known to inhabit – everyone important enough to be targeted is well aware of the impending missile attack and has made alternative arrangements. The attack will only lead to the loss of innocent lives and whatever little working infrastructure Baghdad has left, all of which will be dismissed as collateral damage by the coalition forces.

However, I have become aware, from very reliable sources, of a government plan to fill up what is sure to be one of the targeted buildings with civilians and any Western nationals left in Iraq. The building in question is sure to be selected at random at the last minute, in order to prevent the information from leaking out. The loss of life will ratchet up the pressure against the West to cease their campaign.

Knowing this, to attack these buildings would undeniably lead to a catastrophic and entirely avoidable loss of life.

I will leave it at this. If you do not hear from me again, I wish you all the best. Stay safe.

***

Abdul scheduled the post to be published online automatically in 24 hours.

By that time, he would be safely in Jordan with Sofia. It was also a good precaution to pre-schedule the blog post while the internet still worked – with the impending invasion, the phone lines could no longer be relied upon. Now, the article lived on the foreign website's servers – it would be published at the scheduled hour no matter what happened.

Finally, he could focus on escaping with Sofia. Rafan's plan had been in motion last night and Sofia had played her part really well. She had unplugged the valves under the hood of the Mercedes without anyone noticing. In the morning the driver couldn't start the car to do the usual college drop off. The first deviation from the plan occurred when he phoned another mechanic instead of Abdul. The mechanic quoted a price to send out a tow truck and bring the Mercedes to his garage to be fixed.

Thinking on her feet, Sofia helpfully suggested that the driver should see if they could get it done cheaper by another mechanic. After all, even though they were well off, they should do their due diligence to find out the going rate. Both the driver and her father were pleasantly surprised by the revelation of this new prudent streak in Sofia. Her father asked if the driver knew of any other garage they could call.

The driver thought for a while and said, 'Yes. How about that chap who fixed the bearing in the cooling system, the other day? What was the name? That's right, Abdul's Garage. I'll find out what his prices are.'

Lo and behold. The prices were much more reasonable. Abdul came to the house and picked up the car in a tow truck, letting the driver know the problem would take a couple of days to fix.

'Can't it be done sooner? I must drop off and pick up the boss's daughter and I can't do that without the car. I'm not allowed to drive the other one – the boss's old Bentley. He probably loves it even more than his daughter. He'll insist on going to drop off and pick up Sofia himself. Oh, he won't be pleased!'

Even though Abdul wasn't sure about Rafan riding a bicycle into the front of Mr Aziz's antique Bentley, he stuck to the plan and said, 'It can't be helped. Two days.'

So, that morning, Mr Aziz dropped Sofia off at school himself. Abdul and Rafan followed him to study the route he took, just in case it was different from the one the driver normally used. It was. There was only one place where they could, with some semblance of safety, stage the accident. It was at a steep curve in the road where they could be sure that Mr Aziz wouldn't be going too fast, but also wouldn't be able to see Rafan coming. Rafan wanted to do a test run, so Abdul picked up an old car from the garage and drove it along the same road that Mr Aziz would use. He even put on a hat like the one Mr Aziz usually wore to lend the scene more artistic integrity.

Trial run one ended up with Rafan missing the car completely. Trial run two ended in Rafan banging really hard into the car and breaking the cycle so it was unrideable. But by this time they were already committed to the mission and bought a second-hand bike from a market stall. They just about got it right on trial number three.

Before they knew it, six hours had passed, and the last bell of the school day was about to go off. Rafan waited, hidden with his bike in the bushes near the Aziz household, ready to follow Mr Aziz when he set off to pick up Sofia.

Mr Aziz left earlier than anticipated, but he didn't go to school. Rafan followed him to the post office, where he parked the car and disappeared inside with a parcel.

Rafan made a split-second decision and walked over to the parked Bentley. No one was looking in his direction. He reached underneath the rear left tyre and pulled hard. The car made a small grating sound and sagged slightly. Rafan calmly got back onto his cycle and sailed slowly away, the pedals squeaking at every rotation.

***

Abdul reached the school in the Aziz family's Mercedes – the one which had been sent in for repairs. He wore a crisp white shirt and khaki slacks – something a driver might wear but also something that looked good on him.

He went into the queue of cars leading to the gate of the college. There, each car would be waved into one of six or seven parking bays where the girls would be waiting for their brothers, fathers or drivers to pick them up along with a teacher or a watchman.

If Abdul believed in prayer, he would have prayed that the 'accident' had gone smoothly. He wasn't quite sure of what he would do if Mr Aziz turned up in his Bentley and saw him driving the Mercedes with his daughter inside. But he trusted that Rafan would never let Mr Aziz reach the school, one way or another. Even though Rafan displayed every characteristic of being lazy on a day-to-day basis, when he set his mind to something there was nothing that could stop him. Abdul knew this, and took comfort in the fact.

Before Abdul was let into the school premises, the underside of the Mercedes would be checked carefully with a mirror on a long stick. The boot of the car would be checked by another guard. Car bombs were very much in vogue in this part of the world, and one could never be too careful, especially when children of high-ranking government officials were involved – both Iraqi, as well as the offspring of various foreign diplomats – even if the vast majority of them had already left the country due to the impending invasion. The guard carried a ledger and scrupulously checked every licence plate number and the driver of every car before announcing the arrival of the car to the relevant girl. If one of Baghdad's elites were kidnapped, losing his job would be the least of his worries.

Abdul was very conscious that he was sweating profusely. He realised that he was holding the steering wheel so tight that his knuckles were white. Subversive blogging from behind a screen be damned, being brave in the real world was a lot harder. He was very aware that he would have to make an extra special effort to look unsuspicious as he was not the regular driver.

He looked for Sofia amongst the girls waiting in the glass-encased lobby of the college but couldn't see her yet. He took a deep breath, and his heart rate slowed. His head cleared as the oxygen coursed through his bloodstream. Suddenly, he wasn't scared anymore. He simply couldn't afford to be. It was showtime.

He drove up to the guard with the ledger.

'Sofia Aziz, please,' he managed.

'Sofia... Sofia...' The man ran his finger down the list and then looked up at Abdul. 'Oh yes, she's been missing since lunchtime – run off with some friends no doubt. We have informed the Aziz household of her indiscipline. Why did they send you here? Haven't they found her?'

Abdul was dumbfounded.

Panic rose like bile from his stomach into his throat.

11. Ava

Ava knew that she could not – she would not – let the cars remain in the possession of Uday Hussein. Nor would she let them disappear into the folds of history as the dust settled following the invasion.

She did not know how she was going to go about it, only that she would. She had found a real purpose for her time in Baghdad; it was a chance to procure and conserve a part of history rather than fight a war she did not believe in. That part, she was determined not to do. Not after what had happened to her father.

Of course, Ava's decision to steal two of the rarest cars on the planet presented her with several dilemmas.

First, she would have to find out where the cars had been stored. They would most likely be in one of the many underground storage facilities she had read about, the question was which one and where?

Second, she had to figure out how she would steal them. This would most likely require some local support and a lot of pre-planning and logistics.

Third, she would have to figure out how to get the cars out of the country. She'd probably have to get them into Jordan, the neighbouring country, from where she could fly them elsewhere. This would be every bit as challenging as the actual theft. Luckily, having spent more than ten years in the trade, she had a network of contacts who could help her. Someone she trusted was sure to know someone they trusted in Jordan.

And she had to do all of it while pretending to be a Western journalist, while also pretending to be a spy to her controllers back home. She didn't even speak Arabic besides the few sentences they had taught her during her training.

Ava did not worry about these challenges – she would take it one step at a time. The first step, she knew, would simply be to carry out her mission and gain intelligence on Uday Hussein. In the process, she hoped she would pick up some clues on the whereabouts of the pre-war classics. This meant watching Uday while ensuring she was not noticed – which was easier said than done.

Ava had not known how difficult it was for Western journalists to get permission to enter Iraq, let alone surveil one of its most important occupants. Wars were caused, as well as won or lost, based on propaganda, for which journalists were thought to be responsible.

George Bush and Saddam Hussein both knew this only too well.

Ava's handlers in the army worked with her to come up with a journalist's CV, which had been submitted to the Iraqi embassy in London. Over quiet dinners in various private clubs across London, three selected British newspaper owners had been asked to ensure their people backed up the story if they were asked about Ava by the Iraqi authorities.

Her CV, Ava had been told, would initially be vetted by the Iraqi authorities in London and then, if it was approved, she would be asked to fill out a lengthy form that asked her all sorts of questions about herself, including her religious and political beliefs.

The completed form would then be sent to Iraq, where four different committees would analyse it. If approved, she would be very closely watched by the Iraqi authorities in London and even more closely watched after she arrived in Baghdad.

So, it was no wonder that, after all these steps with so much that could potentially go wrong, she was almost surprised when she found herself in Iraq.

Upon her arrival, a 'guide' had been assigned to her by the authorities. The official explanation was that the guide would help with travel arrangements, as well as the safety and security of the journalist, while they were a guest of Iraq. This was only a half-hearted attempt to disguise the true role of the guide, which was to ensure the journalist did not go anywhere or do anything that would endanger the secrets of the government.

A dual role of the guide, Ava guessed, would be to witness interviews with Iraqis that a journalist may carry out – to say anything negative against the government was punishable by death, as spelt out in the constitution of Iraq. The presence of the guide would ensure any 'anonymous' accounts of governmental transgressions would never be uttered by those who had become disillusioned by the Saddam regime.

When Ava eventually landed in Iraq, she was taken directly to a government facility for a full briefing, where rules that had been made clear to her several times by the Iraqi embassy were once again underlined. She was to apply for permission to travel anywhere outside her hotel. She must be accompanied by her 'guide' at all times. She must get permission from the authorities to interview anyone. She must not do anything to endanger the reputation of the government. In short, she was not allowed to do anything a real reporter would need to do to maintain his or her integrity. Of course, this wasn't of much concern to Ava as she wasn't a real journalist, she was a spy. And truly, she wasn't a spy either. She was, and always would be, a car thief.

However, these rules would certainly get in the way of both of her unofficial tasks. But if there was one thing Ava was good at it was breaking rules. And, if there was another thing she was good at, it was surveillance of people or cars without being noticed.

Ava's guide was a young Iraqi called 'Fahad'. Despite his rather large dimensions, Fahad was exceptionally sharp. Ava noticed this when Fahad's eyes travelled quickly up and down her body making an appraisal, looking for strengths and weaknesses. Either that, or he was simply ogling her figure.

From the moment they were introduced, Fahad never left her side – he even moved into the hotel room opposite the one Ava had been booked into. The two struck up an uneasy friendship, the kind two people might inculcate when they know circumstance has forced them to spend time in each other's company. Fahad had tried to win Ava's trust by telling her about his girlfriend. He mentioned that he rarely got to see her these days due to his work as a government guide. He proudly likened her personality to that of a lioness. Ava was not sure if this was a reference to her bravery at tolerating the sight of an undressed Fahad, or her ability to find suitably calorific prey in this rotund government official.

Ava was not worried about giving Fahad the slip – that would be easy. However, she knew that if she did it enough times it might result in her expulsion from the country.

Her first opportunity to do so arrived earlier than Ava expected.

The day after she arrived, Fahad had taken her around the city to get her acclimatised. To her surprise, everyone from the street vendors to the hotel staff seemed friendly and treated her with the utmost respect, despite the widening schism between Iraq and the West. She recognised the landmarks she had read about – from the massive sculpture called Victory Arch, to the numerous beautiful domes of mosques dotted around the city. She was also pleased to realise she could orient herself quite well due to the long hours spent pouring over maps of Baghdad before she arrived.

Despite the obvious undertones of tension, she was enjoying the sights, smells, colours and people of the loud and busy city. The food had also been a revelation – she thrived on the spicy chargrilled fish and meats, the fried patties of ground meat, the casseroles, stews, the flavoured rice and salads - while avoiding the hummus and pita bread, which are just as much a staple in every English supermarket. Many times, she had sweets and sealed bottles of water thrust upon her by vendors and shopkeepers with payment refused. Ava decided that hospitality to visitors was part of the Iraqi DNA.

However, inevitably, something she had eaten disagreed with her system and she woke up the next morning feeling slightly ill. Fahad had knocked on her hotel room door, having heard the loud retching sounds which Ava made no effort to subdue. Ava opened the door, genuinely looking pale, and Fahad had offered to call the doctor.

Ava refused, asking Fahad if it would be OK to cancel the day's activities so that she could rest and recover. Perhaps Fahad could use this time to catch up on the paperwork he often complained about. 'Paperwork, yes,' Fahad said, clearly revelling in the thought that he would be able to call his girlfriend to spend the day in his hotel room. Ava knew he could not leave the hotel while the foreigner was there - he would be disciplined for an infraction of his duties - but she also knew he wouldn't be able to resist having a bit of fun if he was to be cooped up inside.

As soon as Fahad had shut the door, Ava had a hot shower and called for some scrambled eggs. Although she was genuinely ill, the breakfast and the warm water made her feel slightly less weak. It was then that the thought occurred to her that she could try and give Fahad the slip - the realisation eradicated any remaining traces of nausea as a surge of adrenalin went through her body. Her first-floor hotel room window overlooked a small and dirty courtyard behind the building, in which she had never seen anyone. The ledge outside her window was wide enough for her to edge her way to the drainpipe and shimmy down. But she still wasn't sure if she would get enough time to herself. What if Fahad decided to check up on her?

Just then, she heard a woman's giggle through the walls from the room opposite his. Fahad had wasted no time in inviting the lioness to his room. That made up her mind. Judging by his weight, Ava was pretty sure Fahad did not have the sexual longevity of a lion, but he would be preoccupied for a while, nonetheless.

She threw a bottle of water, her identity documents, her passport and a camera into her bag, slinging it across her shoulder. Gingerly, she stepped out of the window and onto the ledge, while gripping the windowsill, lest the ledge give way underneath her. In a smooth movement, she made the transition over to the drainpipe and crawled down it. In a few moments, she found herself in the street. Free.

Without wasting any time, she hailed a rusty old taxi asking to be taken to the fashionable and expensive Boat Club. After that, she would visit the Mansour Club, and, if she still had time, the Alwiya Club. Each one had been included in her many briefings as places where the infamous dictator's son and other members of the upper echelons of Iraqi society hung out.

Although Ava was a seasoned traveller of far-flung places, she hadn't been to Baghdad before. Still, she felt a distinct sense of weary anxiety in the air. The taxi driver, the guards at the Boat Club, the people in the street – all seemed grimly determined to go about their business, despite the looming threat of the war.

'If God wills it, it will happen,' said the taxi driver, making a dismissive gesture when Ava asked him about the invasion. 'It is best to make the most of today, in case tomorrow never comes.' Ava got the feeling the taxi driver had seen many hard times, perhaps even harder than those yet to arrive.

She had not found out much at the Boat Club, but she had run into a wealthy gentleman who became talkative after several Johnny Walkers. Ava posed as an eccentric Western thrill chaser, who had come to Baghdad to experience 'history in the making,' slowly transitioning the conversation to a love of all things exotic, including cars. The Iraqi gentleman bit immediately, proudly bragging about the cars owned by the Hussein family, the rulers of his country. He knew of the existence of the famed 540k and the 770k but also revealed that no one but Uday knew where they were kept.

Ava knew she should get back to the hotel in case Fahad decided to check up on her but the fatalistic attitude of the taxi driver seemed to have infected her. After all, if Fahad discovered she was missing, he would hardly admit to the authorities that he had let Ava get away. That would be a punishable offence for him.

Ava's next stop was the Mansour Club, but she decided to take a short detour through the Baghdad street market. She heard that Uday often prowled through this area in a fancy car, looking to coerce young girls into coming home with him. Who knew, perhaps she might catch sight of this detestable human she had read so much about.

If possible, she hoped she might even follow the car in case Uday went to a secret garage after he was done with his day's activities. Perhaps it might have even been the same one the 540k or 770k were located in. Normally, two cars of such a high value would be kept in different locations to reduce the chances of losing both if one location was breached. But this was Saddam Hussein's male heir – a man whose audacity and stupidity were only exceeded by his fearsome reputation.

Ava decided to rest her feet in the patio section of a busy café facing the market and ordered a cup of traditional mint tea ('Good for the stomach,' her friendly waiter had told her). The café's tables and chairs spilt out onto the street, sheltered from the harsh sun by a canvas canopy held up by poles. Potted plants on either side of the café provided further shade to the local Baghdadis who sat inside drinking tea and eating kebabs, salads and wraps. It was one of the few spots from which one could observe the hustle and bustle of the main street, line of sight unhindered by the numerous stalls and carts that lined the road. It would be impossible to miss an ostentatious car driving into the market from this vantage point. She looked at her watch. It had been three hours since she had last seen Fahad. She would leave for the hotel after an hour, just to be safe.

Ava spotted a man walking up and down the street. He wore sunglasses and a large moustache, an assault rifle slung casually across his shoulders. When the waiter came to her table to ask if everything was satisfactory. She motioned towards the moustached man and looked at the waiter questioningly. The waiter bent down and whispered one word in Ava's ear: 'Mukhabarat.' Of course, the fact that they visibly wore arms made the 'secret' part of 'secret police' a little redundant. Ava realised the policeman might be checking the market for threats before Uday Hussein drove in.

That's when she noticed the young Iraqi man sitting next to her. The man looked like he had a muscular but light frame. He wore sunglasses and had a goatee. A Stephen King book lay open in his lap, but he did not seem to be reading it. Ava's keen eye picked up what looked like automotive grease on his shirt and trousers, something she was very familiar with.

In fact, he seemed to be waiting for something to come down the road, just like Ava had been. That's when Ava realised the young man was wearing a jacket, which was odd considering the afternoon heat. The man also seemed edgy – his attention seemed to be divided between the Mukhabarat agent and the road leading into the market. Ava was almost inclined to think the young man was about to do something stupid.

That's when he lifted his hand to adjust his sunglasses. His jacket rode up slightly, and from the corner of her eyes, Ava noticed the handle of a gun tucked into his trousers. Only secret police were allowed to carry guns in Baghdad, and judging by how this gentleman was nervously glancing at the Mukhabarat, he was unlikely to be a member of the same feared tribe.

It occurred to Ava that the young man might have chosen this vantage point on the patio of the café for the same reason she had – to spot Uday Hussein as he drove into the marketplace. Had the man *actually* planned to shoot Uday? With a handgun? In broad daylight? With three SUVs full of guards with automatic weapons itching to fire at the slightest provocation? It seemed mad. Perhaps the young man had not been thinking straight or did not understand what he was getting into.

The first thought that ran through Ava's mind was that if Uday was killed, the secret location of where the two cars were stored might be lost forever. The second was for her own safety – if the man in the café shot at Uday, there would be a whole lot of automatic guns fired in the café's general direction. Life was cheap in Baghdad, and no one would give a damn about a foreign journalist killed in the crossfire – another Iraqi infraction would make no difference to the planned Western military action. Even if she escaped, the city would be on lockdown, and she would have to answer very uncomfortable questions about how and why she happened to be there without her guide when she was supposed to be in her hotel bed with an upset stomach. Last, but not the least, she felt sorry for the young man. His life would almost certainly be cut short regardless of whether he managed to kill Uday or not.

Just then, Ava heard the distant roar of what could only be the engine of a classic Porsche. The young Iraqi had clearly recognised the sound as well – Ava noticed the man had broken into a sweat and started fumbling under his jacket.

Iraq's least favourite son was coming towards his possible doom and, along with it, what was sure to be the doom of everyone sitting in the café.

Ava decided to act quickly. She got up and tapped the goateed man on his shoulder, who nearly jumped out of his skin. She looked into the Iraqi man's sunglasses and said, almost under her breath, so no one else would hear, 'Do you know how hard it is to hit a moving target with one handgun? And do you know how easy it is to hit a stationary target – like you – with 20 fully automatic assault rifles at close range? Be smart. Don't waste your life.'

The man realised his cause had been discovered but seemed adamant. 'Please. I do not care. Move away. I will not miss.' Ava thought this was unlikely considering how the young man was shaking but decided not to point this out.

Instead, she said, 'I've been shot at three times. Each time I was driving away in a car like that. Each time the bullets did not touch the chassis, let alone my body. There are better ways. More effective ways. I can help. Put it down. Please.'

However, the man seemed adamant to carry out his mission. Uday's 1975 Porsche Carrera, flamboyantly painted in gold, appeared on the horizon.

'Fine. You wish to die. That is your call,' said Ava. 'But think of all the other innocent people in the restaurant. You know what will happen if you open fire, right? All 20 Mukhabarat accompanying that bastard will open fire back in your direction, their weapons switched to fully auto. None will be spared.'

A glint of surprise seemed to register in the man's eyes. Clearly, he hadn't thought about that. But Ava wasn't sure it would be enough to make him reconsider.

After what seemed like an eternity, which was actually perhaps three seconds, the Iraqi man brought his hand out from beneath the jacket as the Porsche zoomed past.

There was no gun in his hand.

Ava decided she had better find a restroom quickly. The situation had an influence on the scrambled eggs she had eaten, which were suddenly looking for a way out of her body and they did not seem to care whether they used the entrance or the exit. 'I'm Ava, by the way,' she said looking around for a toilet.

'My name is Abdul,' said the Iraqi.

12. Uday

Uday felt a surge of electricity going through his body when he read the text message. Finally, the girl from the market had been caught. He had been denied satisfaction for far too long. He was immediately excited.

He exited the Ministry of Information, leaving behind the poor souls inside, who were working feverishly to try and trace Whistler's identity. Uday then drove at top speed, across the city, in his favourite gold 1975 Porsche Carrera and parked it erratically on the front lawn of his palace.

Parking erratically was one of his hobbies – he loved pushing the boundaries of what he could get away with, regardless of whether it was his property or someone else's. He told himself it demonstrated power to those around him. Once, he had driven his car *into* the lobby of a fancy hotel in Iraq and parked in front of the reception desk. It made him smile every time he thought of the expression on the face of the concierge – shock and anger simmering under the surface as he forced himself to be servile and polite to Uday for fear of his life. Sometimes you just had to show the peasants who was boss. But who was he kidding – there wasn't often an agenda behind his indiscretions. He did things because he enjoyed them. He was guided by the maxim that one must live in the moment instead of worrying about the past or the future.

His short-wave walkie-talkie buzzed, and his brother Qusay's voice came through the speaker. 'Brother! Where are you?'

'I'm at my house, why?'

'Have you seen Whistler's blog recently?'

'No. Why?'

'Have a look. Father is not going to be pleased with you for dragging your feet. Over and out.'

What now, thought Uday. He could almost detect the glee in his brother's voice as he taunted him. He went into the mansion and booted up the computer. Once he loaded the blog he was enraged. Whistler had revealed his father's primary tactic to galvanise the Iraqi people against the invading Crusaders, while also pitting those outside Iraq against their enemies.

They had even drawn up lists of prominent Baghdadis and foreign journalists to place them in a building that was sure to be bombed by US forces in their initial onslaught.

Now the entire plan was ruined. If any citizens or Western journalists were killed in the bombing, fingers would be pointed at them instead.

Once again, he had disappointed his father by not completing his task in time, and once again, he had been made to look ineffective compared to his brother. For that, Whistler would pay. In fact, resolved Uday, Whistler's entire family would pay, and his family's family, and all their friends, and anyone associated with him, and all their pets too. The lions would have a banquet.

But how had Whistler come across such privileged information? Only a small number of Saddam's top ministers were aware of their strategy. He could count them on his fingers – Majid, Barzan, Izzat, Hamdani and Aziz. He had underestimated this man – he obviously had an inside source, close to Saddam. Father would not be pleased with this development; he prided himself on knowing traitors before they even knew themselves.

Anyway, first things first. He needed to let off a little steam, so he could think straight.

'Kasim! Where is she?'

'In the Red Room, sir.'

His victims were usually brought into the basement of his palace, where they were shut in a small room until he was ready to lavish his attention on them. The room – floors and ceiling included – was painted bright red. Uday had purchased (or taken) a human skeleton from Baghdad University, and placed it inside this room, on the bed, tucked under the sheets. He enjoyed the horrified look on his victim's faces as he violated them on the bed next to the skeleton.

During Christmas, Uday enjoyed placing a Santa hat on the skeleton as a festive act of merriment for those who enjoyed its company.

His butler opened the door for him as he strode up to the bedroom to change into a tracksuit that he could throw away later if it got too messy – one of many that lay folded and new in his cupboard.

A toolbox was handed to him by the butler as he descended the stairs to the basement. It included an electric jigsaw, a drill, a sledgehammer, pliers, surgical blades and a set of oversized dildos. A wet wipe and a brandy would be presented to him on the way out. His staff knew the routine.

He was properly aroused now, inflamed with lust and anticipation. Calm down, he thought, or it will all be over too soon. Got to make it last. Deep breaths.

His radio buzzed again. It was one of the officers at the Ministry of Information.

'We have something, sir.'

'Yes?'

'Well, at first, we tried to track down Whistler's IP address, but that led to a dead end. Then we got in touch with the owners of the platform in America, to ask for the location of the user, but they were unable to give it to us.'

'Did you threaten them properly? With their children?'

'Yes, sir, but they said they were calling the police, so we hung up. Then we tried to hack into the account ourselves, but it proved impossible. But then, young Behar here managed to intercept the private messages that were being sent to the writer of the web blog. Those we could access; they were not encrypted very securely.'

'And…?'

'Well, sir, we were unable to discover his identity, but we found something interesting. It seems our man has a lady love he has been corresponding with.'

This was an unexpected twist, thought Uday.

'Sir. It seems her IT security measures aren't as good as his. We have a username that could be her first name.'

'Well, what is it?'

'Sofia. Her name is Sofia, sir.

'Good job. You boys get the bottle of scotch.'

'Thank you, sir. One more thing, sir. It seems like they were planning to meet, but she did not arrive at their rendezvous and Whistler's last few messages have gone unanswered. In fact, it seems she hasn't been online since last night.'

'OK. Monitor the messages closely. I want you to forward each one to my personal email.'

With that, he turned off the receiver.

Had she stopped responding because she knew he was onto her? Perhaps she had been detained somewhere, he thought as he walked towards the room in which the girl from the marketplace was held. At least he knew the name of Whistler's girl. Sofia. This was progress. Uday's mood improved as he entered the room.

The girl from the market was sitting on the bed, a defiant look on her face. He smiled at her ominously. 'Do you know,' he said, 'when I go to the market, I usually never fail to return with my shopping?' He drank her in with his eyes as he continued. 'Especially when I see such firm and juicy melons.' He was proud of his wordplay.

She looked at him with distaste. He failed to detect the usual fear he saw in his victim's eyes. He would just have to teach her a lesson 'Do you know who I am?' he asked her.

She did not reply.

'Well, let us find out who you are first,' he said, reaching for the bag that she had carried to college the day before.

He opened it and extracted her college ID Card. He read her name. Then he re-read it. And read it again and again.

Could it possibly be true, he thought to himself. Clearly, she was the daughter of Tariq Aziz, one of his father's advisors. It made even more sense – Tariq would have been one of the individuals who had access to Saddam's plans. It seemed he had, in one stroke, obtained leverage over Whistler, and also discovered the source of the leaked strategy to galvanise the Iraqi people against the invaders.

Immediately, he convinced himself this was purely due to his brilliance, and not sheer dumb luck. And heck, if it was luck, wasn't he due for some of that too, after his brother had stolen it all from him?

A devious smile crept over his face.

'Do you know something? My father can be quite precious about those closest to him. He's disallowed me to interfere with the daughters of his ministers, like you. But it's no secret, that the thing he despises the most is traitors. Like your family. This he likes to punish in the harshest possible way.

'So here is what I am going to do. I am going to invite your family and also your boyfriend, Whistler, to my suite at the Kadhimiyya Women's Prison. We will go there ourselves tomorrow morning. Yes, I have quarters there – I often visit to keep those poor women company. Prison can be quite lonely. And then, when those closest to you are comfortably seated on the sofa, I will bring you in, strip you of your clothes and punish you in front of them. I can be quite creative in this regard. Almost an artist.' He motioned towards the toolbox and the oversized dildos he had brought in.

'It will be fun. And when I have finished, I will order my personal guards, all 75 of them, to have their way with you while your family watch. By the time they are done, there will not be much of you left. And for the first time, my father will actually thank me for having some fun. Your father, on the other hand, may not thank me much. That is OK, after the performance, I will throw all of you to the lions. And then it will be my turn to watch the performance.'

And with that, he left the room, locked it behind him, went to the study and booted up his computer. He had a message to write to Whistler. In fact, it could even be called a special invitation.

VIP seats, to watch him perform.

13. Abdul

At first, Abdul did not know what to make of the woman who tapped him on the shoulder in the café. She was clearly a Westerner, and she seemed to be utterly and completely calm in what was quite clearly a tense situation. That made Abdul take heed of what she was saying.

But more than that, it was the look in the woman's eyes. Something told him she knew what she was talking about. Despite being a stranger, she seemed to be genuinely concerned for him and the other people in the café.

Abdul had always known he would be shot to death after his attempt at Uday's life, but he had not cared. The last 24 hours had been the worst of his life. When Sofia hadn't been waiting for him at the Baghdad College for Girls, he immediately sensed that something was seriously wrong. He drove straight to Sofia's family home, desperate to know if she was there or something more sinister had happened. He was stopped at the gate of the large house by the watchman.

'Are you here to return the car? Is it fixed?' The guard's eyes scanned the length of the vehicle.

'Er… yes… is the chauffeur here?' Abdul replied.

'No. You can leave the car just here, inside the compound.'

'Thanks. But I need to collect payment.'

The guard looked irritated. 'Listen, man, we will send you the payment later, everyone is a little busy right now.'

'Oh? Hope everything is all right?'

'Boss's daughter is missing'

He left the repaired car behind and ran home, all the time feeling sick with worry. They should have been at the Jordanian border by now.

As soon as he was home, he booted up his computer. He forced himself to check if the blog revealing Saddam's plan had been published, as many lives hung in the balance. He also wanted to see if there had been any message from Sofia.

It seemed the blog had indeed been published safely. Already, many debates were raging about it online. Abdul did not have the inclination to weigh in on any of them but as he scrolled through the comments, one of them made his blood run cold:

The_Lion_Of_Baghdad_69: I have Sofia. Report to Kadhimiyya Prison tomorrow. We will let her go if you submit yourself and your computers and the password for your blog. If not, she will suffer.

Abdul was absolutely certain that giving himself up would not result in Sofia's release. If it would have, he would have gladly done so. It was simply a ploy to get him too, and then they would both be doomed. There only seemed one course of action open to him. He realised he would rather die than allow Uday to harm the woman he thought of so fondly. Taking the gun he kept under his bed for dire situations such as these, he set off for the café he knew that Uday would drive past as he exited his Palace. That was when he ran into the foreigner, Ava.

In retrospect, he realised he had not been thinking straight. His plan had not been practical and its chances of success, as the foreigner said, were close to none.

After a quick visit to the restroom, Abdul's new friend, Ava, asked if there was a safe place where they could talk. Rafan's house was not far from the café, so they walked towards it, trying to ignore the anti-aircraft guns and armoured vehicles that dotted the streets in preparation for the impending invasion. In stark contrast to the hustle and bustle outside, Rafan had been sleeping when they arrived, as usual.

When he heard the story, Rafan went over to the Englishwoman and wrapped her in a warm bear hug. 'Stupid as he might be, I would have lost my best friend if you had not been there, Ava. I owe you, and Abdul does as well, the stupid bastard. And, speaking of stupid bastards, what brings you to this part of the world at a time like this?'

'I'm a war correspondent for *The Independent*. Got in a few weeks ago. In fact, I'm doing a story on Uday and Qusay.'

Abdul remembered Ava's earlier quip about being shot at while driving away. He remembered the woman's calm demeanour a few seconds before bullets were about to fly. That certainly fit the bill for someone who was a war correspondent, but Abdul sensed that there was more to the lady. Ava simply did not strike him as a journalist. At the same time, there was something about her that made Abdul trust her.

A pot of tea was produced from Rafan's kitchen. Abdul felt a little better as he sipped the warm liquid and slowly told Ava and Rafan about Sofia's capture. He could see Ava's face harden, as he spoke about Uday's misdeeds.

'What a bastard!', she exclaimed when he was done, an expression of pure rage on her face. For a few moments, everyone was silent. Her rage gave way to a look of contemplation. Then, as if she had come to a decision in her mind, she said, 'I have an idea'.

14. Uday

Uday was on top of the world.

Firstly, he had Whistler cornered. Secondly, he still had the girl to look forward to violating in the morning – the fact that he would have an audience at the prison only increased his anticipation of the event tenfold. He would bask in their fear and revel in their pain. There would be anger too, no doubt. But that was good – he would enjoy watching the light fade in all of their eyes as they realised the helplessness of their situation; as they realised his complete dominance over them.

All these happy thoughts made him decide to visit Sofia in the basement again before the morning arrived. A few starters before the main course, he thought as he made his way towards the red room. Patience was not one of his strengths.

He was about to enter the small cell in which Sofia had been imprisoned, when he heard the doorbell of his palace ringing. He wasn't expecting anyone and wondered how anyone had dared to arrive unannounced.

He was furious but restrained himself when he realised that it was one of the two people in Iraq he had to answer to, at least to some extent – his brother Qusay. But he couldn't fathom what on earth his brother was doing in his palace.

Qusay looked uncharacteristically anxious. He simply said, 'CNN. Now,' and disappeared into the hallway.

He had taken the liberty of switching on the television in the living room. An image of a grave-looking George Bush filled the screen, speaking from his podium at the White House.

'Last September, I went to the U.N. General Assembly and urged the nations of the world to unite and bring an end to this danger. On November 8, the Security Council unanimously passed Resolution 1441, finding Iraq in material breach of its obligations, and vowing serious consequences if Iraq did not fully and immediately disarm.'

This was nothing new, Uday thought.

'Today, no nation can possibly claim that Iraq has disarmed. And it will not disarm so long as Saddam Hussein holds power. For the last four-and-a-half months, the United States and our allies have worked within the Security Council to enforce that council's long-standing demands. Yet, some permanent members of the Security Council have publicly announced they will veto any resolution that compels the disarmament of Iraq. These governments share our assessment of the danger, but not our resolve to meet it. Many nations, however, do have the resolve and fortitude to act against this threat to peace, and a broad coalition is now gathering to enforce the just demands of the world. The United Nations Security Council has not lived up to its responsibilities, so we will rise to ours.

'In recent days, some governments in the Middle East have been doing their part. They have delivered public and private messages urging the dictator to leave Iraq so that disarmament can proceed peacefully. He has thus far refused. All the decades of deceit and cruelty have now reached an end. Saddam Hussein and his sons must leave Iraq within 48 hours. Their refusal to do so will result in military conflict, commencing at a time of our choosing. For their own safety, all foreign nationals – including journalists and inspectors – should leave Iraq immediately.'

Uday looked at Qusay, and only then noticed that he was wearing a bulletproof vest under his jacket. Keys to the Jeep parked outside dangled in his other hand.

A realisation dawned on Uday – in precisely 48 hours his palace, a primary target, would be reduced to a smouldering pile of rubble by American jets.

But the House of Saddam had planned for something like this. Palaces could be rebuilt. For now, the important thing was to fall back to one of the many safe houses dotted throughout the countryside.

He would have no time to transfer Sofia to the women's prison from his palace; he wouldn't even have the time to enjoy her.

He, along with his brother and father, were the most wanted men in the world, with the entire might of the American and coalition armed forces against them.

Suddenly, Uday realised that he was no longer aroused.

They were officially at war.

15. Abdul / Ava / Rafan

Bush's announcement had slowly started to become public knowledge in Baghdad, but its spread was hindered by the lack of satellite TV in most households. The United States and Iraq would soon be at war unless Saddam gave himself up – which was about as likely as George Bush being awarded the Nobel Peace Prize.

Ava had heard rumours from journalists in the hotel before the media had trickled out of Iraq. A massive US and coalition military force had collected at the Iraq-Kuwait border, and there were rumours of US parachute regiments being deployed in Northern Iraq. The veteran journalists had explained the obvious next steps to Ava, urging her to leave too. A massive aerial bombardment would precede ground troops entering Baghdad. Even if she somehow avoided the violence, she might be captured by the residual Iraqi government for use as a human shield.

At the time, Ava hadn't taken the warnings too seriously, even though everyone knew war was imminent. The idea of a full-blown war in the hustling and bustling city had seemed unlikely. She had also been clinging to hope she could still find the cars before she got the phone call to evacuate. Now she knew differently. Bush's announcement had not only made it official but had also affixed a timescale to the invasion, making it only too real.

As a safety precaution against being taken by the government, Ava had resolved not to return to her hotel at all – one of Rafan's many guest bedrooms had been put at her disposal. Fahad could take the fall for letting her escape, and besides, they were unlikely to look for her now - Saddam's spies and henchmen had other far more pressing things to worry about. It seemed that whichever way you looked at it, the city would be a smouldering pile of rubble in less than 48 hours.

Abdul's blog revealing Saddam's plans to martyr a group of civilians and journalists had created waves in the international media once it had, been published. And it had caused a stir in Baghdad, too. When Ava shared the warnings she'd been given about being used as a human shield, Abdul told her he was certain that the Baathist Party would have to refrain from carrying out the plan, unless they wanted to be blamed for loss of life and incur a civil war atop the regular war.

Hundreds of innocent people would die when the bombs fell regardless. Collateral damage, they called it. Thousands more would die when the ground forces arrived following the air strikes. Sofia would die horribly at the hands of Uday Hussein, and he would die trying to rescue her. He could not think of a bleaker moment in his life.

Then, in his darkest moment, Ava had an idea.

Surely, the coalition forces' primary goal would be to eliminate the top three people in the government hierarchy – namely, Saddam and his two sons. Perhaps, if coalition forces could be convinced that the Husseins were holed up in one of the palaces, they would divert the first barrage of cruise missiles towards that target in an attempt to bring a swift end to the war. They wouldn't even need to deploy the rest of the cruise missiles if they had decapitated the leadership.

Perhaps, if they did choose such a specific target, the Americans would pause after the initial bombing of the palace to verify if the Husseins had been killed before they carried on with their bombardment plans.

This would buy everyone some more time. It would also, perhaps, create the confusion needed to preoccupy Uday just enough for them to spring Sofia from prison.

'Guys, I have an idea,' Ava said. 'Our press office has a contact in the government. It's nothing special; all publications with journalists on the ground in warzones have one, just in case they come across anything that could be a useful source of intelligence. How about I send them an encrypted email now, urging them to convince the US forces to bomb Uday's palace first? I can say that I've cultivated a reliable source amongst the Husseins' domestic help, who has told me the Husseins are holed up there, making it clear that it would be a great opportunity to wipe out the leadership in one swoop. That might create enough of a diversion for us to go and spring Sofia from prison during the confusion.'

Abdul and Rafan exchanged a glance.

Once again, it struck Abdul that Ava might not be quite who she said she was. But regardless, he wondered if it could work. And why was this woman helping them?

'It's worth a shot,' he said.

Ava didn't have to be told twice. She pulled Rafan's keyboard towards her and logged into her secure email account. She typed out a message that would eventually find its way back to HQ in England, and then, hopefully, to the central command centre of the war in the States.

She sent the message.

None of them knew what to think, really. Would they be able to find Sofia in time and then find safe refuge from the inevitable military action? Would the upcoming invasion work for them or against them? Surely Uday's attentions would be diverted by the war? Anyway, it was time for action.

Abdul took a bag from a shelf in Rafan's garage and filled it with anything that could be used as a weapon – a large spanner, a wrench, an electric torch and a tyre iron. Rafan topped it off with a few bottles of water and a bag of peanuts for sustenance, as well as his hefty Dell laptop, which he never went anywhere without. These were tossed into the back of Rafan's SUV.

Abdul got into the front seat and Rafan sat next to him. Ava sat in the back with the bag of 'weapons'. When they hit a checkpoint, she would have to hide. English women, or indeed any foreigners, were probably on the list of things that Iraqi soldiers had to keep an eye out for.

Their plan was to drive toward the Women's Prison and figure out the next steps when they got there. If they could somehow grab Sofia or bribe their way to her amidst the confusion and chaos of impending war and get out of the city, they may be able to get to safety. It wasn't much of a plan, but it was all they could think of. They set off into the dark streets outside the garage – all the city's streetlamps had been turned off.

The tension on the streets was palpable. Shops and businesses were all clearly shut – most had welded sheet metal or nailed planks of wood over their doors and windows. Some had even been bricked up. The few people who were still outdoors walked quickly with their heads down. Soldiers and police were everywhere. Anti-aircraft guns, which had lain under tarpaulins dotted around the city over the last month, were now gleaming, naked, in the moonlight. Teams of heavily armed soldiers were clustered around each one. Tables and chairs adjoined each outpost and held banks of equipment along with what looked like radar screens.

To Abdul, the measures of resistance he saw on the streets seemed comically futile. He knew about the technology used by American forces, and he had read about the doctrine of 'shock and awe' developed by the US Secretary of Defence. This basically involved bombing the target with tonnes of ordinance, and then, if anything was still alive, sending in ground troops to advance as quickly as possible into the battleground with guns blazing. He remembered laughing aloud when he had read that the strategy was purported to have been created, in part, to reduce civilian casualties. For the millionth time, he tried to recollect why he hadn't packed his bags and left Iraq long ago. He held no romantic patriotic notions about his homeland.

But then he remembered the smell of the trees at dusk. He remembered all his friendly neighbours, who remained stoic and generous with what little they had, even in the face of UN sanctions and Saddam's wars. He remembered the many high-end automobiles he had the opportunity to tinker with in his garage. He remembered his blog. He remembered Sofia, whom he would never have met had he left. No. There were still things worth fighting for.

They sped towards the prison with Abdul at the wheel.

16. Sofia

The little red room in the basement of Uday's mansion would have been suffocating for many people, but Sofia wasn't claustrophobic. Her overriding fear was that of Abdul or her father doing something stupid to rescue her, or even worse, submitting to Uday's demands to give themselves up.

They had taken her in the middle of the afternoon when the sun was high in the sky. It was the break between advanced maths and physics, and she had been strolling to the coffee shop at the corner. Two men had walked up beside her, brandishing guns. They grabbed her shoulders and before she had time to react, threw her into a van with blacked-out windows before speeding away.

When they removed her blindfold, she was in the red room.

She knew instantly who had sent the men, of course. At first, she had been frightened, but she had managed to calm herself down, she had looked around her. All the walls of the room had been painted red, as had the floor and the ceiling. A small hole in the ground served as a toilet. The only piece of furniture in the room was a bed on which there was a mattress and a duvet. Under the duvet, she calmly noted, there was a human skeleton.

Then Uday had made an appearance. He had looked at her ID and somehow made the connection between her and Abdul; she had no idea how. Then, after threatening her, he had left. She knew she should be scared, but somehow, Uday struck her as a slightly comical figure, like a Bond villain. In any case, she knew that worrying wouldn't help her.

And then, she heard a commotion outside. She couldn't hear much after the door to the basement area had been shut, but she could sense a lot of hustle and bustle.

Then it went deadly quiet.

She wondered what on earth was going on. It was almost as if the entire palace had been evacuated.

She waited for several hours before she got impatient and decided to bang on the door. No response. She tried looking through the keyhole but, of course, she could not see anything as the key had been left in the lock.

She sat for hours, taking small sips of water from the bottle left on the floor beside the bed. All the fatigue and anxiety eventually caught up with her and she drifted into a dreamless sleep.

On waking up, she drank some more water and then did some more banging on the door. No response. Now, instead of worrying about Uday walking through the door again, she started to worry if anyone would ever open the door. Panic set in.

That's when she remembered a trick she had read about in a children's novel a long time ago. The hero, having been incarcerated in a small room, had taken a hairpin and pushed the key back out of the lock, which fell onto a sheet of paper that had been slid under the door so the detective could drag the paper back to his side.

Of course, she did not have any paper or a hairpin, and this was reality, not a detective novel.

But she didn't have anything to lose by trying.

She took the duvet cover off and slid it under the door slowly, till a significant portion of it was on the other side, directly below the key. She needed something to slide into the keyhole to jiggle out the key. She gave the room a once over but could find nothing. She looked inside her pockets for the hundredth time. Then she had a brainwave.

She quickly slipped out of her dress, took off her bra and slipped the dress back on. She turned the bra over in her hands and then picked at the stitching – there was a thin and flexible wire inside of it.

Once she had it out, she folded it over several times and slipped it inside the lock, jiggling the key loose, slowly and patiently. After a minute or two, it dropped onto the cloth.

Sofia couldn't believe it had actually worked. She slowly pulled the key back towards her until it touched the door. Then, as she withdrew the cloth into her side of the room, it got left behind as the gap between the floor and the door was too narrow. She was about to despair when she remembered the wire from her bra. Straightening it out again, she made a little loop at the end and slid it under the door. Miraculously, it hooked onto the key and she pulled it under.

She hugged the key to her chest for a moment and then put it inside the lock. She turned it. It worked. She was free.

Cautiously, she looked around the door. No one in sight. She went up the stairs and into the lounge. The huge TV screen had been left turned on but was on mute. She was clearly in Uday's huge palace.

It looked like they had left in a hurry. All the lights were on. The carpets on the floor were aligned and streaked, as if many suitcases had been rolled across them. Someone had knocked over an ornate porcelain vase and hadn't bothered to clean up the mess.

It was cold, and she felt very aware of the fact that her bra was missing. But she was also hungry. She made a beeline for the bar in the corner of the room and found a package of cookies, which she gratefully consumed. She considered having a shot of whisky to calm her nerves but decided against it. She needed her wits about her.

Sofia stared blankly at the television set while eating a cookie, vaguely observing at the back of her mind how funny Bush looked with his large nose. He was making some speech from his perch at the White House. With the volume off, she couldn't tell what it was about, and she was too harrowed to care. A countdown timer in the corner of the newscaster's screen said, '1 hour and 27 minutes to deadline.' The ticker at the bottom mentioned something about air strikes. She didn't think much of it and turned her attention to her immediate surroundings – which were more than she could process under the circumstances. It was so silent; it could have been a tomb.

Slowly, she worked her way through the palace. There was a gym with a lot of equipment that looked unused. The bedroom had a super-king-sized round bed with an ornate golden eagle above it. It seemed to have been modelled on the symbol of the Nazi Party. Sofia wasn't sure what to make of it. In fact, it reminded her of the house of the man her parents had selected for her last year, a wealthy Sunni businessman's son. Her parents had insisted they meet him, and he had received them in the living room of his mansion.

He was courteous enough, but the first question he asked her was what she liked to cook. The second was how many children she would like to have. Sofia, who enjoyed talking about politics, history and literature, did not cook. Neither had she ever thought about children.

'Horse meat,' she replied, 'have you ever tried it? It's even better than pork.' The man's eyes widened. His parents' jaws dropped.

'And as for the children, I would like to have at least three.'

He looked slightly mollified at that.

'But ideally with different husbands. You believe in equality of rights between men and women, don't you?'

That one sealed her fate. Even though everyone laughed at the obvious joke, it was a very strained laugh. She never received any proposals after that. In fact, the men of Baghdad gave her a very wide berth – just as she desired.

However, it also had another unintended consequence. Her parents decided she enjoyed too many freedoms and was far too wild. They doubled down on her restrictions and her traditional upbringing became a downright imprisonment. All her books were taken away; she could only read what she had hidden from her parents. The TV in her bedroom was also disconnected and taken away. None of that bothered Sofia, as her parents still let her keep the computer for 'schoolwork' – their wealth allowed them to buy expensive trinkets for their daughter, without too much of an understanding of how this emerging technology worked. They only had the vaguest idea of what the internet was.

Over the next few months, Sofia seemed to do a whole lot of schoolwork and not much else.

Her father had felt a tinge of guilt, she knew – he had quite enjoyed the rebellious spark in his daughter, who no longer fiercely debated the merits of democracy with him. Perhaps he thought she had become a realist, as he had when he reached adulthood. Perhaps he thought she would now find a good husband. At 18, she was already an adult and most women her age had already been hitched. But she marched to a different drumbeat and had never found anyone she liked. Until she found Whistler's blog, that is.

At first, it was rebelliousness; reading subversive writing under her parent's roof gave her a thrill. But slowly, she realised it was more than that. She could really relate to this person – he seemed like a rational and logical voice when all she ever heard was posturing to the party line and the rare, muted whisper of dissent at school. Soon, she started admiring his bravery in finding a way to speak out. After a few months, she started thinking of what he might look like, how he might behave and what his thoughts were like outside of the writings on his blog. She realised she had a crush on him, despite never having met him.

There was no question of his belief in equality, his derision for all things dogmatic. That was within the very fabric of his words. He was young and well-travelled. That was apparent when he described the music he listened to, and his ability to relate to foreign readers.

When she realised he was the young man in the garage, she was not disappointed. He had kind eyes and a warm smile. He had spoken of reading books, not of cooking and babies.

Then, when she had stolen away to meet him in his apartment, there was a very pleasant sort of tension between them. She could tell he liked her. Despite the gravity of their conversation, or perhaps because of the shared experience, she felt much closer to him. More recently, when she was alone in her room at night, she tried to imagine what it would be like to kiss him. She had certainly felt like doing it when she was at his apartment and they were whispering in each other's ears over the sound of Massive Attack coming from the speakers.

Now that she had been abducted by a known murderer, she wished she had. She worried she may never get another chance. If she did, she resolved she would take it. Perhaps she would do more than kiss him. Life, especially in Iraq, was far too short.

She was shocked back to her present circumstances in Uday's palace when she saw a room that held stacks of pornographic magazines on numerous coffee tables. What looked like medieval shackles lay discarded in a corner. Eventually, she came to what looked like an office containing an executive leather chair and a sturdy oak desk. On it, was a computer and a telephone. Finally, she could send a message letting Abdul know where she was. That way, if she couldn't escape the premises, at least there was some hope of them being reunited.

She tried the phone first, but it seemed the line was dead. This was not uncommon. Over the past few months, the telephones had only worked intermittently, just like the electricity, water and every other public and private service in Iraq.

Then she booted up the computer. She was surprised to see it had no password. But, when she thought about it for a moment, it seemed to make sense considering Uday's arrogant and careless personality.

As she waited for the PC to boot up, she leafed through a leather-bound journal that lay open on the desk. She glanced at the open page. It read:

1068. Ferrari, F40, Location: Saba Abkar Car Park. Condition: Good. Source: Import. Price: 200 gallons, crude.

1069. Ferrari, Modenna, Location: Al Arabi Car Park. Condition: Brakes faulty. Source: Kuwait Team Three 3. Price: None.

1070. Ferrari, Spyder, Location: Gejara Street Car Park. Condition: Fair. Source: Import. Price: $258,000.

On it went up to number 2355 – presumably the number of cars that Uday had in his possession.

She knew Abdul would be interested in the journal if she ever saw him again. She was aware of his passion for cars. She slid it inside a satchel that lay under the table and slipped it around her shoulders.

The wardrobe next to the desk was also left half open and seemed to be filled with packages of white powder and what looked like bottles of vaccination that were labelled 'Zoetis' Fel-O-Vax IV+'.

Finally, the computer fully booted up. She opened the email program to try and send a message but, of course, there was no internet connection – the computer relied on an active phone connection. In any case, she typed out a quick message to Abdul. It would be sent automatically the moment the phone lines were active again.

Suddenly, she heard a sharp and loud whistling sound that seemed to be getting louder, coming from the nearby window. She had scarcely had time to consider what it could be when there was a very loud bang. The office exploded in flames and she was knocked clean off her feet. The force of the explosion hurled her across the room and her flight was stopped only when her head hit the concrete wall.

17. Abdul / Ava / Rafan

They were speeding down the highway, only two minutes away from the women's prison, when the first bombs started to fall. Abdul had his eyes glued to the road, swerving around potholes, people, anti-aircraft guns and anyone who was still foolish enough to be outdoors. The first thing they heard was the scream of missiles as they travelled through the air, fired from invisible F-117 Nighthawk stealth planes, followed by a tremendous bang when the four satellite-guided 2,000-pound GBU-27 'Bunker Busters' hit the ground. Their car shook even though they were miles away from the point of impact.

Then, complete silence.

Even though it was not unexpected, Abdul could feel the six million residents of Baghdad collectively gasp. Instinctively, he knew the city would not survive 50 more of these attacks.

But after the initial barrage subsided, they noticed, not without some satisfaction, two thick columns of smoke wafting out from the general area near Uday's palace. Rafan and Ava looked in all directions but could not spot smoke anywhere else. It seemed Ava's email to her handlers had worked.

They could sense the chaos at the prison even before they parked the car. Two huge anti-aircraft guns were at the entrance to the prison complex, however, it seemed that no one was manning them. Neither were there any prison guards to be seen.

When they walked into the prison, the reception area was completely devoid of any form of authority, aside from one very harried-looking guard, who, for some reason, was not in uniform. He was barking furiously into the telephone he had glued to his ear. Abdul, Rafan and Ava heard part of the hurried Arabic conversation:

'I know I said 7,000 dinars. That was before. Now I don't need bloody useless dinars, I need rations. Flour. Rice. Sheep. Potatoes. Or US dollars. And I need them now, in the next thirty minutes, or I leave your wife to rot behind bars. All the other guards have left already, but I'm still risking my neck by sticking around. You should know, I have orders to flood the prison and drown everyone if the situation deteriorates.' He slammed down the phone and was about to dial another number when he noticed the trio looking at him 'Yes? What do you want?'

'Er… we are looking for a prisoner called Sofia Aziz?'

'Yes,' the guard said immediately, 'anyone asking about Sofia was supposed to be arrested immediately. But as you can see, I have neither the interest nor the means to arrest you. Now, if I were you, I would make myself scarce, very quickly.'

'Thank you, sir,' Abdul said, 'but we can't leave without Sofia. Do you know where she is?'

The guard looked out of the window towards the columns of smoke before he said, 'Rumour has it she was supposed to have been brought here by Uday himself from his palace. He had something nasty planned. Although, something tells me they will not be arriving here at all.' Then, noticing the look of abject horror on their faces, he added, 'You may still be able to get there before the place burns down if you hurry. Uday's probably on the run, and I doubt he's taken your Sofia with him. He's got more important things to worry about now and, to be honest, so have I. Leave.'

The guard didn't have to tell them again. In less than a minute, they were speeding towards the palace, towards the thick grey columns of smoke that spiralled into the heavens.

As they neared, Abdul could see several figures running from the palace – he figured they were members of Uday's staff who had been ordered to stay behind.

It took a lot of courage to keep the SUV pointed in the direction of the palace, knowing it was being used for target practice by American jets. They stared ahead in silent determination as they hurtled closer.

As the car sped forward, it quickly became apparent that the palace had been spared the main impact of the bombs – one had missed the complex entirely, and the other three had hit the palace walls. So much for the satellite-guided accuracy the Americans claimed would prevent the loss of civilian life in times to come. But today, they thanked their stars the bombs had not found their target.

Even though the palace had not taken a direct hit, they could see that some of it was on fire, perhaps due to the embers from the compound walls that had been decimated by the missiles. The fire was clearly spreading. If there had ever been any guards, there weren't any now.

The first obstacle was the huge wrought iron gates of the compound. It was clear they didn't have time to try to unlock them. Abdul glanced at Rafan, who nodded, checking his seatbelt and glancing behind to check if Ava had hers on too. He stepped on the accelerator of the large, reinforced SUV.

The front of the car shattered, the airbags deployed and the SUV was stopped in its tracks. But the car had created a huge gaping hole in the gate.

They got out, went through the bent iron bars and jogged towards the palace. Abdul was wondering how they would get through the front door when he realised it had been left open.

He ran straight through it, Rafan and Ava hot on his heels.

The ornate décor combined with the haze of the smoke and the smell of explosives gave the palace a surreal feel. The temperature also felt significantly higher inside, and the building was clearly losing the battle against the fire. They would have to hurry.

They started shouting Sofia's name but only heard the sound of the flames in return. They would have to search the palace as best they could, and so decided to separate in the interest of time. Ava would take the west wing, Abdul the east and Rafan would search the middle.

The bulk of the damage from the explosions, as well as the fire, was in the east wing. Abdul got to work, being as systematic as possible as he moved from room to room. When he came to a locked door, he took the heavy chairs from the dining table, lifted them above his head and smashed his way through. The urgency of the situation gave him a strength he did not know he had.

Then he reached an oak-panelled room that looked like a study. The room was filled with thick smoke, and Abdul could see flames everywhere. He looked around. And then, he saw her. A wave of relief washed over him.

Sofia lay on the floor in her dress, with a leather satchel around her shoulders. She seemed unconscious.

There was no time to waste, so he dashed towards her and picked her up. That's when another explosion occurred, coming from the rear of the mansion, that rocked the palace down to its foundations. Perhaps a gas cylinder in Uday's kitchen or garage had exploded. Abdul fell over with Sofia in his arms. They landed in a heap on the floor. It must have been the shock of falling down that woke Sofia up. She opened her eyes and found herself in Abdul's arms, on the floor, his face a couple of inches from hers. For a few seconds, she smiled a confused smile. Then she looked beyond Abdul's face, realised where she was and screamed.

Abdul looked around in desperation. Miraculously, an unbroken jug of water sat perched on a table. He stripped off his shirt, drenched it in the water and tore it into two. He wrapped one half around Sofia's face and the other half around his own. Then he picked up the semi-conscious Sofia, threw her over his shoulder and ran down the corridor to the exit.

It had become exceedingly hard to see anything due to the smoke but somehow he managed to make his way back to the living room, all the time shouting for Ava and Rafan.

Thankfully, his friends heard him and emerged from the smoky interior of the house. Rafan ran over and grabbed Sofia, putting one of her arms around his neck as they ran out of the door. But when he saw the ruined BMW they had arrived in, now mangled into the palace gate, Abdul thought they would have to run all the way home.

'Wait here,' Ava said, 'I'll be right back.' Clearly, she had seen something during her search that she thought would help them in some way.

Two minutes later, they heard the roar of a large engine coming to life, and Ava emerged from around the corner in a highly polished two-tone Bentley, presumably part of Uday's collection. Shining in silver and blue, Abdul recognised it as a 1958 S1 Continental, a big and powerful car.

They piled in and Ava pulled away, just as another explosion rocked the ground, coming from the direction of the garage. Shrapnel flew everywhere. Their faces asked questions they couldn't put into words. Another American bomb? A gas cylinder from the kitchen or an extra fuel tank going up in flames? They had no time to find out. Piles of burning rubble lay on the path ahead, along with many purpose-built wooden barriers that had been strewn across the grounds to prevent enemy vehicles from entering.

Abdul and Rafan could immediately see Ava was a very skilled driver. She seemed to know her way around the Bentley, almost as if she had been driving it for many years. She pulled away, driving fast, weaving between the piles of rubble and the wooden barriers at top speed. Soon they were out of the palace grounds and in the street.

Just when they thought they had escaped, a black SUV pulled up behind them. The flag of the Fedayeen was perched on top of it. The tinted window rolled down and a hand with a machine gun emerged. A stream of fire erupted from the gun, sending bullets slamming into the body of the car. The side mirrors of the Bentley disintegrated into a thousand fragments.

Ava did not hesitate; her foot was firmly pressed to the floor. She had never driven a vintage Bentley Continental before but felt quite at home. She had driven many exotic sports cars for the first time in difficult situations, usually trying to get away from whomever she had stolen it from. But this time, the consequences of failure wouldn't be a cushy prison cell in England. Capture would mean certain death. Not her death – if the Fedayeen were wise, they would keep her as a hostage. But they would certainly kill the others whom she had gotten to know over the last couple of days. She had to get them away from danger.

Ava felt that her whole life had been a training session for this moment, although, if someone had told her she would be racing a vintage Bentley through a war zone in Iraq she would never have believed them.

Her focus was absolute, and even though she was going at over 100 miles an hour, she felt as if everything was in slow motion. In a split second, she took in a thousand little details about the path ahead: the debris and potholes to avoid, the roadblocks, the closed side streets and parked military vehicles. As she had done in her racing days, she was so focussed on gaining distance that she didn't even bother to look at the car behind her. She desperately wanted to ask Abdul and Rafan for directions, it was their city after all. But she was concentrating so hard that she didn't dare make the effort to open her mouth and ask a question.

She coaxed every bit of speed that she possibly could out of the 4.9-litre Rolls-Royce engine. The debris on the road was another problem. The suspension and the undercarriage were already ruined, she was sure of that, but she just hoped the car would hold together until they reached safety.

Thankfully, Abdul realised Ava did not know where she was going and started directing her. The plan was to get onto a long and straight stretch of road that Abdul and Rafan knew to be smooth and well-made. This would give them a definite advantage over the SUV, and they could leave their assailants in the dust.

They wove through the obstructions on the road, and, for a while, it seemed like they would actually make it. Ava was cornering very sharply, expertly drifting around buildings on the narrow streets, and getting the huge car back under control when the rear tires slid out a bit more than intended. Their pursuers didn't stand a chance, and the gap widened until they eventually disappeared.

The tyres kicked up a thick fog of dust and dirt, churned up due to weeks of neglect by the government sanitation team. Then they made an especially sharp turn, which Abdul had estimated would bring them onto a main road that had not been bombed.

They turned the corner with such force that if they hadn't been wearing seatbelts, they would have all smashed into one side of the car. Suddenly Ava slammed the brakes. At first, Abdul, Sofia and Rafan had no idea why. Then, when the dust cleared, they realised that a manned roadblock lay ahead, and the barrel of an anti-aircraft gun was pointed directly at their car.

18. Uday

There were many things that Uday could do well but running away and being scared were not on that list. The only time that he could recollect being genuinely frightened was when he had angered his father by murdering one of his men due to a disagreement, the cause of which he could hardly recall today.

Saddam had put him in a cell for 40 days before slowly letting him integrate back into aspects of family and government life. As further punishment, Saddam had burned 50 of his sons' cars in an underground garage.

He recalled the incident with bravado rather than fear – that bastard he killed had gotten what was coming to him. Father had been upset, true, but he had gotten over it.

Even now, in the nondescript Fiat with his older brother Qusay, Qusay's 14-year-old son, Mustafa and a bodyguard, Uday did not feel scared. They carried with them a small arsenal and they were well protected by the Fedayeen who followed behind in unmarked vehicles. US ground forces were still miles away. There was no way that US forces could possibly know where they were in order to target them.

The bombs had started to fall – the first target had been his palace. All the other palaces, ministries, Baathist Party buildings, all known government buildings and, indeed, any building likely to have been bombed had all been evacuated long ago. When Bush's announcement had been made, they left the palaces to meet with their father one last time before parting ways with him.

They had known this day would come, of course. They had planned for it as well as they could. Many safe houses, scattered all over the country, had been pre-selected for them. Now it was a matter of staying on the move, light and fast, while remotely encouraging the Fedayeen fighters on mobile and radio communications. Qusay would do the same with his Republican Guard and the Iraqi Army – he was on the phone now, the steering wheel in his other hand and a map laid out in his lap – it sounded like he was asking a battalion leader to move troops to a new location.

Uday's Fedayeen militia was comprised of individuals who had been hand-picked for being fanatically loyal. These individuals were then further educated by one of his father's most trusted imams, whose objective it had been to convince each pupil of his holy duty to fight to the death against the foreign aggressors or anyone against the royal family. If they succeeded in this endeavour, they would receive their reward in heaven. They were cheap to train, self-motivated and completely expendable. Convenient, really.

Uday had never claimed to be the most intelligent person, but even he could not fathom how people could possibly be stupid enough to believe in the rhetoric, much less give up their lives for it.

The official objective of the militia, was to maintain internal security in Iraq and defend the Royal family. Unofficially it had been created as a counterbalance to the

Republican Guard. However, Uday had decided very early on to use them to advance his own causes.

The official party line, across the board, was 'fight till victory, or fight till death.' Uday thought hoping for victory was foolish; he did not share in the delusions of his father and brother. He had no intention of dying – he was even going to keep the fighting part to a minimum for himself, if possible. After all, there were so many imbeciles who were only too happy to do so on his family's behalf. He was the commander of the forces – he needn't dirty his hands.

Even his brother, usually pragmatic and the voice of reason among the two of them, seemed intent on fighting to the death. He did not seem to have any fall-back plan for himself or his son.

For once, Uday did have a plan.

When the time came, he would reach out to Kasim, whom he had trained to contact a Jordanian man who had been on the US payroll for years. This man would approach his contact in the US chain of command and broker a deal for his safe surrender.

If he could somehow get immunity from trial, he would be happy to give up his brother, Qusay, and any other government personnel he happened to know the whereabouts of. In this way, he would escape death. His father would be deeply shamed by his actions, more so than ever before, but since when did he care about that? There was a good chance his father would be dead anyway.

Uday would have no regrets about selling his family to the American forces.

In fact, the only regret he had – and it was a big one – was that he had instructed his commanders in the Fedayeen to burn his entire collection of cars as soon as coalition troops set foot in the city. If he couldn't have them, no one would.

That was the hardest thing he had ever done in his life. It had taken him decades to amass the collection, which he considered to be the largest and the most valuable in the entire world – it had always been his biggest brag, his proudest claim.

He would find a way to live with the collection being destroyed, for he did not care much about automotive history or destroying objects of beauty, even if some of them were the only surviving models of their kind. Because what he simply wouldn't be able to cope with, would be the collection – *his* collection – falling into someone else's hands.

His other major regret was the fact that he had missed out on having fun with the girl from the market. He had left her locked in the red cell, he recollected. He could, of course, have let her go before he left himself. But again, if he couldn't have her, why should anyone else, least of all that bastard, Whistler?

Fuck them all.

That was just how he rolled.

19. Abdul / Ava / Rafan / Sofia

The moment they saw the Iraqi National Guard's anti-aircraft gun, they knew it was all over. There was no room to swerve around it; concrete barricades surrounded the huge, mounted gun. These barriers had been placed in strategic locations, each with a crew of about 10 soldiers. The encampment covered the entire space between two buildings.

Abdul took in the set-up, desperately searching his mind for ideas on how to pass. That's when he realised the soldiers were looking confused. Even though he could not hear what they were saying, he noticed a heated exchange between the man at the trigger of the massive gun, and another soldier of similar rank. They both looked conflicted. Why hadn't they been shot or ordered out of the car yet?

Then the penny dropped.

They were driving a car that every man, woman and child in Iraq knew could only have belonged to Uday Hussein. And since the windows were so strongly tinted, the soldiers did not know who was inside the car. As far as the soldiers knew, it could have been the crown prince of Iraq, Uday Hussein himself, and they would lose their jobs and possibly their lives for pointing a gun at him. Or it could be one of Uday's close friends – how else would someone be able to get their hands on that car? Of course, the erratic way in which the car had turned the corner might have suggested that something was amiss – but the first-born son of Saddam was known precisely for his erratic behaviour, especially when behind the wheel of one of his sports cars.

The Fedayeen in the SUV behind them would catch up any second now and they would be trapped between the two military forces. They had to make themselves scarce, and quickly too.

As this thought occurred to him, he noticed one of the armed soldiers was cautiously approaching the car. At the same time, he noticed something that looked like a handheld radio perched on the dashboard of the Bentley – the kind where you have to press a button to talk. He spotted a wire from the handset that disappeared behind the dashboard. On an impulse, he picked it up, pressed the red button with his hand, and coughed into it.

An amplified version of his cough emerged from under the bonnet of the car and boomed across the street.

The soldier stopped in his tracks and looked nervously at the car, one hand on the butt of his holstered pistol. Then a high-pitched voice suddenly pierced the air.

'Are you mad? Do you dare to stop the prince of Iraq? Get out of my way you fools. And be quick about it. Now! Now, god dammit, now!'

Even though the soldiers could not have been sure it was Uday, the voice seemed to fit the description of the son of their commander-in-chief. It sounded like Uday sounded on TV. They had no reason to doubt it. After all, there was only one two-tone Bentley in Baghdad.

After a moment of hesitation, the soldiers scrambled to move the concrete barriers. It took all the strength of 10 soldiers to move one of the barriers, which left just enough room for the car to scrape through. As soon as the barrier was moved, Ava stomped on the accelerator and the Bentley lurched through the narrow gap.

Just then three black SUVs came speeding around the corner. A member of the Fedayeen jumped out waving his arms, but it was too late. The gap in the barrier was not wide enough for their SUVs, and by the time the soldiers had recovered from their shock and helped the team of Fedayeen to move the barriers, the Bentley was long gone.

***

Baghdad had always been far too politically unstable to go without a bomb shelter, Abdul remembered thinking at some point during the Iraq-Iran war. Evidently, Saddam had thought the same thing, and the government had given loans to anyone who wanted to build shelters on their own property at the time.

Luckily, the garage he had bought had come with a basement. Over the years, with the help of a government loan, Abdul had worked on the little room until he was happy with it – re-enforcing the walls and ceilings enough to withstand the weight of the small building on top of it, and then some. It had basic plumbing, electricity and, most importantly, an efficient electric ventilation system, with a backup secondary system. He put in a sofa bed, painted the walls and topped it off with a framed black and white poster of a Mercedes Benz 300SL, shot from the rear, with its gull wings opened out – one of the most beautiful cars ever made, in his opinion. Candles, canned food, water, his computer and several good books were added.

A crate of beer and two bottles of scotch went in the corner. Lots of booze and no windows. The perfect bomb shelter, Abdul thought.

Today, Abdul was glad he had the room. The bombing of Uday's palaces had only provided a brief lull in the aerial campaign, after which it had re-started with gusto. Two houses on his street had been reduced entirely to rubble. They had, unfortunately, happened to be near a government building, which was clearly the target. Many other buildings on the street were missing walls, windows or doors. Automatic gunfire had become a constant part of the background noise.

Everyone had known the war was coming for a while, yet, when it finally came, it seemed almost surprising. Even though everyone had stocked up and secured their premises, no one had really wanted to believe that their city would come under attack. For Abdul, Ava, Rafan and Sofia, it reminded them how fleeting life could be.

Rafan had dropped Sofia and Abdul off at the Garage so they could take refuge in the bunker, before driving himself and Ava to his own house, where there was more room to hide and take apart the bullet-riddled Bentley. Rafan had his own bunker.

Abdul opened the garage door and then the trapdoor in the floor. He let Sofia climb down first before he shut it and drove an SUV he had been fixing over the square in the floor. Then he rolled underneath the big car. The trap door opened just far enough for him to wriggle into the basement bunker.

Sofia was sitting on the sofa bed staring into space, as the adrenalin dissipated. Grey soot covered her face, and her clothes were charred from the fire in Uday's palace. When he handed her a glass of water, he noticed her hands were still shaking. He returned to the fridge to collect another for himself and it briefly crossed his mind that he may not have a fridge for long as electricity might soon be cut off. He looked at his hands, only to realise they were shaking too.

He went to the basin in the corner of the bunker and soaked the corner of a towel with water. Bringing it back, he gently wiped the soot away from her face, working his way down to her neck. Under her dress, her shoulder was badly grazed, perhaps due to the fall in the palace.

'Are you OK?'

She nodded. 'I think so,' she said, finally coming out of her trance. 'I wouldn't have been OK if you hadn't come to look for me. I still don't know how you managed to find me. But I'm glad you did.'

'No problem,' he smiled and told her about how he had met Ava, their successful but mistaken attempt to re-direct the bombing to Uday's palace, and the women's prison. Her eyes widened when he told her he was going to attempt to shoot Uday in the market. For some reason, Abdul thought she looked lovelier than ever; her tousled hair fell over her soot-stained face and her torn clothes.

'You're crazy. Could you clean my shoulder? It stings.'

'Yeah,' he said, slipping the towel under the wide neck of her ragged dress. She realised the angle wouldn't work. And she needed to get out of these burned clothes.

'You have a spare shirt somewhere here, don't you?' she asked, slipping the dress over her head, and wrapping the bedsheet around herself, almost in one fluid motion.

Abdul brought out a bottle of anti-septic and dabbed her shoulder with the clean part of the towel. She turned her head towards him.

'When I came over to your place the first time, to tell you about the files I found in Baba's study, that wasn't the only reason I came over, you know.'

'What was the other reason?' he asked, daring to hope.

'I thought you were cute,' she said, smiling shyly. 'Besides, I haven't met anyone else in Iraq who likes Stephen King.'

Abdul smiled. To his surprise, he leaned forward and put his lips on hers. She kissed him back with a desperation neither of them had expected. But then, nothing that day had been as expected.

Suddenly, everything else disappeared and they were the only two people in the world. He drank in her smell, smoke and all, revelled in the feeling of her soft hair on his face and the sweet taste of her mouth. They fell back onto the sofa bed, and Abdul put his arms around her as they kissed, their bodies pressed together.

He could feel her chest on his through his thin t-shirt. She held him even closer, straddling his thighs with hers. Suddenly, the cotton barrier between them no longer seemed tolerable, they both reached for his shirt at the same time, tugging it over his head.

His mouth travelled to her ear. He kissed her earlobe. Tracing his lips against her skin, he explored her neck. As she gasped with pleasure and excitement, his lips went further south, until they reached the valley formed between her breasts, down her stomach and between her legs.

She moaned softly, every sound turning him on even more, spurring him on to caress her harder, to consume her, to drink her in, like a tall, cool glass of apricot juice on a hot summer's day.

As the bombs fell outside, they had never been happier.

***

Then, two weeks after the bombing of Baghdad, US troops began to flood the city and a deadly game of hide and seek between the Fedayeen and the US Army commenced, with both sides treating all of Baghdad as their playground.

Sporadic machine-gun fire and explosions could be heard throughout the city. Most Baghdadis thought it was best to stay out of their way and let them get on with it; the sooner the idiot Fedayeen were exterminated, the sooner they could all get on with their lives.

The Americans were mostly quite friendly, as long as they were sure that you didn't belong to one of the many insurgent organisations that formed part of the resistance. However, there had been instances when they had not been sure, and the results had been dire. 'Shoot first and ask questions later' seemed to be the policy for some of them. Not for the first time, Abdul had to weigh up what he wanted more – the ousting of Saddam and subsequently the possibility of democracy or not being bombed or shot to death.

The war re-aligned Sofia's priorities. She told her mother about Abdul, and that she was spending the war in his bomb shelter, rather than their family's plush underground facility. Her father had disappeared without telling anyone where he had gone – a wise move as a senior Baathist Party official in Saddam's inner circle. Given the circumstances, it was best that no one knew where he was, especially his loved ones.

At first, her mother had been angry, but she calmed down when she realised Abdul had Sofia's best interests at heart, and that he knew what he was doing in terms of supplies and precautions. This was highlighted by the fact that Abdul's ventilation system was functioning perfectly when the expensive German system in the Aziz family basement had already started to malfunction.

Abdul sealed the deal when he risked his life by making his way over to the Aziz household to fix the system. He returned to the basement laden with chocolates and cooking supplies that had been forced upon him, as well as a bag of Sofia's clothes and belongings.

Sofia's mother also realised that, as higher-ups in Saddam's government, their home might be a target – it was sure to be under surveillance, either by the coalition forces or by Saddam's people keeping an eye out for traitors. It was safer that Sofia spent the war with someone else who cared for her. So, as it was a matter of life and death, she swallowed her traditional values and made do with phoning Abdul's bomb shelter for as long as the phone lines were active – which wasn't very long. Within days of the first bombs landing, you could only get through to people occasionally, and even then, only if both parties belonged to the same telephone exchange.

The Iraqi state TV channels were still running – footage of Saddam greeting ministers and drinking tea with his council was aired almost daily as if to show that he was still alive and well. The Information Minister came on screen daily too, assuring the people of Iraq that there were no American soldiers in Baghdad yet. However, on the next channel, Al Jazeera, there were shots of American soldiers clearly inside the city, almost everywhere in fact.

The internet service had long since been disconnected. In fact, the last email he received had been a very strange one indeed. It had been from a random email address he did not recognise, and it was in Arabic. It read:

Do not resist the American forces, it said, they are your friends. Do not store weapons in your house or go near where weapons are stored. Stay in your homes and don't shelter government forces or venture near government buildings. The Americans will not harm you.

Then, nothing. Complete ISP silence. Someone had pulled the plug as soon as that email had been sent out. Abdul had heard similar leaflets were being air-dropped on cities in Iraq, and some had claimed to hear a similar message on the radio and even over phone lines when receivers were lifted to make calls. Super spooky. But Abdul was inclined to listen to the advice and stay at home. The trips he had made outdoors since the start of the war had been exciting enough.

It seemed that the army had just vanished into thin air. Iraqi soldiers literally got out of their army vehicles, took off their uniforms and left their posts, walking home to their families. They had no interest in fighting at all, in part because they hadn't been paid for the last four months. Of the many insurgent organisations, only a few Baathist Party members and the crack-pot Fedayeen with their death wish remained active, forming some semblance of resistance.

The night before, the bombs had been dropping again, when Rafan and Ava were visiting.

Ava had long since told them the truth about her past as a car thief, and how she had been recruited to work for the government. The Iraqi trio accepted this; Ava was one of them now – they did not know how they could ever repay her for her role in Sofia's rescue. It was too late for her to leave Baghdad now and, in any case, she was still clinging to the thought of stealing the cars, although those hopes grew dimmer and dimmer by the day. She even jokingly mentioned this to Abdul and Rafan. As Iraqi car-nerds, there was a good chance that they might have known the whereabouts of the two ultra-valuable vintage Mercedes – but alas, that was not the case.

With four people inside the bomb shelter, it seemed a bit crowded. But they were glad they were all together. Rafan brought along a crate of nuts and tinned fruit from the seemingly inexhaustible stockpile in his large house. Ava was also glad to see Sofia again – the two women, despite their vastly differing backgrounds, had a lot in common beyond their obvious inclination to colour outside the lines.

Abdul wondered how many other bomb shelters held such an eclectic mix of individuals – rich and poor, Sunni and Shia, Western and local. War was awful and mostly tore people apart but, sometimes, it did bring people together.

The pattern of the bombings seemed to consist of the wail of a high-speed aircraft, then a whistling sound and, finally, a loud bang before the sound of the aircraft resumed once more. It was impossible to think or do anything amidst the sound of that din, especially the time between the wail and the bang, as you were left wondering if the approaching bomb had your name on it. And then, all you did was wait in anticipation of the next wail and wonder how far away the last explosion was. Everyone's nerves were frayed, their minds ready to tip over from survival to sheer insanity.

'This is so fucked up,' Ava announced. 'How can they possibly refer to this as Operation Iraqi Freedom?'

'I think they mean freedom in a more philosophical sense,' said Rafan. 'The same way that when you're dead, you're free from the shackles of life. That kind of freedom.'

'It does sound like whoever named the operation was trying just a little too hard to sound altruistic,' said Abdul.

'Well, they couldn't possibly call it Operation Fuck Shit Up In Iraq. That's not quite as PR friendly, in my humble opinion.,' retorted Rafan.

'My dad was a solder,' Ava found herself telling them, partially to her own surprise. 'In the 1960s, he was sent to Aden.'

'Was it as fucked as this?' asked Sofia.

'I don't know, but when he came home, he was in a deep depression. The only time he seemed a bit alive was when he was behind the wheel of his E-Type.'

'Nice!' chimed Abdul and Rafan at the same time.

'In fact, I didn't realise the level of his fucked-up-ness at the time. One day, when we were out for a drive, he told me why he was depressed. Said that I had a right to know what had fucked him up, why he was behaving the way he was.'

'What was it?' asked Sofia.

'He shot a child by mistake, during a raid. Told me the child was my age. Even looked like me, just a bit darker, he said. The father of the child was there too. Dad said the father looked like he loved his daughter as much as he loved me. Told me not to forget that. That he loved me.'

Everyone was quiet.

'That was our last evening together. The next day, he hung himself. And that is why I hate war.'

No one moved or said anything for a few seconds.

Tears were flowing down Sofia's face as she looked at Ava. Rafan and Abdul were trying very hard not to be visibly upset and were failing miserably. All three of them got up and ensconced Ava in a hug.

Suddenly, to everyone's surprise, Ava stood up, opened the hatch of the shelter and went out. They were starting to worry, when she popped her head through the hatch again. 'Grab this stuff, will you?' she said, lowering Abdul's speakers and amplifier through the hatch.

Next, she connected the system to a portable music player she produced from her bag. Loud jazz filled the basement shelter. The sound of trumpets all but completely drowned out the explosions, and the upright bass drowned out most of the machine gun fire. Only explosions from heavy ordnance could be heard above the music.

Next, Ava brought out the whisky. 'I propose a drinking game,' she said. 'It's quite simple – every time a bomb falls, we do a shot.'

No one disagreed.

That's when Rafan brought out a plastic bag saying, 'I have been saving this for a special occasion. I think now is the time.' It turned out to be a piece of hashish.

He proceeded to roll a small joint, and everyone had a puff or two. Ava turned the music up louder still, and soon they couldn't hear a thing happening outside their four walls, which had become filled with smoke.

They had about four shots each before they started to think that the bombs were almost in tune with the music, and the cymbals seemed to go off immediately after the sound of explosions.

Hours passed and, for the first time in a while, their troubles started to feel just a little bit distant. They started to relax a bit and chat about random subjects.

Abdul was describing, in detail, how it was theoretically possible to produce a completely electric supercar in the next 10 years when Sophia suddenly remembered the leather journal she had picked up from Uday's desk – the one that listed all the cars. It was still in her satchel.

'Oh, I totally forgot, I think I have something that might interest you guys,' she said. 'I was in Uday's office when I picked up this journal. It has the names of all his cars inside it. I know you guys were talking about Uday's cars. Wanna see?'

She had been expecting a reaction, but certainly not to this magnitude – all three of her friends' jaws had dropped at exactly the same time.

20. Rameez

Rameez was sitting in a darkened room on the outskirts of Baghdad. His well-built frame was hunched over a rickety table strewn with wires, hand tools and various large jars that held nuts and bolts, nails, screws and even ball bearings. A bare light bulb shed a narrow circle of light over his desk. Every now and then, he stopped whatever he was doing and stroked his voluminous beard or adjusted the rimless glasses that sat perched on his nose. He had to proceed with caution, even though he had done this several times before.

The furnishings in his house were sparse, cobbled together from various bits and bobs he could salvage from the rubbish he found outside wealthy homes. He had always been thrifty. He needed to be. After all, he had eight mouths to feed – seven children and one wife, all asleep in a single room upstairs.

As Rameez worked his mind drifted to other things. Rather than distracting him, this, in fact, helped him to concentrate. What he was doing was meditative. He thought of his career in the Fedayeen over the last three years. The force had been created as a counterbalance to the Republican Guard and reported directly to the royal family, bypassing the military chain of command.

Even though he had risen through the ranks, this was not a job that paid. People joined the fedayeen for two reasons – power to do as one pleased without fear of the law, or loyalty to the regime and to Iraq. Rameez belonged firmly to the latter group.

Two weeks ago, a man of his position in the Fedayeen would not have been hiding out at home, constructing improvised explosive devices. That would have been taken care of at a large facility in the next town, with proper equipment, systems and expert supervision. However, even though the bomb factory churned out dozens of IEDs every day, they lacked a crucial element – creativity. To be a good bomb maker, you had to be creative. You also had to know what you wanted to achieve, in what sort of geography and at what time.

Now, of course, the bomb factory was shut. It had, in fact, been bombed.

But then what hadn't been? Shock and awe had been difficult for all Iraqis – many thousands of people lay dead in the streets, in houses, in shops and American detention facilities. Basically, everywhere besides the morgue. The number of dead that would fit there was a tiny fraction of the total, but whoever was supposed to be running it had locked up the premises and vanished.

He did not feel pity for the common Iraqi, his fellow man. In fact, he did not feel much pity or respect for anyone who didn't fight the war against the invaders. The fact that it was a losing battle was beside the point – it was their duty to do so.

Of course, if the leader of the Fedayeen – Uday Hussein – had run away with his tail between his legs, how could he have expected his followers to do better? No one had really expected Uday to lift a gun in the heat of battle, utter a war cry and run towards the bullets. That had been clear from the outset. Unlike Saddam, thought Rameez, Uday was completely and totally devoid of any moral fortitude. In fact, Rameez absolutely detested Uday. He hated him with every iota of his being.

However, this time, he was preparing for a direct order by Uday, one that he himself believed in.

Uday had stated that in the event of the city falling, when defeat might seem certain, the Fedayeen were responsible for destroying his car collection. Uday's motives were purely selfish – if he couldn't have the cars, then no one could.

However, the exercise was cloaked in an aura of selflessness – Uday was willing to 'sacrifice' his prized collection to prevent it from falling into the hands of the enemy. Rameez would have gladly destroyed the cars even without the order – he hated them with a passion too. They stood for everything he was against: unnecessary luxury, opulence and Western corruption.

There were approximately 15 different car parks where Uday's cars were located, and each one had been assigned to a particular Fedayeen leader to destroy. Rameez was proud to have been assigned the most prestigious one, located in Saddam's Al-Sijood complex.

His mind snapped back to the task at hand. He went through a mental checklist. Making a bomb when they still had the factory had been easy; there were prescribed routines and formulas to follow. However, the bomb being created today, in his home, was not a run-of-the-mill job.

An improvised explosive device usually has five components: a switch or activator, a trigger or fuse to set off the device, a battery if required by the trigger mechanism, explosives and a container to hold everything together.

Recently, his team at the bomb factory had become fairly sophisticated, using infrared triggers, motion sensors, lasers and various step-on triggers. The explosive itself differed according to the objective of the bomb.

Initially, he had thought of simply dousing the car park with petrol and using a conventional incendiary bomb made with kerosene, but that would not have done a thorough job of destroying some of the solid, old German automobiles. And Rameez was nothing if not thorough.

This particular bomb would be packed primarily with a substance called thermite, made from aluminium and ferric oxide. It took very high temperatures to ignite, but when alight, it could burn through solid steel. Thermite was particularly effective in enclosed spaces, creating an intense burst of heat and high temperature. It was used during World War Two to burn through heavy armour plates, so would have no trouble destroying a fleet of cars in an underground parking lot. It might even be adequate to bring the entire building down atop the underground garage. Now, that would be thorough.

This particular device was the last one of nine others that Rameez had built for the task, to be placed strategically in the area to be destroyed. However, it was the most important one as it contained the trigger mechanism to set off all of them. As thermite required extremely high temperatures to ignite, traditional fuses could not be used. This bomb would carry a magnesium strip, created specially from a large stock of sparklers, one of the most common hand-held fireworks available.

As he finished and carefully put away the device, alongside its eight other siblings, he thought the sparkler fuse was especially fitting.

After all, this would be a celebration.

21. Abdul / Ava / Rafan / Sofia

Rafan had been drinking a beer when Sofia had produced the journal, but now most of it was all over his shirt. Ava looked sceptical. Abdul's mouth was agape.

'Why didn't you tell us about this journal before?' exclaimed Abdul.

'Hmm… Let's see… Because I was still recovering from escaping a kidnapping, a bombing, a fire and a high-speed car chase?' Sofia replied.

'Well, show it to us!'

Sofia went to the corner in which she had piled her things, disappeared behind the shawl hung up on a clothesline which had been installed for privacy and rummaged around. Eventually, she returned with a large leather-bound journal. 'Are you looking for anything specific?' she asked.

'Yes!' they replied in unison and told her about the 540k. They did not, at this point, mention that Ava had wanted to steal it.

She put it on the rickety dining table of their bunker and opened it to the first page. Each line on the ruled page held the manufacturer, model, registration number, location and, finally, the cost of the cars. The first page, which had 45 lines on it, consisted only of E-Class Mercedes Benz cars. The next page had more 1990s Mercedes. Then the next page had a number of Porsches. All in all, there were close to a hundred pages that had writing on them in the journal. They realised they would have to go through every single line until they found the 540k Special Roadster, the jewel in the crown.

They took it in shifts. A large pot of coffee was brewed and a flat stick served as a ruler, so they could go line by line. Halfway through, Abdul decided he may have missed the car and started again. This time, he ticked each car off as he read the name. He read aloud so that Sofia, Rafan and Ava could hear too. There were a few low whistles when he went past the Ferrari and Alfa Romeo section. But still, no 540k.

Soon he reached the end of the journal. Sofia took over and repeated the process, just to be sure. She realised that there was more to the story than her friends had told her, but she didn't ask. There had to be a reason why they had put so much effort into going through the journal to identify the car, more than the mere fact of ascertaining if Saddam or Uday had owned it.

But no luck. It just wasn't to be found. After spending about six hours searching through the journal, they decided it definitely wasn't there. Sorely disappointed, they put it away and went to bed.

When they woke up the next morning, they all felt the aftereffects of their drinking game, followed by the excitement of Sofia's discovery of the journal and the crash of disappointment when the 540k wasn't listed. But still, they had to make the most of it – they had their health and they had their friendship. Things could certainly have been worse. A hearty breakfast was cooked up by Abdul. Sofia asked them why they had been so keen to find the 540k and Ava told her all about the legendary car.

The hours they spent in the basement bunker turned into days, and they found ways to amuse themselves. Abdul started making complex technical drawings of machines. No one was sure what sort of machines they were, least of all Abdul himself. Ava started whittling little cars from a piece of wood and cut open her finger which had to be tightly bandaged. The bombs still fell. The machine guns kept firing.

They did their best to forget the cars, but they were never very far away from any of their minds. One day, they were sitting in a circle, drinking the last of the bottled beer in Abdul's house and debating how long they would have to put up with the armed conflict around them. Abdul explained why he thought it would be a matter of years and not months and Ava listened attentively, peeling the label off her bottle – a habit she had developed in her student years.

Suddenly Abdul stopped talking and looked at Ava's bottle, with the label half removed.

'What's the matter?' Sofia asked, sounding alarmed.

Instead of answering, he responded with a question. 'Can I have Uday's journal, please?'

He looked so serious, that Sofia fetched it without persisting with her questions. Abdul laid it on the table and turned to the last page, which had no writing on it at all. However, the inside of the leather-clad back cover of the book was also ruled, which seemed slightly odd. Abdul put his fingernail under the corner of the last page, which seemed to have been stuck on the hardback cover. He managed to prise it loose, just a little. Then he got a knife from the counter and slid it between the page and the hardcover, slowly working it free. It could be nothing, of course, he thought. The journal might have been designed that way, with the last page, stuck on the leather cover of the book. Or it may have gotten stuck due to heat and pressure. It took him a whole ten minutes to work the whole page free. He turned the page open, expecting to see a blank sheet of paper.

Instead, he saw six lines of child-like writing in pencil.

Each line held a description and location of only the rarest of rare vintage sportscars and their location:

> Mercedes-Benz Special Roadster 540k – Al-Sijood Compound
> Mercedes-Benz Tourenwagon 770k – Al-Sijood Compound
> 1935 Duesenberg SSJ – Al-Sijood Compound
> 1931 Bugatti Royale Kellner Coupe – Al-Sijood Compound
> 1939 Alfa Romeo 8C 2900B Lungo Spider – Al-Sijood Compound
> 1957 Ferrari 250 Testa Rossa – Al-Sijood Compound

The four of them stared at the page, mouths agape. No one said a word. They were all too stunned to react.

But Ava asked the million-dollar question. 'So, can someone tell me, where the fuck Al Sijood is?'

'That makes sense,' Rafan said, 'Al Sijood is one of the eight original palaces Saddam built. It's in the south of Baghdad, on the north banks of the Tigris. Quite a pretty building, with lavish grounds and a big turquoise dome. It's the Hussein administration's nerve centre – both Uday and Qusay's palaces are near it too.'

'It makes sense that the cars are there as it's highly protected,' said Abdul. 'Of course,' he said hesitantly, 'it's probably empty now due to the bombing campaign – likely a key target. I wonder if the cars are still there.'

'Only one way to find out,' said Abdul. 'Let's go check it out.'

Sofia looked a bit dubious as she glanced at the trapdoor, from which the muffled sounds of bombs could still be heard. 'Are you sure it's worth the risk?'

Ava picked up the journal and looked at the page listing the cars thoughtfully. A moment later, she looked up and said, 'Forty-six million. That's the total prize if we manage to get just two of these cars to Jordan. Split four ways, assuming you're all interested, that comes to twelve million each. It's worth the risk for me,' she said definitively, looking at her three friends.

'OK,' said Sofia sensibly. 'We know the prize. Now let's calculate the risk. First, we have to figure out what the conditions are like outside the bunker – nothing is worth dying for, however precious. Secondly, we have to figure out how we are going to get to Al Sijood, which is all the way across town, without getting into a gunbattle. Then, I suppose, we may have to break in, or even create a diversion that is big enough to distract anyone still guarding the building.'

Ava smiled, 'I like the way you think. That's a good idea, depending on the situation. I would propose we simply watch the building for as long as possible first – who's going in, who's coming out, how they are armed.'

Rafan looked thoughtful.

'Then we have to locate the cars and somehow escape with them. We can't assume they are in a driveable condition, although, I'm willing to bet we have enough mechanical expertise amongst the three of us to get them running, at least briefly. Still, I think it's obvious, but we cannot drive pre-war machinery across the country given all the violence out there.'

Abdul had been quiet, using his computer while listening to the others talk. One window held architectural drawings, the other a spreadsheet with calculations. 'I have an idea,' he said. 'It's a bit unorthodox, but I know how we can get away with all the cars intact. But, even then, we will likely still need some help to get away with our bounty – this project may require more than just the four of us.'

Sofia jumped back into the conversation. 'Why don't we take it step by step? See where we get to? I don't know about you guys but if I sit here any longer, I'm going to go crazy.'

So, with absolutely no belief that they could pull it off, not quite believing they would even try, and because they literally had nothing better to do, they decided to take the first steps, dividing up the tasks. Ava would pop her head out of the bunker and see what the situation outside was like. Abdul would get together the equipment and transport needed to steal the cars and design a getaway strategy. Sofia would look at a map and plan their routes to and from Al Sijood, including multiple contingency plans. Rafan would design a diversion to be used at Al Sijood or en route if required. He and Abdul also needed a few days to make arrangements for their escape.

For the first time in many days, they felt purposeful and alive.

***

The preparations had taken longer than they thought.

While the phone lines had only briefly worked for a few minutes intermittently, after lots of effort and special software, Rafan had managed to get online just long enough to find the website of the foreign architectural firm that had built Al Sijood. He downloaded the case study that proudly mentioned the skilful construction of a large subterranean facility below the administrative building. If they ever managed to break into the building, they would start by looking there.

A four-wheel drive BMW from the garage had been selected for the excursion. The owner of the car, who had handed it in before the invasion for a mere change of hubcaps, would be surprised if he ever got it back. Abdul had affixed metal plates onto the insides of the car in an effort to armour plate it and the suspension had been modified to account for the extra weight. Thankfully, the car had a massive V12 engine that produced 700 horsepower, which would normally be used to pull trailers with boats on them. It would easily withstand the weight of the extra armour plating and the supplies they wanted to carry.

The car had been stocked with food, water, tools, makeshift weapons, a diesel generator to use as a power source should they need it (given the grid was down), extra fuel and, most importantly, large capital letters spelling the word PRESS were painted onto all four sides, as well as the roof.

Each of them carried a backpack with some personal possessions, documents and a change of clothes. It was unclear if they would ever return to the bunker after their mission. If all went well, they would be in a foreign country soon. But at the moment, everything was theoretical. First, they had to actually go through with it.

They set out cautiously, with Ava at the wheel and Sofia sitting in the front passenger seat. Now that the Republican Guard had melted away, the Iraqi troops manning the checkpoints had been replaced by US Marines. They hoped that after seeing a woman in the front seat of an expensive car, especially one with PRESS written all over it, coalition troops might be deterred from shooting first and asking questions later. If they did come across any troops that stopped them, Ava would tell them she was a reporter and show them her press pass. She had already prepared a story in advance, something about being a reporter looking into the administrative functions of Saddam's government, and the lack of public services available to Iraqis during the invasion. She would vouch for everyone in the car as her local team. Even if they were stopped from proceeding, at least they would not be in any trouble.

The streets were eerily silent; it was clear they were the only ones out and about. A murky haze made up partly of dust, partly of smoke from burning oil fields in the countryside and partly from expended artillery hung over the city. Mountains of rubble and rotting garbage lay in the streets. There was no outward sign of the Iraqi National Guard or the Fedayeen, but the four of them knew that they still controlled some small pockets in the city. They had to assume that either the coalition forces or Iraqi national forces had control of the Al-Sijood complex, as it was such an important building.

Finally, they arrived at a checkpoint. They could see that a soldier on top of an armoured vehicle had been tracking them with his roof-mounted machine gun from the time they had emerged from the fog. Three other soldiers had their automatic weapons trained on the car. The one with stripes on his arm motioned for them to stop with one hand while keeping his finger on the trigger of his weapon with the other.

Ava rolled the window down, poked her head out of the car and smiled, 'Do you mind if we shoot you, gents?' She brandished a small digital camera.

'Funny. Stop where you are and put your hands out of the window, or it will be you getting shot. Where's your military escort?'

'We don't have one. I'm independent. Been here since before the shit hit the fan. This is my local team.'

'You were in town during shock and awe?'

'Yeah.'

'Christ,' he said, revealing both shock and awe on his face. 'Didn't you get the memo?'

'I got the memo. Decided not to evacuate. Zara here didn't let me.' Ava smiled what she thought was a love-struck smile, reached over and tucked a strand of Sofia's hair behind her ear, in what she hoped would be seen as a tender gesture. Sofia, for her part, beamed lovingly back at Ava, batting her eyelids.

'OK. You lot are legitimately crazy. Pass over your creds, please.'

Ava showed them her press pass.

'Hold on, I've got to check this out over the radio.'

'OK, but don't be long. We're holding up all the traffic,' she said, motioning towards the empty highway behind her.

The soldier smiled. 'There hasn't been any traffic for a while. Just a few Haji's taking a pop at us now and then.' He glanced at Sofia, then quickly said, 'Whoops, pardon my language ma'am. Be right back.'

He turned around to head towards the radio in the armoured vehicle with Ava's press pass in hand. Just then, the sound of a single round from a high-calibre weapon shattered the silence. The soldier with Ava's press pass, who had been standing by the armoured vehicle, was now face down on the ground, his body lying on an expanding pool of blood.

For a moment, everyone froze. Then one of the three other soldiers shouted, 'Incoming! Incoming!' They all scrambled to take cover behind their car. Ava did not wait around to see what happened, she stomped on the accelerator and the huge BMW darted forward. Another shot rang out, but they did not wait around to check who it was targeting. All four of them were trembling.

Ava repeated the word, 'Fuck,' under her breath like a mantra as she steered. Sofia gripped the armrest so hard her knuckles were white. Rafan and Abdul at the back were just doing their best not to throw up from the fright and the rapid movement of the car.

Five minutes later, they noticed a convoy of five military vehicles driving towards the checkpoint they had just left. It was possibly a reinforcement or a medical evacuation team. The convoy completely ignored them and sped towards the checkpoint.

They drove on in silence. The harsh reality of the situation they were in had suddenly made itself very apparent.

Finally, the turquoise dome of the palace in the Al-Sijood complex appeared in the distance. As they drew closer, they could see that the carefully manicured rose gardens and palm-tree-lined drive contrasted vividly with the damage from an aerial bombardment. The main palace building seemed to have escaped unscathed, but the administrative buildings that flanked it seemed to have borne the brunt of the bombing. None of the glass in the building remained intact. One whole side of the complex had collapsed into a mound of rubble. Ava brought the car to a stop behind a clump of trees and let out a long sigh.

Sofia dug out a flask of tea with shaky hands and passed it around. Abdul looked at the steam emerging from the top of the flask and considered what it might have been like when the buildings were freshly bombed and smouldering. Had everyone evacuated? Had the person pulling the trigger known about the priceless car collection deep underneath?

Abdul thought both answers were no. The windows were rolled down, and they took turns observing the building with a pair of ancient binoculars that Rafan had found in his house. They were looking for access points, as well as any activity by soldiers on either side. The sun began to set as it was Abdul's turn to monitor the building.

As he peered through the binoculars, he noticed a glint of sunlight in the corner of his field of vision, near the eighth or ninth story of the building. He trained the binoculars at the flash of light he had seen and turned the dial on the bridge to focus. Suddenly the image in front of his eyes became laser sharp. It was a man in a Fedayeen helmet with a sniper rifle. He was looking through the telescopic sight intently. And the rifle was pointed straight at them.

22. Kasim

As the bombs fell around his humble apartment on Al Rashid Street, Kasim started to feel philosophical, as some did when confronted with their own mortality. What was it that they had written over the gate to the Nazi concentration camps, Kasim thought to himself. Thats it. Work will set you free.

It ought to have been written over the servants' quarters in Uday's palace, for if you displeased him, you would indeed be relieved of your duties and, of course, your life – both in quick succession. If you were lucky, your family would be spared.

The chaos of war was an interesting time for Kasim. He wasn't quite sure how to deal with it. On one hand, he was under orders from Uday to stay in Baghdad and continue to look after the zoo. And, of course, to wait for the special phone call which his master relied upon so very much. On the other hand, he had never come across a better time to escape Uday's clutches.

He hadn't seen Uday since the invasion. Kasim felt the Hussein family would somehow emerge from the conflict victorious. Having been confronted with the god-like power of the family on a daily basis, even if from a lowly servant's position, he couldn't imagine anything different. That, of course, did not stop him from hoping they would be destroyed.

Kasim stood at the crossroads of a decision he needed to make. One road led to a sensible destination, carrying out Uday's final orders would ensure he and his family could live. And it was easy enough to do – possibly the easiest task his master had set for him.

The other road meant disobedience. This would mean he would most likely suffer Uday's retribution if he didn't conclude the task – while the maniac was alive, he commanded enough resources to disappear Kasim's entire family. But, under the circumstances, would Uday ever know if he slipped away?

Kasim reflected on the recent past to try and help him make up his mind.

Kasim had gotten a promotion, of sorts, after the successful transportation of the three lions to Uday's personal zoo in Baghdad. He had been elevated from the position of chief mechanic to the esteemed position of Uday's chief mechanic *and* secretary.

Frankly, Kasim could not have wanted the job less. He was looking for an 'out' and had been for a long time. But not unlike the mafia, once you were part of the organisation, it was nigh on impossible to ask to be relieved of your duties.

The events of that night were burned in his memory. They had been in Uday's study in the palace when Uday looked up from his desk with a very serious expression on his face. 'Kasim,' he said, 'I am promoting you to the position of my private secretary. You must work very hard to make up for the fact that you are not a hot bitch like a secretary in the movies with the teacher glasses and the short skirt and the high heels.'

He motioned towards the room in which he kept his pornography.

'It has been a great sacrifice for me not to have a hot bitch for a secretary, who can suck my cock whenever I want. I hope you realise this is a difficult decision for me and will work extra hard. Eh? Or maybe I should make you wear a skirt and heels, eh, you bloody fag? Eh? Hah!' He laughed at his poor excuse for a joke. Then, just as quickly, his famously temperamental mood changed to one of seriousness. 'You will do everything I say. You will feed the lions and take care of the zoo. You will continue to manage the care of all the cars. And, most important of all, you will make up for the fact that you are not a whore by bringing me plenty of whores!', he laughed.

'Come, Kasim, let's celebrate,' he said with an evil look in his eyes. 'Go to the bar and bring us the 40-year-old Laphroaig.'

Kasim did as he was told and fetched the eye-wateringly expensive whisky.

'Good, good. Now, pour two glasses.'

Kasim obliged.

'Excellent,' he said with an evil glint in his eye. 'These are both for me. You can have that cheap rum sitting in the cabinet. Bring the whole bottle. You are happy, yes?'

'Yes, sir,' Kasim replied.

'Good, if you are happy, I want to see you drinking the whole bottle. No, no need for a glass.' He caught Kasim looking at the couch. 'And don't you dare sit down next to me, you fag – who do you think you are? Eh? Eh? Drink the bottle. Now. I command you.'

Kasim knew Uday was serious. He had seen this happening before – many of Uday's 'friends' had suffered the same fate. Once, Uday had held a gun to a man's head and told him to drink an entire bottle of hard liquor in one gulp. If the bottle left his lips for even a second, he would pull the trigger.

To Uday's partial credit, he would observe the effects of these little experiments with a near-scientific curiosity. He would glance at his watch while the liquor was being consumed and say, 'Quick, quick, you must beat the standing record!' Next, he would memorise the time the bottle was emptied. Then he would wait for things to happen with childlike anticipation. Sometimes the victim would vomit, sometimes pass out, sometimes die. Sometimes all three.

Of course, Uday was the first one to admit he did this mainly for entertainment. The scientific merit of the experiment was merely an added bonus, as he would put it.

Kasim imagined, not for the first time, that Uday would have made an excellent Chief of Experiments in a Nazi concentration camp. He would have positively enjoyed it. As they say - choose a job you love, and you will never work a day in your life. Kasim sincerely felt he should have done a better job of choosing.

He knew the situation had the distinct possibility of escalating and he wanted to avoid it. He wasn't ready to be 'set free' quite yet.

He drank the bottle, steeling his nerves, determined not to vomit. He knew that violence would ensue immediately if he threw up on Uday's Persian carpets.

He became dizzy. He was not sure what happened next. He remembered falling down. He remembered Uday laughing uproariously. He remembered vaguely that Uday had guided him to a chair and sat him down. He had passed some sort of a test, he imagined. Uday then took out some hashish and rolled a joint. He puffed on it contentedly. Then he offered it to Kasim, who took one look at it and retched. Uday hastily withdrew his hand from projectile vomit range, along with the offer of the joint.

Then, to his immense surprise, they watched Star Wars. Or, to put it more accurately, Uday watched Star Wars, while Kasim struggled to stay conscious. He vaguely remembered Uday giving him a running commentary on every scene. Through the haze, he recalled Uday's excitement would reach a fever pitch when Darth Vader or the stormtroopers would appear.

What happened next was even more surprising. At the time he thought he was imagining it all but, later, he realised it had actually happened.

'Papa is putting me back in charge of the Fedayeen,' Uday said, puffing thoughtfully on his third joint. 'And my first task is to design a uniform. I feel inspired by the movie,' he said. 'First, I was going to copy the Nazi uniform. But then I thought it was too smart, too good for those fanatical bastards. I want something more… scary. Not nice to look at.'

A determined look came over his face.

'Kasim, as my secretary, your first task will be to prepare and make stormtrooper uniforms for the Fedayeen. You have one week. If you fail, I will have you feed the lions. No, not with beef. With yourself. Get out.'

And, just like that, he was Uday's personal secretary.

Kasim only remembered the next couple of days as a haze of vomit, diarrhoea and splitting headaches. Through it all, he worried about his first task. He appealed to Uday for more time but was denied. But, luckily, salvation came from one of the most unlikely places: Saddam himself.

Uday had mentioned his new uniform design to Saddam, who, after looking at a Star Wars poster, was not amused. He asked Uday to drop the ludicrous idea. He said the Fedayeen would be a laughingstock if they wore those outfits. But the stormtrooper helmets, the helmets Uday could keep. They were sufficiently commanding and intimidating. So Kasim posed as a memorabilia collector and ordered a Star Wars stormtrooper helmet from a Hollywood store and had it shipped over to Iraq. The Iraqi army's head of livery was then given the helmet and asked to replicate it. The squad of irregular troops would live up to the phrase and wear black jumpsuits underneath the stormtrooper helmet.

Kasim wrote it off as just another Uday-ism that no one would ever believe if he survived employment long enough to write a book.

As the days passed, tensions with America seemed to escalate more and more. Uday had spent more time with the leaders of the Fedayeen. In reality, Saddam had ordered the leadership of his own irregular forces – The Royal Guard – to ensure the Fedayeen were trained properly, possibly because he did not trust Uday to get the job done.

Surprisingly, as the weeks wore on, Saddam himself seemed to withdraw increasingly from public life. Rumours were flying around that he spent hours locked up in his room, feverishly writing a book. It was almost as if he wanted to finish writing it before America took military action.

However, it made no difference to Kasim what Uday and Saddam did. He had to go about his duties as usual. Uday, despite being away, had a surprising knack for knowing when any of his servants were slacking in any way. Kasim had figured everyone informed on everyone else.

So, he ensured Uday's huge automobile collection was kept in as good a shape as possible, kept the lions fed and stole young girls off the streets of Baghdad for his boss. He now had 20 people working for him, as well as extra help from the National Guard when he required extra firepower to abduct a young girl or transport the lions safely. He developed a reputation as someone who got the job done for Uday, who himself even noticed the efficiency with which Kasim carried out his missions. Throughout this time, Kasim learnt a lot of secrets about his boss.

However, he was under no illusions. Now that he had so much sensitive information about Uday – from the girls he raped, to where the most precious cars were kept – he knew he was not safe. He was only more at risk of being shot if he was even mildly suspected of betraying his boss.

However, one day, he was told a secret that he wasn't expecting to be told.

He had received the call at midnight. Uday told him to collect the new Porsche from one of the numerous car parks around the city, to prepare it to be driven before dawn and to meet him outside the palace with it.

When Kasim arrived at the palace just before dawn, a party being hosted by Uday was in full swing. Slowly, as the rays of the sun filtered through the tall trees around the boundary of the property, the guests started to leave.

Finally, Uday staggered out. He had clearly had lots to drink and nearly lost his footing as he descended the stairs.

'Kasim! You are here. This is good! You are always here for me. Keys! Give me the keys!'

Kasim handed over the keys. He wasn't overly worried. Uday drove drunk more often than not. As it was a well-known fact to everyone, he would not be blamed if Uday had an accident and died. In fact, Uday had wrecked countless cars while drunk driving. One could even say it was a hobby. However, he had always seemed to escape unscathed.

On this occasion, Uday looked more drunk than usual. Kasim hoped that Uday would finally kill himself in a car accident. It would be great for everyone concerned, especially him. He would finally be able to leave this soulless existence and disappear for good, never to see a member of the Hussein family again.

So, he handed over the keys to Uday without a word of protest.

'Good,' Uday had said as he slipped into the driver's seat. 'Now, get inside the car with me.'

Kasim felt a surge of terror pass through him. This was not what he had been expecting. In fact, it had never happened before. But he had no choice; it was a direct order. So, he slipped into the passenger seat.

Uday revved the engine, and the Porsche surged forward. They veered straight off the driveway and onto the lawn, but Uday did not seem to care. He drove towards the huge wrought iron gates at the end of the property, over the carefully manicured rose garden, ruining countless hours of work by the head gardener.

The car had shown no sign of slowing down as it approached the gate, Kasim recalled. Thankfully, the guards on duty saw what was happening and opened the gates for their master in the nick of time to avoid a crash. A grinding sound was heard as the side of the new Porsche scraped against the gate as it shot past. Kasim shuddered to think what would have happened if the guards had been asleep.

Nevertheless, Kasim had been sure the guards would be blamed for the huge gash across the side of the car.

They drove through the sleeping city at breakneck speed. Uday, of course, knew the surroundings like the back of his hand, which was good, because if he had not been working on pure muscle memory, they would surely have crashed.

Uday cornered at top speed, the tail end of the car skidding and often touching the sides of the buildings as they passed them.

'OK. Listen carefully,' Uday shouted over the roar of the engine, 'I will say this only once. There is a man. He lives in Jordan. His name is Ali Masood. He has connections to the American Embassy in Jordan. I know this man.'

There had been a pause as Uday swerved around a pothole, mounted the footpath and smashed a handcart some poor street vendor had left there. Uday didn't even pause. It was almost as if he were playing a video game and had received extra points for colliding with the cart. Or maybe he hadn't noticed the collision at all. Kasim wasn't sure. Uday just kept his foot on the accelerator, the same glassy distant stare in his eyes.

'I will email you Masood's number. You will keep it with you, night and day. Tomorrow, a tattoo artist is coming to the palace – he will tattoo a secure phone number and the email of this man onto your hand, so you will never forget it.'

Kasim had many questions, but he knew better than to interrupt at this point. In any case, he was too scared to think of much beyond the next looming turn in the road or obstacle in their path. He held on for dear life.

'So,' Uday continued, shouting at the top of his voice to be heard over the noise. 'This man is very important, but no one must know that I know him. Not Qusay, not Papa, not the Fedayeen, not The Guard and not anyone in Iraq or abroad. No one. It's top secret. I don't need to tell you what happens to people who give away my secrets. Understand?'

Kasim had just about mustered the will to nod as they missed a lamppost by inches. Not that Uday needed an answer. It was a rhetorical question, really.

'So, if the time comes, and the infidel forces enter Iraq, I will phone you and you must contact this man. You will tell him that I am ready to talk. That is all you must tell him – that I am ready to talk. Ask him if this is possible. Then, after some time, perhaps a day or two, he will ask you to send me a message. It will be a simple yes or no.'

The obvious question occurred to Kasim, and he managed to ask it as the pace of the car continued unabated. 'Sir. No problem, sir. But wouldn't you prefer to speak to him directly?'

Uday laughed. 'If I ever ask you to contact this man, I will be in hiding. And I will not be able to speak to anyone – except maybe you. Also, I cannot speak directly to this man. It is dangerous for me. He cannot know where I am until he comes back to you with his answer. He is my insurance policy. If the answer is yes, the insurance will pay off. If the answer is no...'

Just then, they came to an abrupt halt as the car collided with a house – head-on. A small pile of bricks fell onto the bonnet. The car was finally stationary, and the engine silenced. Nothing stirred for a few seconds.

'I think we have finished this drive,' Uday said.

23. Abdul / Ava / Rafan / Sofia

Abdul jerked back, nearly dropping the binoculars.

None of the others knew what he had seen, but everyone jumped at his reaction. 'Sniper. Up there. Window. Fuck,' Abdul managed to spurt. 'I thought he saw me.'

'Unlikely,' said Rafan. 'We are behind very thick bushes.' But he slid a little further down in his seat nevertheless.

'How many are there?' asked Ava.

'Not sure,' said Abdul. 'I just saw one.' He hazarded another look out of the window with the binoculars and heaved a sigh of relief. 'Yeah, I don't think he's seen us. But I can see some shadows moving behind him. Definitely someone else up there with him. Motherfucking Fedayeen. What shall we do? Wait for nighttime?'

Of all of them, Ava had the most experience in these situations. Now she took charge. 'OK. Here's the plan,' she said. We will wait till nighttime. But the cover of darkness won't be enough. There will be more than one sniper, and they may have night vision so we can't risk just walking into the building. Rafan and Sofia, you can trigger the diversion you've planned and stay in the car. Abdul and I will make a break for that entry point – see the doorway near the left there? Once we get under that awning, we will be safe as the sniper will not be able to see us. We will break the door and enter. Then we will look for the subterranean parking lot. When we find the cars, we will click three times on the radio. When you hear three clicks, Rafan and Sofia, you two can drive, full tilt, to the exit point. Hopefully, we will be there with the first two cars. Then we initiate the brilliant escape plan Abdul has so carefully devised.' All three of them nodded. 'OK, get to work Rafan – it's your show – it will be dark in half an hour.'

Rafan came to life immediately, as he did whenever he put his mind to something. He worked quickly and methodically as if he had been through the routine many times. First, he flattened the back seats of the SUV, so they formed a platform in the rear of the large car. Then, he removed a heavy bag from under the seat and, with a grunt, placed it on the platform. It took up about half the space. Next, he unzipped the bag to reveal part of a remote-controlled helicopter. It said 'Kyosho EP Concept' across the fuselage. Then, he removed three slim and aerodynamic rotor blades from the bag and fitted them onto the main body of the craft. Sofia had to clamber into Abdul's lap in the front seat to make room. Finally, Rafan attached the undercarriage with a small screwdriver before opening another bag that held the remote control – a rather large device with a telescopic antenna, two toggle switches and several buttons.

'Is that thing going to be able to fly so high up?' Ava asked. The sniper was at the top of the building. Rafan nodded and said, 'Yes. Not out of the box. But I have made so many modifications over the last few days – it's like a different product altogether. Now, it has a brushless motor and double nickel cadmium batteries so it can fly faster and higher, and modified cedarwood rotors for more precise controls. Oh, I also re-moulded several of the metal parts from plastic in my factory, so it's much lighter. Changed out the radio so its got way more range too. See that wire trailing down from the back of the undercarriage like a tail? That's an antenna. Oh, and here is the best part: its got a payload. 60 grams of Rafan's Blend, which consists of dynamite, sulphur and phosphorus. This will be the chopper's last mission. A suicide chopper. This button on my remote sets off the payload.'

For a moment they just stared at Rafan, not knowing what to say. Bored out of his wits in the basement shelter, it was clear he had enjoyed himself.

'That,' said Ava, 'is precisely when we will break down the door to enter. When everyone's eyes and ears will be on the fireworks.' They all nodded. It was a good plan. They broke out some sandwiches and, even though no one felt like eating, Ava and Abdul forced down half a sandwich each and washed it down with some lukewarm tea from the flask.

Soon, it was dusk. 'OK. Showtime. Let's keep this plan moving. Abdul! You ready mate?' Abdul didn't respond. He was looking at Sofia, who was still sitting on his lap. He leaned towards her and kissed her hard. Sofia kissed him back. Abdul looked at Ava and, with steely determination he did not know he had, he said, 'I'm ready.'

They each shouldered a backpack that held all manner of hand tools from Abdul's garage, along with a bottle of water. They each had a switchblade in their pocket and a headlamp on an elastic band on their heads. Ava glanced at her watch. 'OK. Give us two hours precisely. If you don't hear the clicks in an hour, try to reach us on the radio. If you can't reach us on the radio, leave. We will meet you back at the garage. Do *not* leave the garage after that point. Understood?'

Rafan and Sofia both nodded their agreement.

In their minds, each of them had already quietly decided they wouldn't leave the premises without their friends under any circumstances.

24. Rameez

Fedayeen translated to 'Saddam's Men of Sacrifice'. And men of sacrifice they were – even though there were many ways in which Iraq could fight and eventually expel foreign forces, the Fedayeen had always been designed to fight to the last man, to eventually be destroyed. The Fedayeen knew and accepted this.

Some of them were driven to devotion on religious grounds, defending the holy ground from the crusader, at any cost. Some were aided in their philosophy by the political belief that the Baathist Party truly was what was best for Iraq. Some of them, quite literally, did not think at all. While they were alive, they had been respected and feared. And for the average Fedayeen, who was recruited at the age of 16, that was more than enough.

It was one of these individuals that Rameez was with, inside the crumbling Al-Sijood complex. They were in a small room on the ninth floor of the building, just under the huge turquoise dome. Plastic bottles of water, packages of dates and almonds lay beside them, serving as their sustenance. The firebombs Rameez had prepared at his house lay packed carefully in a huge rucksack.

They had come there two days ago, their mission two-fold. They would protect the complex and any remaining secrets it held from imperialist forces. Secondly, and more importantly, Rameez was there to destroy the underground car park before the imperialists found it.

Rameez had originally planned to bomb the car park the very day he had arrived, but he had been waylaid – they had spotted an American patrol approaching the complex and had to deter it from coming closer.

His colleague had been selected for this mission as he was one of the few good shots in the Fedayeen. Most had only received basic small arms training, the leadership preferring to focus on the conditioning of the mind. However, Rameez had noticed the young student's prowess with the famously inaccurate AK-47 and had personally selected him to have special arms training to become a sniper. He was one of the few individuals that Rameez and other members of the leadership had selected to defend some of the most valued government buildings during the invasion.

It was a futile exercise of course, with no real practical benefit to anyone. The buildings had been emptied of all important or secret documents long ago. The buildings had already been bombed and were of highly dubious structural integrity. The stand was purely symbolic. After all, Saddam couldn't very well allow them to be taken without any fight at all. It was understood that the individuals who were left behind to protect these buildings would die with their sniper rifles in their arms, at their posts, after taking with them as many imperial forces as possible.

Of course, the individuals in question always knew they had the option of surrendering and escaping with their lives.

They kept that idea in their back pocket. Rameez knew this. He was good at anticipating people's emotions and he knew how to motivate them. For example, with this young man, he had spoken about glory. He had told the young man, who prided himself on his marksmanship, that he would go down in history as the man who defended the Al-Sijood complex. He may eventually be killed, but he might be known forever as the person with the record for the highest number of US Marines killed. If he tried hard. If he wasn't scared.

Sure enough, the young man looked as if he was ready to die. A steely reserve could be seen in his eyes, and he gripped the rifle close to his chest as if it were his lifeline to being admitted into the history books.

So far, they hadn't killed anyone – a sniper's job was far more about being patient and staying alert, even after many hours of duty than it was about being a good shot.

The young Fedayeen had shot at the one US patrol they had spotted approaching the complex. He had missed. The Marines had beat a hasty retreat. Rameez and his disciple had expected them to return with armoured vehicles and heavy weaponry to lay siege to the complex. They had dreamt of going down in a blaze of glory, like real men, defenders of their holy land.

Now it looked increasingly like the Americans had decided not to bother – no one had returned. Yet.

Ah well, thought Rameez, there was still always hope.

The young recruit was lying prone on a rectangular dining table on his stomach, facing the large window. The telescopic sight of his precious Druganov SVD long-range rifle was glued to his eyes. The Iraqi army did not have snipers or sniper rifles, and Rameez had acquired the 1950s Soviet Union-designed rifle for his disciple with difficulty.

‘Something is happening, Emir,’ he said. ‘I can sense some movement in the dusk. I hear a sound.’

Rameez strained hard to find the source of the sound. And suddenly, he saw it. At first, he could not believe it. What was a remote-controlled helicopter, this wealthy children’s toy, doing in the middle of Iraq? It could only have come from the U.S. Army Special Forces. Perhaps it had surveillance equipment on it. Or worse, perhaps it was a bomb.

Shoot it, he ordered the recruit. The young man took aim and fired the gun many times, but the helicopter was moving too fast and too erratically to make itself a target.

The buzzing sound of its engine and rotors became louder and louder.

Rameez unholstered his handgun and removed the strange military helmet each member of the Fedayeen had been issued. He did not know which idiot had designed it, but it was impossible to aim a gun accurately while wearing it. As a consequence, most Fedayeen had resorted to removing the helmet when they were in a firefight.

Rameez took aim. The pilots of the craft, wherever they were located, were clearly very skilful – not a single shot had penetrated the fuselage of the small toylike craft.

That’s when Rameez suddenly remembered there were highly explosive materials located in the room with them: the firebombs intended for the garage. If the toy held its own explosive charge, which he had the imagination to realise might be the case, then it may set off his own explosives.

Rameez convinced himself that it was not a fiery death that he was scared of – it was the fact that he had not completed his mission. Yes. Yes, that was it. How could he forgive himself if he did not finish the job and destroy the garage?

The helicopter came closer and closer.

In a few moments, the helicopter would be level with them, and only a few feet away from the window. Without a word to his colleague, who was getting increasingly frustrated by his lack of success in shooting down the chopper, Rameez holstered his pistol, grabbed the heavy rucksack full of the thermite explosives, and quietly left his colleague hunched over the rifle. He ran downstairs, taking two steps at a time. The heavy rucksack bounced on his back, likely causing permanent damage to his spine.

When he was perhaps three flights of stairs away, he heard a loud explosion above his head. But Rameez was focused. He did not pause. He knew exactly where to go and what to do.

Minutes later, he was on the ground floor, his black jumpsuit drenched in sweat, and his back curved under the backpack. He sought out and found the hidden trapdoor leading to the underground facility where the cars were kept.

It was exactly where they had told him it would be in his instructions – hidden but unlocked. Carefully, he descended the staircase and looked around. The subterranean facility was far larger than he had ever imagined – there was a chance that even the explosives he had devised might not be enough. But his eyes lit up with joy when he saw what he had been looking for – the petrol pump by the workshop. It made sense really, if you were to store scores of cars there, you needed a fuel source, Rameez supposed. Very convenient. It was also very convenient if you were looking to blow the place sky-high.

He got to work, setting down the backpack and laying out the packages of thermite. The one with the main charge and trigger went next to the petrol pump, a wire led to the next one, amidst the 30-odd black Mercedes, another next to the older looking cars, followed by the sleek looking ones, and finally the long black ones that looked as if they could seat eight people. He had no regrets and held nothing but contempt for what he saw as symbols of Western corruption.

Finally, he fitted the mechanical alarm clock onto the first package, setting the timer for midnight.

At that time, one best be far away. Rameez had no plans to hang about. However, the climb down eighteen flights of stairs with the heavy backpack and the precision with which he needed to plant the bombs had taken its toll.

Rameez felt a bit dizzy and tripped over his own feet. He caught himself just in time. He knew, at that moment, he wouldn't get far unless he ate or drank something quickly. Sure, there was a massive incendiary bomb below him and a fire raging above, but the only thing he could think of was a cup of hot, sweet tea.

As a bomb-maker, he prided himself on his cool, calm demeanour in stressful situations. His self-image was one of a devil-may-care hero. Besides, what a story it would make when he told it to his compatriots over the campfire later. Just imagine, planting a bomb and then going to make a cup of tea while the fuse had been lit! He would secure his place amidst Fedayeen folklore!

So, he made his way to the kitchen.

25. Abdul / Ava

Abdul and Ava were waiting for the fireworks.

They had laced up their shoes and shouldered their backpacks, ready to jump out of the SUV and run towards the side door that would serve as their access point into the Al-Sijood complex. Ava had a heavy crowbar, ready to use on the door if required. Everyone watched in admiration as Rafan expertly flew the remote-controlled aircraft straight out of the back of the car. Abdul worried that the sniper would shoot it down prematurely, and the payload would go off close to them, injuring them all. He needn't have worried; no shots rang out until the helicopter was level with at least the third story of the building. They could tell immediately that the chances of it getting shot were minimal as Rafan had quickly developed a technique of jerking the controls, making the chopper swing from side to side. Finally, Rafan took a deep breath and, squinting carefully through the binoculars that Sofia held to his eyes, used the small joystick on the control pad to navigate the helicopter directly over the head of the Fedayeen soldier, who had now resorted to holding the barrel of his rifle and swinging it in wild arcs at the toy helicopter as if he were trying to swat a particularly irritating mosquito. Then, Rafan pressed the button to detonate the charge. At first, nothing happened. But after a few seconds, it exploded.

A huge fireball had emerged from the window that the helicopter had disappeared into. Rafan's blend had delivered in abundance. The suicide chopper had done its duty and was now in helicopter paradise. Far more than a diversion, they had probably eviscerated every living creature in that part of the structure of the Al-Sijood complex.

Abdul and Ava stood there, mouths agape, staring up at the devastation they had caused. The building was properly on fire, no doubt about it. Whether they had enough time to recover the cars and make their escape was anyone's guess. Amongst the debris that showered the road below, a blood-soaked Fedayeen helmet crashed to the ground and bounced several times. In an effort to stay focussed, Ava grabbed Abdul's arm and motioned towards the door. They ran towards it and, when they reached it, Ava smashed open the lock with a crowbar. Abdul gave it a few strong kicks and it flew open. Inside, there was only darkness.

Abdul glanced at his watch – it was 10 p.m.

26. Kasim

None of the senior leadership were left in Baghdad, of that Kasim was now certain. The Hussein family had been spirited away long ago. He would see Saddam on Iraqi state TV now and then. The man always appeared to be happy and cheerful, as if to say, 'Look! I am still alive and well. This invasion thing is nothing but a minor distraction, everything will be back to normal soon.'

These images were interspersed with images of the Iraqi Minister for Media, who had a penchant for high drama and blatant lies. One line that stood out to Kasim was, 'American soldiers were committing suicide by the hundreds at the gates of the city, rather than facing the brave Iraqi forces who are successfully defending their motherland.' Kasim remembered diverting his attention from the TV set to the window, just in time to see US troops in the heart of the city, casually strolling around with not a single Iraqi soldier in sight.

These were truly interesting times.

The easy freedom seemed within Kasim's grasp. He could go underground; disappear into a hazy sandstorm, into the fog of war, never to be seen again.

But Kasim was too scared. A lifetime of obedience to the Hussein family was very hard to break. He hated himself for it. When freedom was finally there for the taking, he was too afraid to grab hold of it. Deep down, he hated himself for being a coward – and he hated Uday even more for making him feel that way.

Kasim had visited the palace immediately after the bombing had subsided, before the first wave of looters had arrived. The auto garage and paint shop behind Uday's palace had also completely caved in under the barrage of missiles. There were still small fires here and there.

Uday's zoo itself had also been bombed. Many of the wild and endangered animals had been killed. The ones whose cages had not been bombed were literally mad with anxiety and foaming at the mouth, throwing themselves against the bars of the cage, bleeding from open sores.

There was no sign of the lions.

Their cage had been broken by a missile. Kasim could see that part of it had disintegrated and there were scorch marks all around. But, ominously, there were no carcasses. Just a huge gaping bomb crater where part of the cage was supposed to be. A feeling of terror had crept up on Kasim, and he suddenly wanted to be as far away from the zoo as possible.

Kasim ran back home as quickly as he could, all the time looking over his shoulder.

He was contemplating the idea of three ravenous lions roaming the streets of a war-torn Baghdad when his satellite phone went off, the one Uday had told him to keep with him at all times.

Ring ring.

Kasim did not answer. He watched the phone ring. It could, of course, mean only one thing. Uday wanted to trigger his insurance policy.

Even though courage was not his strong suit, Kasim was clever – he knew that the fate of Uday Hussein lay in his hands. He understood that Uday's contact in Jordan, Masood, whom he had been asked to call when Uday told him to, would negotiate Uday's surrender to US forces. Uday would probably want a guarantee that his life would be spared in exchange for state secrets, perhaps his father's or brothers' locations. Kasim did not doubt that Uday would give up his family for even an instant; that was Uday. That was probably why Uday did not want anyone to know about Masood.

The phone continued to ring.

Kasim watched it ringing until it went silent.

Then it started ringing again.

Kasim could not take it any longer. Hating himself thoroughly, he picked up the phone.

Immediately he regretted it.

'Kasim? Do you dare make me phone twice? Where were you, you bloody fag? I'll strip you naked and feed you to the fucking lions, you bastard.'

'Sorry sir. I was in the toilet.'

'I don't give a fuck where you were – you keep the satellite phone with you at all times. Now, tell me, where are you, really?'

'At home, sir.'

'OK. Call Masood. And then call me right back. Tell me what happened. Is that understood? OK. How is my palace? You have not touched my liquor cabinet, have you? And how is the zoo? I swear to God, when I come back if I find one scratch on my lions, I will have you strung up and shot on the spot. Call Masood now.'

Click. The line went dead.

Kasim stared at the phone for a moment. Then he stared at the wall. A rage bubbled up inside of him. That bastard! He was depending on Kasim, quite literally for his life. And after everything Kasim had sacrificed for him, he did not even have the courtesy to ask him how he was faring in the fucking warzone.

Fuck Uday's phone calls, Kasim thought to himself. Fuck his insurance. Fuck the zoo. Fuck his cars. And fuck him.

The call was just what Kasim needed. He took the phone, switched it off and put it in a brown paper bag. Then, in large lettering, he wrote on it, in English, 'Trace my calls'. If he was going to escape, he would have to make sure Uday did not. Or else, he would be in for it. The only way to proceed was to ensure Uday was caught or killed by American troops.

Kasim then ran up to the nearest US checkpoint. It was deserted; the soldiers were probably on patrol and would return soon. Good. He placed the brown paper bag on the military field table and ran back home.

As soon as he was back home, he instinctively felt as if he had made the right move. However, one thing was clear – he could no longer stay at home. They might be able to trace the phone back to his house. Or not. Kasim did not know how these things worked. He did not care. He felt as if a burden had been lifted from his shoulders. No more lion taming. No more accessory to rape. No more fixing beautiful sportscars to see them being abused by that monster. No more abuse.

He put on his shoes, grabbed a backpack and melted away into the night.

27. Abdul / Ava

The first thing that Abdul and Ava noticed as they walked over the threshold of the Al-Sijood complex was the smell.

The smell was revolting. It smelled like a cross between a wet dog and rotting faeces. It reminded Ava a little bit of the smell of the wild animal enclosure at the zoo. As expected, there was no electricity. They switched on their headlamps and explored the complex in the darkness. The whole administrative wing of the palace was a mess. Empty filing cabinets lay on the floor, their drawers strewn everywhere. Chairs and tables lay overturned. Wires and cables hung from the ceiling. Many of the fluorescent tube lights and ceiling fixtures crunched under their feet as they walked. There was no indication of the fire that raged some distance above their heads but Abdul knew it was only a matter of time before the lower floors filled with smoke and surrendered to the flames.

The structural integrity of the building had already been compromised due to the bombing. If the fire spread, it might not stay standing. They needed to act quickly.

Then Abdul noticed a trail of muddy footprints leading from one room to another. He walked over to them and turned his head at an angle so that the beam of light was focused on them. He realised they weren't footprints. They were paw prints. A dog perhaps? If it was a dog, it was a very big dog indeed.

Just then, Ava called out. She had found a staircase leading downstairs. Even though they had some architectural drawings of the building, the entrance to the subterranean facility had not been included. They had planned to get to the lowest part of the building, to check if that was where the entrance was. If it was not to be found there, then they would have to start looking for a trapdoor or a secret entry point.

They were, of course, both frightened. Who knew if there were more Fedayeen in the building? It would not be surprising if Uday had buried some of them alive in the parking lot, like ancient Egyptian slaves entombed in the Pharoh's treasure chamber, to ensure the safety of their master's possessions in the afterlife. One thing was certain, they needed to be in and out as quickly as possible – even though the flames from the helicopter bomb had been several floors above, one never knew if the entire building would go up in smoke.

They reached the bottom of the stairwell and looked around in the darkness. The door exiting the stairwell seemed to only lead into another office, this time with rather shabby décor but not too much bomb damage. Abdul guessed this was where the domestic staff and services for the complex were based. Sure enough, they found a room full of brooms and cleaning liquids. Another full of staff uniforms. And then a huge kitchen with many stoves, cabinets, pots and pans.

But no sign of a car park and no steps leading further down. The two of them got to work looking for a hidden entrance to the garage. It was exceedingly slow work in the dark – the narrow beam of their headlamps only illuminated the area directly ahead of them, and they kept tripping over various bits of debris that lay strewn all over the floor. They tried to proceed carefully, having no idea what lay around the next corner. Ava noticed that it was getting colder – she wasn't sure if it was because they were now below ground or because the sun had set a couple of hours ago. When, at last, they had looked for an hour or so without any success – in the kitchen, supplies room, administrative floor, utility room and a room with a hive of bunk beds – Ava suggested they go to the kitchen and make a cup of tea, as she had noticed a box in the kitchen when she had been searching it.

Abdul smiled – the stereotype of the English who made a cup of tea to deal with all forms of strife seemed to be true. The place was well and truly deserted. Surely, Saddam wouldn't begrudge them a cup of tea in his complex. Confident that no one was around and lulled into a sense of security by not seeing any living creature since they entered the complex, Ava hummed softly to herself as she filled an ancient wrought iron kettle and put it on the stove.

At first, Ava thought Abdul was keeping time to her tune by beating his palm on the counter. Then she realised that Abdul's hands were in his pockets. She listened carefully, a worried expression creeping onto her face. Seeing her expression, Abdul became alert as well. At the same moment, they both realised it sounded like footsteps in the distance. Whoever it was, wore heavy combat boots. And the sound was getting closer. Abdul and Ava were filled with a sudden and intense dread.

For a few moments, they stood, rooted to the spot, listening, thinking of how to react. Then things happened very quickly. Ava turned off the stove and darted to the corner of the vast kitchen, motioning for Abdul to do the same. She opened the stainless-steel doors of an industrial kitchen cabinet, and they both crept inside and shut the door, leaving it open a crack.

Through the crack in the cabinet doors, Abdul noticed that thin whisps of steam were coming out of the spout of the kettle on the stove. If the intruder came into the kitchen, it would be hard to miss the steaming kettle and consequently be alerted to the possibility of someone else's presence. The footsteps seemed louder as if the person was coming closer to them – but they did not seem like they were immediately outside the kitchen. Yet. Abdul made a split-second decision. He dashed out of the cabinet, leapt two paces towards the stove, picked up the kettle and leapt back into the cabinet. He shut the door of the cabinet, leaving it open just a crack as it had been before. He had done so in the nick of time; just as he swung the cabinet door shut, the kitchen door swung open and a flashlight beam swept the room.

A tall man stood there, dressed from head to toe in a black jumpsuit, the uniform of the dreaded Fedayeen. His ridiculous helmet swung to and fro on a strap attached to his belt. He had the thick, long beard of a religiously observant man. A pair of rimless glasses were perched on his nose, which gave him scholarly air despite the pistol in the holster at his waist.

He strode straight over to the area near the stove – thank goodness Abdul had snatched the kettle away – and rummaged around in the drawers below the counter. At first, Abdul wasn't sure what the man was looking for. Then, he heard the man mumbling to himself, 'Cha? Cha? Cha? Cha?' Should have known, thought Abdul. The only people who loved a cup of tea more than the English were his fellow countrymen.

Then, the man walked over to the first cabinet amongst the row of cabinets in which they were hiding, and started to throw open the doors, one by one.

Abdul counted as he peeped through the gap in the cabinet door – there were six cabinets to be opened by the man before he reached theirs. Just as he reached the fifth cabinet, the bearded man's body language changed – his body seemed to tense up, and his nostrils flared. He sniffed the air. He sniffed again and softly mumbled a single word to himself in surprise. 'Cha?!'

Abdul knew the cat was out of the bag. In a split second, he knew what he would have to do – he motioned for Ava to hold up the spanner in readiness. He took the lid off the large wrought iron teapot. Even more steam emerged. The Fedayeen soldier, following the smell, approached their cabinet and, putting the torch in his mouth, in one quick motion, threw open the doors with both hands.

Abdul flung the steaming tea straight towards his head and then hurled his own body towards the light behind it. The Fedayeen soldier cried out in pain and surprise. Ava jumped out behind Abdul and smashed the spanner in the Fedayeen's head, and they heard the sharp crack of metal on bone.

Wordlessly, the man sank to the floor with a deep, red gash on his head. A puddle of blood appeared underneath him. His leg twitched slightly for a few seconds, and then he was deadly still.

For a while, they both stood over his body in silence, shaking.

Then, from somewhere in the depths of the building, they heard the unmistakable roar of a lion who had just smelled blood.

28. Sofia / Rafan

Rafan remembered that in the old Hollywood detective films he used to watch - the undercover cops would stake out a building for hours on end. They made it look dangerously glamorous. Cigarettes were smoked and hip flasks were swigged under neon lights, while the policemen peered out of the window above a newspaper, into the hazy outside world, waiting for their suspect.

Having been inside a stationary car over the last hour or so, he did not feel the least bit glamorous or dangerous. He felt tired and stiff and grimy.

Sofia seemed to be her usual calm and cheerful self, but Rafan could tell that she was just as anxious as he was about their two friends inside the complex.

There had been no sign of Ava and Abdul. They had tried reaching their friends on the radio, but they'd had no luck – perhaps the government building had taken precautions against the transmission of radio frequencies for security purposes.

They both knew that neither of them was going anywhere until their friends emerged from the building, regardless of whether it had been two hours or ten.

They were, however, getting very nervous. The fire from the diversionary explosion had travelled from the third floor of the east wing to the west part of the second floor of the sprawling Al-Sijood complex. The cladding on the building seemed to have been constructed from a very flammable material – their friends needed to get out, and quick.

A rumble in the distance made her snap out of her thoughts. It sounded like a truck, or rather, a convoy of trucks. And it sounded like it was heading towards them. Rafan jumped into the driver's seat and put his hand on the ignition, just in case they needed to make themselves scarce at short notice.

Sofia jumped out of the car and ran to the corner from which the road approaching the Al-Sijood complex could be seen.

What she saw shocked her – a long trail of powerful headlights was heading in their direction. She could tell they were US military vehicles. Perhaps they had seen the explosion, she thought. But then why were they appearing on the scene so late?

It did not matter now. What mattered was that they were here. She ran back to the SUV and jumped in next to Rafan, telling him what she had seen.

In about two minutes, the convoy would come across them. Rafan desperately tried to reach Ava and Abdul on the walkie-talkie radio but to no avail. They were clearly in a location where radio signals could not reach them.

They looked at each other. In an instant, they knew what they had to do, even though it probably wasn't the smartest move on the planet. Silently, they slipped out of the SUV and darted towards the building, crouching low to make themselves smaller targets for any snipers that might still be in the building, or for the coalition forces behind them.

They entered through the same door as Ava and Abdul, determined to find their friends, warn them about the military convoy approaching the complex and all escape together before the fire consumed the building. To hell with the cars. The danger level of the situation was well past the acceptable mark and the risk-reward ratio had changed.

The inside of the complex looked like hell. They took in the stench, the lack of electricity, the overturned tables, the pieces of paper everywhere. But most crucially, they noticed that the smoke had now reached the level that they had entered.

Quietly, they crept forward into the darkness, shining the beams of their torch ahead of them.

They reached a sparsely furnished room near the stairwell, where the smoke seemed to be at its thickest, and scanned it with their torches – they could see it was empty.

Then, from the centre of the room, they heard a squeaking sound. Rafan and Sofia quickly switched off their torches and retreated behind the door frame.

Sofia hazarded a quick peek into the room. And then she gasped.

A very large, bearded man wearing a black jumpsuit seemed to be pulling himself out of the floor itself with a great effort. A tired grunt emerged from deep inside his body. Rimless glasses were perched askew on his nose, and he supported his back with one hand.

The smoke, heat and darkness all contributed to the surreal visual. To Sofia, it seemed like a creature breaking out from the depths of hell.

The man, now standing up inside the room, stumbled straight past the doorframe behind which Rafan and Sofia were hiding. He didn't even notice them amidst the chaotic environment.

He seemed to know where he was going and disappeared behind a corner. His footsteps receded into the distance and, in a few moments, they couldn't hear him anymore.

Sofia and Rafan, with their hearts pounding, crept into the room the man had emerged from, looking at the spot where he had seemingly crawled out of the solid floor. They noticed what looked like a thin ridge, a few centimetres wide and deep, built into the floor. Rafan put his fingers into the ridge – immediately he realised it was a handle and pulled reflexively.

A trapdoor opened. Clearly, the bearded man had come out from whatever lay underneath.

Rafan glanced at Sofia. In his expression, there was a question – shall we go down and check it out?

They opened the door and climbed down a ladder. When they reached the bottom, they stood there, stunned.

One would never have thought that such a humble trapdoor in the basement level, could have led to such a sprawling underground facility. The chamber seemed to have its own power source, as lights flickered on automatically as soon as their feet touched the ground.

Marble columns rose from the ground, meeting the triple-height ceiling above, contrasting starkly with the industrial lighting and exhaust system suspended on a metal framework. The lights were bright and the fans turned lazily.

On one side was a garage and workshop and, on another, a petrol station. In the far corner, there was a spray-painting workshop and, next to it, an industrial elevator in which at least four vehicles could be lifted, presumably to the ground floor level. There was a suspended walkway all around the periphery of the facility.

In between all this, there were about 80 gleaming vehicles in a grid system. They seemed to be a mixture of vintage and modern cars. They could see a section with military and armoured vehicles, a section for SUVs, a wide section of modern saloons from Jaguar, Cadillac, Bentley and BMW as well as a fleet of identical 1980s E-Class Mercedes, all painted black.

Another section held cars that were clearly used by state officials for government business and parades. Amongst them, there was a 1946 Rolls Royce Silver Wraith, a 1936 Rolls Royce Phantom 3, a 1939 Packard 1708, a 1956 Bentley S-1 and a 1956 Excalibur Classic.

And next to them were the almost mythical Mercedes 540k Roadster and 770k Tourenwagon.

Rafan then noticed the wires and the ominous-looking packages that had been arranged on the floor of the facility. He followed the wire to see where it led.

It terminated in a parcel that lay near the petrol filling station. On that parcel was an alarm clock with wires protruding from within it. The alarm had been set for midnight – roughly forty five minutes from now.

'Fuck,' he said, 'it's a bomb.'

29. Uday

Fear was not an emotion Uday had experienced. He thought back to all the times in his life he ought to have experienced fear but did not.

There was the time in Monte Carlo, when he and his friend, high on cocaine and amphetamines, had gone on a rampage of sexual assault and violence in a five-star hotel and casino, resulting in the death of a police officer. There had not been a hint of fear in them that night – a team of lawyers and fixers had been flown in and local politicians and friends in the French and Monaco police force had been bribed, coerced or promised favours to stage a massive cover-up. The next week, they were back in the same town at another hotel raising hell all over again.

Then there was the time his father had slapped him and gone so far as to imprison him for killing his aide with an electric bread knife. Uday had been returning home after an evening of heavy drinking, only to discover that there was a loud party in a hotel en route to his palace.

How dare a loud party be held near his palace without an invitation to him, without his blessing? After all, he had a reputation to maintain for hosting the loudest and most raucous parties. He strode inside to see Kamel Hussein, his father's aide and chief supplier of prostitutes, presiding over the party. Uday had never really liked the man. He'd always noticed how upset his mother seemed to look when a troupe of girls was being led into his father's study.

Drunk and obdurate, he had angrily walked up to Kamel and ordered him to cease all festivities and pack up immediately. To Uday's immense surprise, Kamel had laughed and told Uday that he only took orders from his father, not him – who did he think he was, walking into his party uninvited? It was clear Kamel had also had a few drinks.

When Uday's shock wore off, he calmly walked to the buffet, seized an electric bread knife and walked back to where Kamel was standing. To Kamel's complete surprise, he snatched the drink from his hand, and plunged the breadknife into his stomach, ripping out his intestines. Then, as Kamel lay writhing in agony on the floor, he calmly sipped from his glass while watching his body bleed out in front of all the guests. Then, he walked back out of the hotel and into his waiting limousine.

This time, his father could not possibly ignore the infraction. He had sent the army to Uday's house, under instructions to seize his son and throw him into prison. When he visited his son in prison, he personally beat him up while an aide held Uday's hands behind his back. Then Saddam ordered 50 of Uday's favourite cars to be destroyed. They were his favourites too; all modern supercars.

When he was finally allowed to return to his palace, Uday felt humiliated and angry, but not scared. Unable to release his anger on his father, he took it out on the people around him.

In the period that followed his return, no amount of money could convince people to work in his palace – and in a poverty-stricken Baghdad, that said a lot. Such had been his reputation for cruelty and violence.

Then there was the time when, in the early 90s, an attempt had been made on his life. He was shot several times. The best medical care available had been flown into Iraq from all four corners of the globe. The doctor in charge of the team dedicated to Uday's care had been promised his weight in gold if Uday recovered, along with dark threats on his family's lives if he failed. Uday survived, but he remained in hospital for over a year. And for a year after that, he was partially wheelchair-bound for a long time.

With every operation, every pill and every painful physiotherapy session, Uday had only felt mounting anger, not fear. There had been plenty of frustration, sure – he had experienced a significant loss of libido along with his physical mobility. But even before he was back on his feet, he used all his considerable resources to track down the people who had attempted to kill him. His team had narrowed down the suspect list, but there were still several potential culprits when Uday decided he could no longer wait to discover who it was. He had all of them rounded up, along with their families and extended families. Then, over the course of two months, they were slowly tortured and destroyed. Afterwards, the videotapes had given him many happy hours as he recuperated in his private hospital.

And today, Uday took pride in the fact that he still was not scared. All his resources had been taken away from him, save for the small group of Fedayeen and the weapons they carried with them.

When his brother had collected him from his house, on that fateful day when he was about to take pleasure in the girl in his red room, he had been asked to pack no more than one suitcase. Such was his arrogance, that instead of practical clothing, Uday had packed his favourite Louis Vuitton ties. Instead of shampoo and a toothbrush, he had packed his favourite Gucci colognes. Instead of important documents, he had packed his favourite S&M porn. Instead of medication and a first aid kit, he had packed heroin, cocaine and a bottle of Remy Martin.

Of course, he had regretted it afterwards – it turned out that it made sense for both him and Qusay to throw out all their normal clothes and disguise themselves. Uday had let his usually carefully manicured 'designer' beard grow long and scraggly. He had shaved his hair off to reduce his chances of being recognised. He told himself it was only for a short time, but recently he wasn't sure he believed it.

Until recently, he had counted on being safe very soon – be it in a safe house, or under the protection and shelter of one of his father's sympathisers, or through his negotiated freedom with the coalition forces via his contact in Jordan, or simply taking off in his private jet for greener pastures. But he had not counted on the tenacity of the coalition forces in hunting him down. He had not counted on the sheer force and the level of technology they employed to track him and his brother, Qusay. He had not counted on the million-dollar bounty on his head, or the fact that his father's friends were no longer his father's friends, now that his father himself was on the run.

He had not counted on the US forces in Jordan shooting down any aircraft in Iraq's airspace they did not recognise. He had not counted on the instant desertion of Iraq's entire army. He had not counted on the complete and utter shutdown of communications between him and the outside world.

Most of all, he had not counted on Kasim ignoring his phone calls. He still could not believe it. That had been his insurance. That bastard would certainly get what was coming to him.

But still, he was free and he was alive, even if it was an uncomfortable existence. Every two days they went through the list of perhaps twenty-two safe houses, each owned by some family still loyal to the Saddam regime, and decided where to go next. But they could not spend more than a few days in each as it was too risky. Now that they were approaching the end of the list, they would soon have to start going back to the houses they had already been to.

Uday could not believe how things had changed in Iraq, and how the power dynamic had shifted so quickly. One of the families they had come to had actually tried to refuse them shelter. He couldn't believe their nerve. They would certainly be on his hit list once the war was over. Another had the audacity to suggest that he share a bedroom with his brother because the family, 'had no other rooms.' Uday had insisted the couple themselves move into the living room and had commandeered their bedroom for himself.

To compound the problems Uday was facing, it had been so long since he had a woman. Sure, he had slowed down after his assassination attempt, but he certainly had never gone for so long without sex.

One of the families they had lived with had a 13-year-old daughter. That was just the sort of age Uday liked; when they were at the cusp of becoming women. He would have had her too, but the father, seeing the look on Uday's face when he introduced them, had hastily sent her away to live with another family. Uday had been enraged but there was nothing he could do. Qusay would kill him if he brought more attention to them by killing the father or trying to track down the daughter.

Qusay always managed to stay polite to their hosts – Uday wondered how he tolerated the peasants.

But even Uday had to eventually become aware of the fact that he was depending on other people's generosity to survive. Qusay had ordered him to behave – after all, there was a pretty juicy bounty on their heads. Any one of their hosts may have been tempted to turn them in and claim it.

Over the last two days, they had been living with another one of their father's cronies, in the town of Mosul. Even though their host had never previously missed a chance to praise Saddam in public, Uday and Qusay did not feel like they could completely trust him to keep them safe. But then, Uday and Qusay had been feeling a little paranoid in general, the result of being on the run from the world's most powerful country.

However, in this case, they might have been justified – their father had even briefly jailed the brother of their host. The man in question had boasted that he was a cousin of Saddam, rather than just belonging to the same tribe. Saddam, who liked to tightly control who was allowed to use the influence of his family name, heard of this and had the man picked up. The brother of their host had repented and begged forgiveness, so Saddam had allowed him to go back home after a few days. This was not entirely out of the kindness of his heart. Saddam had many uses for the man's family – they had, for example, been instrumental in raising support for Saddam amongst a few of the local tribes. In return, Saddam had awarded their family business with lucrative government construction contracts. They had gotten rich, pocketing much of the money instead of using it for bricks and cement. The family had made millions due to Saddam's rule, even after the brother had been released from jail.

Qusay and Uday were counting on the forgiveness Saddam had shown, and the rewards the family had been showered with, to assure their host's loyalty. In any case, they were completely out of options and had nowhere to go. So, on one sunny morning, Uday, Qusay, Qusay's son Mustafa, and one of their bodyguards simply knocked on this man's door.

The man, while initially shocked to see them standing on his doorstep, had not been able to refuse them, so he had let them into the new villa that he had built from the proceeds of the business he had done with the Hussein family.

Uday and Qusay had made themselves at home. Qusay had commandeered the man's son's Nintendo system and Uday had glanced longingly at the man's four daughters before they were ushered away by their parents. Mustafa had demanded Pepsi.

The man obliged them with everything they wanted. But they still couldn't shake that feeling of mistrust. Uday was thinking about their next move when suddenly he heard a knock at the door. For a while, no one answered.

Uday knew their host's wife and children were out visiting relatives. Perhaps this is why the door had not been answered quickly – the womenfolk who usually did this were not at home.

Finally, he heard the door being opened and eventually slammed shut. Uday decided to glance out of the window – just in time to see a large group of US troops leading their host away to a waiting Humvee. They did not handcuff him but led him away and gave him a cigarette.

He looked around at the courtyard.

The house had been surrounded by US special forces.

They had been betrayed.

30. Abdul / Ava

There are few things as terrifying as the primordial roar of an apex predator in the dark, particularly a big cat.

Said to be an assertion of dominance over any other creature within their territory, their roar can be heard up to five miles away. Supersized vocal cords create a low guttural sound that strikes fear and intimidation, not just in the mind, but also within the physical being of all those who hear it.

Abdul remembered the awe with which David Attenborough had spoken about the deadliness of lions – many centuries of evolution had provided big cats with the ability to hunt with supreme effectiveness at any time of day or night, their highly developed sense of smell compounding their ability to see in places devoid of light. Made up of approximately 250 kilograms of pure muscle, lions can cover vast distances very quickly. Their main weapons of choice are their super sharp retractable claws that are approximately four centimetres long and used to tear away large chunks of flesh from their prey, which they proceed to consume with teeth that have a scissor-like function to tackle raw meat.

Statistically, lions are far more likely to attack humans if they have been kept in captivity at some point.

Abdul felt like he was in an absurd nightmare; a surreal mix of smoke and fire, crazed Fedayeen and, now, lions, all within Saddam's mammoth palace. He had no time to reflect on the fact that they had just killed a man. All he could think of was the roar. How the lion had gotten into the Al-Sijood complex remained a mystery to them – although Abdul suspected it might have been something to do with Uday Hussein, who reportedly kept a small zoo of wild animals. At first, they were both frozen to the spot, not quite believing what they heard. Then they heard another roar, louder than the first. Abdul realised the lion would be attracted to the smell of blood from the deceased Fedayeen in the kitchen.

Rather than looking for an escape route, it seemed safer to simply lock themselves in somewhere. But the kitchen had no door. Grabbing Ava by the arm, he led them both quickly out of the kitchen and into the adjacent room, which looked like an office, and closed the door behind him. They weren't sure what their next move should be. They had nothing to subdue the lion with. They had not even had the presence of mind to take the Fedayeen's gun when they escaped the kitchen – the roar of the lion hadn't really inspired rational thought. Abdul kicked himself. The pistol would have proved invaluable. But now it was out of their reach as they could not risk opening the door again – the lion could be right outside.

They could smell the lion approaching from several metres away. The smell was complemented by the clicking sound of the huge cat's claws as it padded closer to the kitchen area. Clearly, the lion had extended them, ready for an attack. Then there was a huge crash – Ava and Abdul guessed the lion had swiped at a trolley full of vessels in the kitchen. When the clamour of the vessels had died down, they heard what could only have been described as a scrunching sound; the sound of flesh being ripped apart. 'Shall we run while it's distracted with eating him?' Ava whispered to Abdul, anxiously. Abdul could tell Ava really wanted him to say no. But he knew what Ava also knew – this would probably be their only chance to escape.

'Yeah. Let's. They don't attack if they are well-fed, anyway. I think.'

'You think so?'

'Yeah, I watch a lot of the Discovery Channel. Once they had this documentary where...'

'OK! OK! Don't need to know. Let's do this. I'm going to open this door extremely quietly. I think silence is the name of the game here. If we can tiptoe past the kitchen door, we can escape. Sound OK?'

'Yeah. Wait. Let me tie my laces.'

'OK. You tie your laces. I'm going to take off my boots; impossible to be quiet in them. Don't breathe loudly once I open the door, OK?'

Abdul looked at her dubiously.

Ava slowly slid back the latch, holding the door shut. She opened the door just a crack and peered out, every movement deliberately slow, deliberately quiet. Slowly, she opened the door. They crept out, terrified that the creature would notice them. They could still hear the gnawing and the ripping sound being made by the lion as it feasted on the dead Fedayeen. They crept, very cautiously, along the corridor. As they were passing, they summoned the courage to glance briefly through the kitchen door.

They saw the behind of a huge lion, its tail swaying merrily as it crouched over the corpse of the Fedayeen. There were blood splatters all over the area. They continued silently, each muscle within their bodies tensed, totally focused on getting away. Soon, the door through which they could exit the floor became visible in the distance. Suddenly, the silence was shattered by the sound of static from Ava's walkie-talkie, and Sofia's voice filled the air 'Hi guys! Where are you? Hellooooo?' The two looked at each other, each one's face mirroring the terror in the other. From behind them, the lion roared in what sounded like surprise and anger. Abdul and Ava both dashed for the exit, which was still a good 20 metres away.

As they ran, they could hear the lion coming up behind them – a kind of scraping, bounding sound combined with its ragged breathing. Abdul looked behind him and nearly lost his footing. It was amazing how quickly the big cat had covered the distance between them, its fangs and mouth dripping with blood. As Ava ran, she was vaguely aware that Sofia's voice continued to talk merrily at them, 'Heloooo! If you can hear me... come to the stairwell... lower ground floor... secret entrance... found... entrance.'

She pushed the transmit button on the walkie-talkie as she ran and screamed loudly, 'What are you doing inside? We're going to try and get to you. There's a lion chasing us.'

The voice of a justifiably stupefied Sofia came over the line, 'A what? Did you say a lion?'

Ava clicked the radio off as they ran as fast as they could towards the place that Sofia had described.

They crashed through a swinging door, the lion just a few feet behind them and gaining quickly. They won a few seconds extra as the heavy glass door swung back and crashed into the surprised lion's face, enraging it further. And there was nowhere to go.

They had led themselves into a small room near the elevators that had no exit. They could see the angry and bloodied animal had backed up slightly as the door had smashed its face. At first Ava and Abdul were frozen to the spot – then Abdul leapt forward and held the door shut quickly followed by Ava who did the same. The lion pounced on the door, its front paws smashing against the glass, cracking it, and causing the door to swing open a few inches. Abdul and Ava did their best to keep the door from opening wide enough to let the animal through.

Ava realized Abdul wouldn't be able to hold the door shut much longer. Desperately, she looked around.

There were definitely no doors, nor any windows, just a ventilation grille built into the ceiling. She wasn't sure it would work, but it seemed big enough to let them through into the air conditioning duct above.

They had no other option.

Ava quickly grabbed a chair and positioned it below the duct. She had to jump a little but managed to push against the grille. It gave way easily, and she managed to push it to one side inside the duct.

Next, she jumped and caught the edge of the duct with both hands, pulling herself up until she could place her elbows inside the edge of the opening. She wriggled into the crawlspace. Pipes and wires of every thickness and colour were everywhere. Everything was covered with a thick black layer of dust. Worst of all, she could smell the smoke even more strongly. However, it was still safer than being in the room with the enraged lion. Abdul had stood on the chair to follow Ava into the crawlspace.

Ava grabbed his hand and pulled him up just as the lion broke into the room and bounded towards the chair. But Abdul was already through the opening. In the darkness, they looked below. Their headlamps shone into the face of the lion, who looked directly at them and roared. They could smell its breath even though they were a good six feet above. The lion paced up and down, constantly looking up and growling at them.

Abdul glanced at the luminescent dial of his watch. It was 11:22 p.m.

31. Copella

First Lieutenant Copella of the 1st Marine Division, 1st Reconnaissance Battalion, had been watching the events unfold at the Al-Sijood complex. Even though he did not know exactly what was going on, he had some theories.

He was lost in thought: Did anyone really believe that the coalition didn't have eyes on the complex at all times? Saddam's main nerve centre of administration? The very reason why it had not been under US guard after its initial search by coalition forces was because he wanted to lull the enemy into a false sense of security. His theory was that, sooner or later, someone from the leadership of the now-defunct government would come by. In such a huge building, it would have been impossible to destroy everything or to remove everything of value. Someone senior would be tempted to enter – either to retrieve or destroy something. And that's when Copella would swoop down and pick them up. After all, these were Hajis they were dealing with – how clever could they possibly be?

Copella was due for a promotion and he was determined to get it. The only reason why he was doubtful it would happen was because his record on civilian casualties so far was not great.

Or, to put it in other terms, it was too great.

His commanders thought he was a bit of a loose cannon; someone who wasn't scared to use too much force.

This could not have been further from the truth. The reason Copella's civilian casualties were very high was precisely because he *was* scared.

He was scared to get shot and he was scared to die. He did not have the sort of experience that would allow him, under pressure, to distinguish friend from foe or to stay calm and follow protocol, even though many of the new recruits seemed to manage just fine. Quite frankly, if there was a risk that he could be shot by someone – man, woman or child – he would not hesitate to shoot them first and ask questions later.

He was conscious this was not the case for many of the men under his command. In fact, he was often dumbfounded by their professionalism, particularly when Marines went to lengths to protect the civilians whose country they were invading (Copella *did* consider it an invasion). Some of them had even put themselves in harm's way, shielding them with their own bodies when bullets flew in residential areas. He understood the moral logic to these actions: the common Iraqi citizen had little to do with the conflict. Indeed, the invasion had been labelled 'Operation Iraqi Freedom' in an effort to position it as one big altruistic effort in favour of the Iraqi populace. But First Lieutenant Copella certainly did not share that sentiment.

Their key task in Baghdad was to, 'Cut the head off the snake,' or, in other words, to hunt down Saddam, his sons and the leadership of the Baathist Party, and to do so as quickly as possible. All other tasks were secondary. To this effect, many teams of Marines had been sent to various locations around the city based on intelligence that came from God only knew where. They were given coordinates and asked to raid a particular flat or house in the city with the vague notion that it may hold a senior Baathist Party official.

It was, of course, one of the greatest absurdities of the situation that none of them would be able to recognise a single party official, even if he (they were all men) were to invite them in for tea – thus, very few had been captured or killed. A bright spark somewhere high up in the ranks had decided that the best way to help the troops ID one of the targeted individuals would be to create a deck of cards with pictures of the targets on the reverse – because of course, all the troops did during their downtime in the 20th century was play cards. However, not a single Marine on the ground in Baghdad had actually received or even seen one of these decks of cards. The shipment probably lay forgotten in some military storage facility – the struggling military supply chain from Kuwait favouring the transport of fuel and ammunition. Ironically, many bullets and much fuel would be wasted due to the absence of a means of identification.

Copella had long since decided he would put the bullets and fuel to better use than chasing Saddam's ministers. He would use the vast means and resources of the US Military to enrich himself as much as he possibly could. Charlie Company of the 1st Reconnaissance Battalion had always been a stand-alone battalion with no parent regiment. Instead, it fell directly under the command of the 1st Marine Division, allowing him more leeway to act independently.

After they had destroyed much of Baghdad and established a new administration, American businesses would be required to step in and rebuild the city. Copella planned to play a vital role in what was sure to be a lucrative reconstruction effort. US contractors would require local knowledge and local contacts to help with their tenders.

He had been on raids over the last few days where they had come under fire and had dealt out more than their fair share of death and destruction within Baghdad.

If the fucking Iraqis did as they were told, stayed in their homes, did not hide weapons, and did not approach the troops, then they would have no cause to get shot, would they?

Copella had seen the activity as it unfolded. He had known, of course, about the sniper on the sixth floor who had been there from the time he had started watching the building. He had known that another Fedayeen, the one with the beard and spectacles, had joined the sniper and brought with him some IEDs – he had seen both of them together in the room on the third floor. This gave Copella hope that perhaps a member of the leadership would walk into the building and he would pick them all up together.

But then, there was a fly in his ointment – for the last few hours there had been some unexpected visitors to the complex. Two men and two women. One of the women clearly looked European, and the other three looked like locals. The three locals were dressed in jeans and t-shirts, the uniform of the westernised youngsters of the Baghdadi middle class.

Then he had seen the explosion and, even though he didn't know what had caused it, he suspected it had something to do with the visitors. He guessed they weren't on the same team as the Fedayeen.

Copella thought they were going to steal something.

He had come to that conclusion after thinking through many different scenarios – the possibility of the woman being a journalist - but then, why would a journalist enter the palace? Or was she in some secret branch of the coalition forces?

Surely, they would have warned him! What about the remote possibility of all of them being part of the Hussein Regime? That seemed too unlikely for a westerner. In the end, the only theory that made sense was theft, a motivation he could relate to.

In the last few weeks, he had received an increasing number of reports of looting from government buildings and ransacking of Saddam's palaces. Their standing orders were not to interfere with these activities – the only building that was to be sealed and guarded by the US Marines was that of the Oil Ministry. They didn't have the resources or the motive to protect any of the other buildings of the previous administration.

But what in the world could these looters possibly be after? The building had been searched already – top to bottom – and nothing had emerged besides a few binders of files highlighting the corruption rampant in Saddam's government's construction and public services contracts.

He made a phone call to his local fixer, a man he had 'befriended' in his first week in Iraq by slipping him a few dollars. He didn't trust the man at all, didn't really trust anyone, but he had proved to be a useful source of verifiable information so far.

He quizzed this man about the Al Sijood complex. It seemed the fixer knew exactly what the thieves might be after – he didn't even have to make any enquiries. It seemed that Saddam and Uday's most valued and precious cars were stored underneath the building.

At that moment, Copella made up his mind to have them for himself.

If he could, he would use his contacts amidst the private military contractors to smuggle the vehicles out of the country. If he couldn't do that, he would turn them over to the soon-to-be elected Iraqi leadership – at least that way he would still get the fame that went with securing the Hussein family's most precious cars and perhaps even a promotion.

So, with that in mind, he rallied the troops, got into his armoured vehicle and made the ten-minute journey to the Al-Sijood complex, along with about 30 of his Marines.

He knew that the man and woman waiting outside the complex had joined their two friends inside.

He wouldn't hesitate to kill them all to accomplish his goal. After all, if they were running around in a war zone, there was a good chance that all four of them would wind up dead anyway. No one would miss them and there would be no inquest or hearing. This was war.

30 soldiers under his command would storm the palace with instructions to shoot and kill anyone they encountered. However, Copella was nothing if not cautious. He placed armoured blockades on every road leading out of the palace and into the city, each accompanied by an M230 chain gun (625 rounds per minute across 4,000 metres as he recalled) mounted on a Light Combat Tactical All-Terrain Vehicle, capable of destroying armoured vehicles and helicopters. A ring of iron now surrounded three sides of the complex, with the fast-flowing Tigris blocking off an escape from the rear of the property.

All the troops had been told four very dangerous armed insurgents, including two women, one of them European-looking, may try to escape in vehicles. He had suggested that shooting first and asking questions later might be the best tactic in the circumstances – who knew what sort of ordinance these determined insurgents possessed? After the vehicles and individuals had been disabled with deadly force, they were not to be approached or opened – there was a chance they were booby-trapped. Copella was to be radioed and he would take over with the explosive experts on his team. Once the cars had been located and those in his command had left him to it, he would have ample opportunity to hide the precious vintage automobiles in his own army trucks, taking them wherever he wanted. His men would comply, they knew what was in their best interests.

With that thought in mind and scant concern for the lives of his men, he exited his vehicle and motioned for the soldiers to enter the burning building.

32. Abdul / Ava

Abdul and Ava appraised the situation they were in. The lion prowled below them as the smoke in the crawlspace seemed to get denser by the minute.

If they knew where their friends were within the complex, perhaps they could use the crawlspace to get to them – it seemed to extend for miles. Or perhaps their friends might be able to help them somehow.

Either way, they needed to get in touch with the rest of their group, and they needed to do it quickly.

Abdul had just tried to reach their friends on the radio. Unfortunately, all they could hear was static – it had been hard enough to hear them even outside of the enclosed crawlspace. Additionally, Abdul guessed their friends might have been in the subterranean part of the facility, making it even harder for radio waves to reach them.

If only they had a better or more powerful antenna on their radio, maybe they stood a chance.

Abdul looked around the crawlspace. All the wiring in the building seemed to travel through it, presumably from its source, to supply every light, computer and air conditioner. A possible solution, Abdul thought, would be to use some of the copper wire that surrounded them to extend the range of the two-way radio. He even had a multitool in his pocket that had a wire stripper, pliers, small shears and a ruler.

The problem was, he wasn't sure which wires were still live and which weren't. Sure, the lights were off but that did not mean all the electrical systems were down. Clipping a live wire might give him a deadly shock. He worked quickly, peering through the smoke to deduce which wires seemed to branch off towards the light switches in the room and were therefore unlikely to carry a charge at that moment. He couldn't be sure, of course, but it was their best chance. He decided to risk it and snipped the wire.

He felt no shock.

Quickly, he cut off a length of the wire, measured it with the ruler on his multitool and cut it down to 17.5 centimetres, the required length for his radio. Next, he removed the belt clip on the back of the radio exposing the screws that secured the clip to the body of the radio. Abdul knew this screw was very likely connected to the ground ring around the antenna, thus extending the size of the antenna by a quarter wavelength and, consequently, increasing its range. He stripped some of the wire and attached it to the screw.

Scarcely had the bare wire touched the radio when the speaker came alive with the sound of Rafan's voice. '…to the stairwell. Once again, if you can hear us, come to the room near the stairwell. There is a trapdoor that leads down to the garage – it's massive and there's an exit to a back door. We will need to use the back door to stop us from getting caught by troops that are now surrounding the front of the building.'

Then, Rafan said something that chilled them to their core.

'There's a bomb here that is set to go off in, like, twenty five minutes. It looks like it's been created to destroy the garage. You guys need to get here quick so that we can get out. Like, right now.'

Abdul looked Ava in the face – while at first, there was a clear expression of admiration for Abdul's prowess with the radio, it soon gave way to a more terrified look. The lion continued to pace below them as they had a quick discussion.

They knew, due to Rafan's guidance, roughly where the room with the trapdoor lay. It wasn't far from where they were. They could crawl through the massive crawlspace, get themselves above the right spot and drop down onto the trapdoor. But the problem of the lion persisted. The creature seemed to follow them as they crawled noisily from one area to another, positioning itself directly below them.

'Listen,' said Ava, 'do you remember which direction the kitchen is?' Abdul nodded. 'I think I have an idea. No time to explain, but tell me – do you think you could find the elevator's wires amidst this mess?'

'Sure, the elevator is only a few feet away I think, if we crawl to the space directly above it, I should be able to identify the wires that branch down into it'

Ava nodded. 'OK. So, could you control the doors of the elevator from up here? Open and shut them? Lock them and so on?'

'Theoretically,' said Abdul, looking dubious. 'I'll have to identify the right wires that complete the circuit to lock the doors.'

'OK. Go figure it out. See if you can do it. I'm going to figure out a way to get the lion into the elevator. You figure out how to lock it inside using the wires.'

Before Abdul could reply, Ava scampered off, crawling in the direction of the kitchen.

In a minute or two, she was above the kitchen and opened the ventilation grille, which she remembered seeing right next to the huge industrial freezer.

She poked her head out of the shaft – there was no sign of the lion yet. Perhaps it had decided to stay and track Abdul. That suited Ava just fine.

Acting quickly, she reached out for the door of the freezer from the open ventilation grille. She had thought she could reach it without descending into the room but she was wrong, it was a few inches too far away. She made a split-second decision, leaving the safety of the crawlspace to jump onto the floor of the kitchen. In a trice, she opened the freezer door. As she expected, a wave of water splashed out – there had been no power for a while, and everything had defrosted. A very foul smell hit her nose – she would only have seconds before the lion sensed it. Quickly she grabbed a massive leg of lamb that lay wrapped in plastic shrink wrap. She hopped onto the counter and back into the crawlspace, the stinking leg of lamb tucked into her waistband. A trail of lamb blood trickled down the inside of her trousers.

Then, she crawled back to Abdul who had, by this time, located the wires leading into the elevator. They had been helpfully labelled in Arabic.

Ava positioned herself near the ventilation grille that was in the ceiling of the small lobby in which the elevator door was housed. She unwrapped the leg of lamb, making the stench considerably worse. Blood from the lamb covered her arms and dripped down the vent into the lobby below. The lion went into a frenzy, growling and attempting to jump up at them.

Ava opened the vent and slowly lowered herself through it, even though every instinct told her not to. Her legs, bent at the knees, hooked around the ledge of the vent, while her head, torso and the arm holding the leg of lamb dangled upside down, directly above the crazed lion, who was now jumping and swiping at her, desperate to get at the lamb.

Her legs cramped due to the stress they were under, and her entire body trembled – half out of fear and half from sheer exertion. She wasn't sure how long she could hold on in this position – a few seconds at most.

'OK. Now! Open the door of the elevator!' screamed Ava.

Abdul crouched over a panel in the crawlspace and touched the two wires together that he'd stripped of their insulation.

Nothing happened. The doors didn't budge.

'Quickly, I can't hold on any longer!', Ava shouted.

Working as fast as he could, he stripped another wire and tried it against one of the two he already had in his hand.

The door opened and Ava threw the leg of lamb straight into it. It landed with a resounding thwack, right inside the elevator. Flecks of watery blood splattered all over the walls of the narrow space.

With one big bound, the lion jumped on it, tearing it to bits with his fangs, which had been dripping with saliva moments ago.

'Now! Now!' said Ava.

Abdul touched another set of wires together and the doors of the elevator shut. These, he twisted together using a strip of insulation to secure them.

The elevator doors remained shut. Muffled scrunching noises could be heard from within and Abdul hoped, desperately, that they would hold.

But they had no time to consider the extent of their safety. Pushing down their instincts to stay amidst the security of the crawlspace, they both jumped through the opening that had held the ventilation grille and ran towards the area Rafan had mentioned. A few moments later, they entered the room that was adjacent to the elevator door – identifying it as the one with the entrance to the subterranean car park.

Sure enough, Sofia's head was poking out of the trapdoor. As soon as her and Abdul's eyes met, she ducked down, giving them room to enter. Abdul jumped in blindly and Ava dove, headfirst, into the cavity in the floor. A prepared Sofia slammed the trapdoor shut behind them, just as she saw a blurred and hairy, brown shape emerge into the lobby from the elevator.

She locked it behind her, her hands shaking, as they heard an angry roar above them. Then another roar, slightly less ferocious and a bit lacklustre. Then, finally, clicking sounds heading back to the elevator.

The four friends stood there for a moment, too shocked and out of breath to say anything.

Then, finally, Sofia managed to get some words out. 'You *did* say lion!'

33. Abdul / Ava / Rafan / Sofia

All four of them fell into each other's arms, but Rafan broke away. They had no time to celebrate. He quickly told Ava and Abdul about the troops surrounding the palace. Abdul and Ava, in turn, reported on the fire that seemed to have almost reached the first floor of the building. The question of how they had seemed to come across a lion was pushed aside - the clock on the bomb showed fourteen minutes until it was supposed to go off.

Despite the looming danger, Ava and Abdul's eyes went wide as they took in row upon row of beautiful cars. Under better circumstances, they could happily have spent many hours in the facility, but they knew they had a job to do. The faster they could get away, the safer they would be.

Rafan, who had the chance to look around the garage while he and Sofia had been waiting for Ava and Abdul to find them, had devised a plan. He felt they could still get away with the 540k and the 770k using the massive freight elevator at the rear of the garage. He reckoned it would take eight minutes to get away safely, with six minutes to spare before the bomb went off. He had done a test run while waiting for Abdul and Rafan, so he knew the exit to the car elevator overlooked the rear gardens of the Al-Sijood Palace.

There were now only fourteen minutes between them and certain death, or them and an escape with the two cars that would make each of them a millionaire many times over.

They decided to try, agreeing that if they couldn't get the cars out in eight minutes, they would leave without them.

They went straight over to the 540k, the focus of their attention and the primary subject of their thoughts over the last few weeks. The car, like the other vintage classics, was conveniently sitting on a trailer platform which had modern road-capable wheels. The front of the trailer could be hitched to a truck or car.

Rafan had already examined the vintage automobile and used straps to secure the vast chassis to the platform before removing the blocks that held the wheels of the trailers in place. He and Sofia had found large canvas sheets in one of the corners of the facility and had used these to drape the 540k and the 770k.

Abdul and Sofia found a forklift and drove it towards what they now thought of as the vintage section, where Rafan and Ava stood with the cars. The plan was to hitch the forklift to the trailers and drive them to the elevator. Once both trailers holding the cars were on ground level, above the subterranean garage, they could think about the next part of their plan.

They were about to get to work and hitch the platform with the 540k to the forklift when they heard the wail of an alarm system from the corner of the facility.

'You guys continue to sort this out, I'm going to see what that is about,' Ava said, as she ran towards the sound. The alarm was coming from a loudspeaker set above the bank of monitors fitted to the wall. Guessing what they were for, Ava threw a few switches on the main console. Some of the monitors flickered to life displaying a blueish static while others remained lifeless. A few displayed images of the building above them and the grounds outside.

She suddenly caught some movement on one of these screens and looked harder. The image was not at all clear, but she could see what looked like a troop of heavily armed Marines storming through a corridor. The Marines disappeared from the screen she was looking at and appeared on another as another camera picked up the fast-moving soldiers.

Quickly, she scanned the cameras outside of the building they were in, as well as those placed on lampposts and trees outside the complex. She could see several armoured vehicles with very dangerous-looking machine guns mounted on them dotted all around the roads leading into the city. Every road in front of the complex had been sealed with roadblocks and armoured vehicles. There were no roads to the rear of the property; it backed directly onto the Tigris, which flowed through the breadth of the city.

The trapdoor to the underground facility was unsecured – anyone who found it would be able to enter without a key. She desperately looked around and her eyes fell on a large storage shelf in the workshop area, the kind made out of a sturdy iron framework, used to store heavy items like engines, tools and building supplies. If placed directly under the trapdoor, it might block the opening for long enough for them to escape.

She switched on the radio so she wouldn't have to shout across the room. 'Need help, come quick, all of you.'

They feverishly started to empty the industrial shelving unit and then, taking one corner each, unlocked the massive castors it rested on and rolled it towards the trapdoor, placing it underneath. It fitted nicely. Ava guessed it would require an explosive charge to get through the trapdoor, blasting away the thick iron shelving unit underneath.

They made their way towards the industrial freight elevator. So far, the cameras showed no military presence behind the complex, where the industrial size car-elevator opened.

Feverishly, they worked to get the two vintage cars into the elevator and pressed the button to take them up to ground level. They could hear some machinery humming to life. Abdul's watch beeped. Their eight minutes were up.

That was when they heard muffled footsteps overhead.

The soldiers were here.

34. Uday

The minute he saw their host being led away by the Marines, he knew the bastard had sold them out. He wasn't handcuffed. Hell, they weren't even holding on to him. He was following them willingly. They led him to a van and sat him down inside. Uday watched from the upper story of the house as the bastard calmly borrowed a lighter from a marine and lit a cigarette as even more Marines took up their positions around the courtyard.

Uday realised he should not have been surprised by this; it had always been only a matter of time before he and his brother were found. For some reason, he was not sure if they would find his father – the patriarch's stores of cunning and guile had always been limitless.

Uday took stock and thought through his options. He could walk out of the house and surrender to the Americans. That would almost certainly be simply postponing the inevitable - he knew that, without a deal, he would be tried and hung. Sure, it may take a month or two, but it would happen.

He held no cards. He could not give up his brother as they had been found together already. He could not give up his father; it would be too public, too obvious that he had done so, unlike the deal he would have struck if Kasim had come through. Besides, he did not know his father's exact location anyway.

There was, however, one card he could try and play – he knew where the money was.

Two days before all hell had broken loose, Qusay had committed the biggest bank robbery in history: four billion US dollars, pretty much all of Iraq's National Bank's cash reserves. It had also been one of the easiest bank robberies in history.

When it had become plainly obvious that the American invasion was inevitable, Saddam summoned Qusay and ordered him to go to the bank and take the money, handing him a letter bearing the royal seal of the House of Saddam.

Qusay had taken three of the largest trucks he could find and driven them to the bank with Saddam's chief secretary, the head of the finance ministry and a few trusted members of the National Guard. Next, he simply walked into the bank and presented the manager with his father's letter, asking for all the money – each penny of it belonging to the people of Iraq – to be loaded into his truck. The bank manager was clearly uncomfortable with what he had been asked to do, but his hands were tied. Even a single word of protest would have resulted in Qusay shooting him in the head without a second thought.

It had taken a team of several men three entire days to pack and load all the currency into the three eight-wheelers. By the time Qusay drove away, it had been dangerously close to Bush's deadline for the invasion.

Following that, all the staff at the bank were sworn to secrecy. Of course, too many people had seen the money being packed and taken away, so there was no way to prevent the news of the robbery from spreading. But they could spread misinformation, seeding out the idea that 'only' one billion had been stolen instead of four.

When the rumour spread, hordes of people went to the bank to try and withdraw their money but the doors had been barricaded and the building lay empty. All of Baghdad was angrily talking about the heist, sharing their theories on where the money would be taken and where it would be hidden. There were rumours that it had been put behind a false wall in one of the Palaces. This was not true. There were several million hidden behind false walls in all the palaces, including Uday's own private reserves, but that had nothing to do with this money.

But Uday knew where Iraq's billions were hidden. Qusay had laughed as he had told Uday. The truth was tremendously underwhelming and, thus, also the last place where anyone would think of looking. One of the trucks, containing exactly one billion in cash, had been driven straight to one of Saddam's palaces, where the cash had simply been stored in a large cupboard for the American forces to find should they manage to get that far into Baghdad. It was all a decoy.

The contents of the other two trucks, approximately three billion dollars, had been spread out everywhere. Some of it had been hidden in the Al-Sijood complex, but thankfully, nowhere near the car park he had ordered to be destroyed. It had been lodged in the ample crawlspace of the building; bundles of hundred-dollar bills, shrink-wrapped several times over, and then each bundle wrapped in nondescript hessian sacking that had been carefully sewn tightly shut.

Uday sighed wistfully as he thought of the cars hidden at the Al-Sijood complex. Those were now only a memory. He had personally ensured the order to destroy them all had been given to a trusted lieutenant of the Fedayeen, but only if it had become certain the Americans had breached the city. As it had become certain, he had no doubt the contents of the underground garage were gone.

But perhaps the money in the crawlspace was still safe and lay there undiscovered. Perhaps he could recover it. Perhaps he could use it to bribe his way out of trouble. After all, everyone had a price. Perhaps he could… Uday nearly jumped out of his skin due to a very loud gunshot that erupted only two feet away from him, near the window.

It was little Mustafa, Qusay's young son. He had a grim and determined look on his face and held one of the royal family's gold-plated AK-47s in his hand. It was pointed out of the window towards a cluster of American troops. Uday had been so lost in thought that he had not even noticed Mustafa coming into the room. Uday risked a glance out of the window and saw that a Marine had been hit. He couldn't be sure if the wound was fatal or not; the fallen man had quickly been dragged away by his colleagues, some of whom, by now, were firing back at them.

All the windows in the room shattered in the first few seconds of the barrage. Mustafa ducked expertly under the windowsill after firing a volley of shots; even though he had quite literally signed all of their death warrants by firing the first shot, Uday couldn't help but feel a flicker of admiration, or even pride, at the young man so expertly handling his weapon, and so bravely determined to go down fighting. Uday could not take any credit, of course. All that had come directly from Qusay's training. Uday had given him quite a different sort of training, taking him to a whorehouse when he turned 13. Still, Uday thought that had been equally important, considering how short the young man's life would now be.

As the shards of glass rained down on him while watching Mustafa, something inside Uday changed. He felt somehow protective of the boy. OK, perhaps protective was a bit of a stretch – Uday only really felt protective of himself. How dare those ignorant peasants come to Iraq from whatever goddamn US village they were recruited from? How dare they come into his country, thinking they could do as they wanted? How dare they fire at him and his brethren? He was Saddam's first-born son, and he was going to show them what he was made of. In any event, there was nothing left to do but make use of the small arsenal they always travelled with. They had enough ammunition to hold out for days, including RPGs, grenades, heavy machine guns and millions of rounds of AK ammo. They could call for backup from the Republican Guard and hold out long enough for them to arrive. Who knows, perhaps they could even blast their way out of the situation. They would certainly try.

By this time, Qusay was also crouched at the window next to his son, holding his own gold-plated AK-47. Two of their Republican Guards were in the other bedroom facing the courtyard, setting up the heavy machine guns. It was confirmed – they were making a stand.

At the first lull in firing, Uday dashed for the cupboard. He opened it and, ignoring the weaponry stored inside, reached for his suitcase. He had been saving his last wrap of cocaine. Now was the time to use it.

He took a large sniff and let out an animalistic war cry as he grabbed one of the AKs in the cupboard and commando rolled to a window. He peeped out, intending only to be exposed for a few seconds. But his jaw dropped open as he saw a huge Abrams tank rolling towards the house, its gigantic gun turret pointed directly at the house. In the process, he forgot to limit his exposure at the window.

Before he could let off a single shot, a volley of hot lead smashed into his body, throwing him halfway across the room.

The last thing he saw, as the life ebbed away from him, was his brother Qusay crouched over him, a familiar expression on his face. It was the same expression Qusay used when he caught Uday dozing off at military council meetings or getting drunk at the boat club at 11 a.m. – a mixture of resigned exasperation and contempt at his ineffectuality.

As his final act, one that required considerable effort for a man in his condition, Uday brought up a glob of phlegm in his mouth and spat it directly into Qusay's face. He lived long enough to see the expression on his brother's face change from contempt to surprised anger.

Many hours later, when the Americans found Uday's bullet-ridden body amidst the rubble, they were surprised to find a peaceful, almost smiling expression on his face.

35. Abdul / Ava / Rafan / Sofia

Starting as melted snow from the mountain ranges of Turkey, the Tigris skirts the border of Syria and continues down the length of Iraq before emptying itself into the Persian Gulf and, consequently, into the Arabian Sea.

The historic river had brought cool relief to the desert-like landscape and had enabled agriculture, trade, commerce and wildlife to flourish since time immemorial. In fact, some of mankind's first cities, like Babylon and Nineveh – and later Baghdad – were founded on its banks.

Under the Ottoman Empire, expertly made wooden rafts, floating on cushions of inflated cattle skins, were used on the Tigris to transport goods throughout the region. However, the Tigris has also been used for slightly less savoury purposes.

Visitors to the British Museum have sometimes wondered how the massive ancient Assyrian bulls made of stone were transported from Iraq in the 1840s – they are surprised to learn that traditional rafts could bear such immense weight and were used to transport them down the Tigris to the British Navy, waiting in the Persian Gulf. A few decades later, Her Majesty's navy also used the Tigris to travel up the river and wrestle Baghdad away from Ottoman rule.

Throughout history, the rich and powerful built homes on the river bank. Whether their wealth was a result of their proximity to the water, or whether their proximity to the water was a result of their wealth is a point of debate.

Saddam continued this tradition, building several palaces along the banks of the Tigris. The Al-Sijood complex was one such palace.

Of course, Saddam had only done so because he enjoyed the view and the clean air – the river had stopped being used for transportation purposes as road and rail took over after the First World War. He had never dreamed that his family's most prized automobiles would one day make the same journey over the Tigris as the ancient Assyrian stone bulls.

The car-elevator's exit was on the rear side of the building, facing the river. Luckily, none of the troops had been positioned there, perhaps as it had been considered a dead end – all roads leading out of the complex were in the front, facing the city rather than the river.

They emerged from the massive industrial elevator and looked out at the beautiful vista that lay before them – the gardens, followed by the riverbank and a jetty from which Saddam could board a pleasure yacht to cruise along the river should he wish to (this had never happened due to security reasons). Any boats that had been moored there had either been stolen or long since stored away somewhere within the complex.

They proceeded towards the jetty. Rafan drove the forklift, pulling along the platforms on which the cars lay in a long train. Looking back, they could see that the entire building was ablaze – it was a miracle the elevator still worked. Rafan paused beside the jetty and pulled out a handheld radio from his backpack before transmitting a message in Arabic.

Over the last few days, they had prepared their escape carefully, going over Abdul's plan with a fine-tooth comb in their basement shelter. Abdul and Rafan had made two reconnaissance trips to the opposite bank of the river to photograph the jetty. The strength of the jetty, its width and length, as well as its distance from the water, had all been calculated. The depth of the river, its narrowest point and the approximate weight of the cars had all been taken into account when the rafts had been designed and the loading process formulated.

Huge, sealed drums, made from re-enforced plastic (taken from Rafan's factory), buoyed up the rafts, making them float an entire two feet above the surface of the water when unloaded – this would reduce to one foot when the weight of the cars had been secured atop them.

The process had given Abdul a newfound appreciation for the British marauders who had stolen and transported the bulls of Nineveh on similar rafts in the 18th century.

Rafan had also made a trip to the dwindling community of fishermen and raftsmen who still existed in Baghdad. He knew that some of them had a side business, using their boats, as well as homemade rafts, to ferry goods from one part of the city to another or, in some cases, to the neighbouring villages along the Tigris. After a few conversations, he offered a job to two men – Ali and Hamza – who seemed capable and trustworthy. Given that much of their trade had come to a standstill due to the war, they gladly accepted even though they were aware the assignment might be dangerous and was obviously illegal.

The raftsmen had been instructed to hide in the darkness under the 14th of July Suspension Bridge, ready to row a few minutes downriver to the palace. One of them had been given a radio and taught how to use it. The two men, determined to earn their bonus, had followed their instructions well and now rowed into sight of the small group on the palace jetty.

They worked quickly, in what had been a fully rehearsed process.

Wooden ramps, reinforced with steel, were placed with one end on the jetty and another on the raft. Sliding the cars across to the raft was the trickiest part of the entire process, with the biggest risk of dropping the precious cargo into the river – needless to say, if they fell, they would be impossible to retrieve.

The edge of the raft, upon which the ramp lay, dipped into the water as the car descended. Abdul wondered with trepidation if his calculations had been correct. Obviously, he had to approximate the weight of the cars themselves – no records of the weight of the custom bodywork existed. Everyone held their breath.

Due to the weight of the cars, clearly far greater than expected, the two feet of clearance of the raft above the water was reduced to nothing. For a moment, it seemed almost certain that the raft would tip over. The front wheels of the gigantic car rolled onto the raft, making it see-saw wildly.

Amidst the delicate operation, a massive explosion shook the ground, and they could see smoke emerging from the bottom windows of the palace. All four of them thought of the US Marines that had entered the building – they hoped no one was hurt.

Distracted, neither Rafan nor the elder of the two raftsmen, Ali, could maintain a foothold on the rocking platform, and both fell overboard with a splash. Sofia, watching from the riverbank, screamed in surprise. However, the cars remained safely atop the raft where their axles were clipped onto the deck with the mechanical holds that Rafan had designed.

Rafan and Ali crawled back onto the rafts, soaked and spluttering, but otherwise well.

Two minutes later, they cast off.

The raftsmen were simple folk, used to ferrying around grain, vegetables and livestock. Most did not know how to read or write – and had certainly never been involved with a heist of such gargantuan value before. When Rafan had brought them to his villa to brief, he had set out lots of time to carefully explain the getaway operation he had devised. Within a few minutes, it had become clear how much he had underestimated them – these were men who had spent their lives on the river that wound through one of civilisation's busiest cities. They had seen and heard it all before.

In fact, when Rafan took them to Abdul's garage, where the rafts were being constructed, Ali immediately shook his head and suggested several changes to the design, including the shape of the rudders and the type of insulation required for the platform. It was Ali who had also suggested they replicate the journey on a small craft first, to foresee any issues the much larger and heavily laden rafts would encounter. But they simply hadn't the time for that. Ali had to be satisfied by looking at maps, something he had never needed to refer to before that point.

Even though the raftsmen had spent their lives on the river, they had seldom ventured outside of the city limits of Baghdad, and only on occasion to small towns and villages nearby – neither of them had been all the way down to the Persian Gulf even in the best of times, let alone during a massive armed invasion.

The six of them floated down the Tigris as minutes turned into hours and dawn broke across the city.

After the excitement of loading the rafts and getting away with their lives and bounty intact, all of them experienced a sudden crash as the adrenaline abated.

They sat, stood or rowed wordlessly, as Baghdad was slowly enveloped in the glow of the rising sun, illuminating the hazy, smoky air. Saddam had ordered the oilfields aflame, to make the task of the British fighter jets more difficult.

The only sound came from the oars as they gently dipped in and out of the water amidst the smog. For a change, they couldn't hear the sound of any machine gun fire, earth-moving equipment, sirens or bombs. It was almost as if the warring factions had agreed to watch the sunrise in peace.

Ava felt like she had run a marathon. As she sat on the last of the three rafts, she realised that she wasn't sure that she had the energy to stand up, much less row. She was glad Rafan had the foresight to enlist the help of the local raftsmen. However, her tiredness was mingled with disbelief at actually having gotten this far. Not for the first time that day, Ava marvelled at the strange turn of events, hardly willing to believe that they had not only found the 540k but had actually escaped with it.

Then, Ava reflected, there was a completely unexpected bonus.

As they had trawled through Al Sijood's ceiling crawlspace during their escape, they noticed several brick-shaped objects wrapped in hessian sacking. In fact, the entire length of the narrow space was lined with a neat row of them – there must have been thousands, considering the crawlspace was an intricate maze that spanned the length and breadth of the level they were on. They could only presume the rest of the levels were also lined with these hessian bricks.

Curious about their contents, Abdul had decided to open one of them. Inside of it was a neatly shrink-wrapped brick of tightly packed hundred-dollar bills.

There was no way they could carry all the bricks with them – but they had emptied their backpacks of all the tools they were carrying and stuffed them with as much of the money as possible before dropping from the hatch in the crawlspace and jumping into the underground car park.

The two bulging backpacks had been hidden safely inside the vintage cars, under the tarpaulin, to be split among the four of them later, after putting aside a hefty tip for the raftsmen, one that would certainly see them through the war and well beyond.

Ava enjoyed the feel of the loose abaya which she had donned shortly after boarding the raft – her jeans, along with Abdul and Rafan's trousers and t-shirts, lay at the bottom of the river. The long-sleeved, loose robes they wore instead reached their ankles. These would not only disguise them as local river folk but would later shelter them from the relentless rays of the midday sun. One of the boatmen had wrapped a cloth around Ava's head like a turban, in line with rural fashion. A 'dupatta' or scarf lay wound around her neck, ready to pull up across her mouth should it become necessary to disguise her Western features. This was considered perfectly innocuous among the local males or working women, who often wore these coverings as they travelled along the dusty roads of the desert-like terrain.

She did an inventory of everything she had left Abdul's house with. It wasn't much – a roll of banknotes amounting to about 2,000 dollars, her passport, a copy of fake press credentials, some credit cards that could be used outside of Iraq, a mobile phone and the radios with which they communicated between the rafts. That was all she would need to make her way back to London. It was much harder for Abdul, Rafan and Sofia. They had left everything behind in their Baghdad homes, with the windows boarded up and all the doors double locked. Still, they wouldn't need to worry about their finances; Abdul estimated there was about a million in cash in each of the backpacks. If they sold the cars, they would have several million each after expenses. It would be more than enough to live elsewhere for the duration of the war, or indeed, as long as they liked, if they were careful.

Sofia rode on the first raft. She had thrown an abaya, the traditional black women's cloak, over her cargo trousers and sweatshirt. A headscarf and veil covered her face. It had been a while since she had worn these – most urban or middle-class Baghdadis dressed in Western fashion under Saddam's rule. She paused to consider if they looked like local Baghdadi fisher folk or boat folk, many of whom had migrated upriver to the city from more rural locations and lived on the breadline in the city. All their clothing looked old and worn out, but clean and intact in line with the norm. It was not unusual for a boatman to be assisted by his wife or children, but still, she hoped they would not encounter any troops.

She knew there was still a very long way to go before she could relax – the first stop would be a small, dusty city called Kut, about 160km south of Baghdad, where Rafan had a trusted business partner whose factory they would be able to shelter inside of. As the products it made required a source of water, it was located on the river itself. In fact, they would float their rafts directly into the factory via a small tributary that had been created expressly to supply water to the factory.

The location was normally only a two-and-a-half-hour drive from Baghdad but would take about six hours on the meandering but fast-flowing river, passing several small villages on the way.

Their next stop after that would be Amarah, a much larger and more urban city. That was where the Tigris would split into two, the northern fork ending in a marshland, and the southern fork going down to another city called Al Qunah, where the Tigris would merge with the Shatat al-Arab, going past Basra to discharge itself into the Persian Gulf. This, in turn, would lead to the Gulf of Oman and, ultimately, the Arabian Sea. The entire journey could take five or six days.

She was jerked out of her thoughts by a buzzing sound. It was the sound of a small engine, getting louder every second. Then, from the hazy distance ahead of them, a small craft came into view. Its bows had been painted in camouflage, and it very clearly had a mounted machine gun. The stars and stripes decorated her hull.

It was heading directly toward them.

***

They had together decided on the best way to disguise their cargo and themselves – they could hardly sail down the river with some of the most expensive automobiles in the world openly perched atop them. That might be far too much temptation for an opportunistic general from the Republican Guard, or even the allied forces – although it seemed that the latter did not have orders to intervene when looting occurred; they were happy to stand by and watch as some of Saddam's palaces had been ransacked by locals. Besides, the doctrine of shock and awe stipulated that they make their way across the country at lightning speed, following the aerial onslaught.

Again, it had been the raftsman, Ali, who suggested a solution. When the rest of them heard it, they instinctively knew it was their best chance of not being stopped by either side.

As the armed craft approached their raft, they swung into action, each of them having pre-arranged roles. Sofia, on the lead craft which the gunboat would encounter first, reached under the tarpaulin and identified a big plastic drum, like the kind being used to buoy the raft. This one could be opened by turning a clasp and unscrewing the lid, which she did. Suddenly, the malodour that clung to the proximity of the drum became an overwhelming, nausea-inducing smell, reminiscent of rotting flesh. It was only with an iron will that Sofia managed not to throw up the bread and apricots she had managed to swallow after they had cast off from the palace. She was glad of the headscarf and veil that hid her face and disguised her as a local of undeterminable age.

Ali, who was posing as her elderly husband, unfurled a white flag, and put his hands up, one of which held a sign printed in Arabic. He made it clear he was unarmed and peaceful, as the craft came within arms distance of the raft – although that did not stop the soldiers from pointing their automatic weapons at him, one of which was a gigantic mounted and belt-fed machine gun manned by two individuals on a platform.

Once the crafts were parallel, one of them shouted, 'Salam. Who are you? What's on the raft?'

'Salam. Juthath… juthath almawtaa!' Ali replied.

'I don't speak Arabic. English? No English?' the soldier asked, never once taking his finger off the trigger or relaxing his aim.

'Umm… body…' said Ali, 'tise… body.' He held up nine fingers. This was followed by a finger drawn across the throat, the global sign of being killed. 'We go… Amarah,' Ali continued. 'For bury. Home village.'

'Is that what the smell is? Jesus!'

Ali motioned for the soldier to come aboard, gesturing to the huge pile covered by the tarp, as if the soldier was welcome to come and check underneath it. 'You. Tea?' he said, pointing towards a big brass teapot that lay on deck, alongside a few dirty glasses.

The soldier, who was now desperately trying not to breathe through his nose, had to make an effort to speak. 'No tea, er, thank you. How'd they die? Bomb?'

'Eh?'

'Kaboom?' asked the soldier, miming an explosion with his hands.

'Ah!' said Ali, a look of understanding on his face. 'No kaboom.'

'Then? How did they die?'

Ali pointed to his stomach, and put his hand on his head, miming a fever. 'They sick,' he said, 'I also sick.' This was distinctly believable, as the gaunt raftsman didn't look particularly robust even at the best of times.

Then, in an inspired stroke of genius, he coughed in the soldier's general direction.

The soldier shrank back.

'Jesus!' he said again. Lowering his weapon he addressed his colleagues: 'God only knows what disease these guys have.'

'Please. We go?' asked Ali.

'You go,' said the soldier, pulling his shirt over his nose. 'And good luck to you, buddy.'

The boat passed them and disappeared up the river, giving the other rafts a wide berth. The throb of its high-powered engine eventually faded into the horizon.

Sofia darted back under the tarp and wrestled the lid on the drum back on, once again sealing up the dead and rotting goat inside.

Then, she took off her veil, leaned over the raft and vomited.

36. Copella

First Lieutenant Copella prided himself on being a determined man – one who achieved his goals by any means necessary. But even he had been shaken by the turn of events. He had briefed the team to be prepared for anything when they entered the complex to hunt down the four unidentified individuals. The Marines had very much considered themselves the 'hunters' in this scenario; as the soldiers of the most powerful country in the world, they often did. They had almost certainly not considered the possibility of being hunted by hungry lions in an underground labyrinth of hidden passages.

At first, the soldiers could only hear the most distant roars, echoing down the dark passages of the complex. This was very alarming at some deep primal level but they told themselves that their firepower and night vision would keep them safe.

As they searched the facility in the dark, the roars became louder and louder – they were very aware that the animal had their scent and was following it. Then they heard a pounding sound as if the huge animal was running toward them. Finally, they could feel the floor vibrate to the time of the pounding and could hear the click of its claws as they struck the cold tiles of the vast complex.

When the lion finally emerged into the passage the soldiers were in, their nerves had been frayed to breaking point. Muzzle flashes filled the air, and three Marines were injured due to friendly fire. It was almost a miracle that no one died. The lion disappeared down a corridor, unscathed.

When they finally stumbled upon the trapdoor that led to the massive basement garage, it had been too late – the four unidentified individuals had somehow blocked it from opening. They had laid an explosive charge to blow it open when suddenly a massive explosion below them rocked the foundations of the building. The heat, even without the trapdoor open, was oppressive and, combined with the level of smoke from the part of the building that was already on fire, made the already toxic environment completely unbearable. The Marines beat a tactical retreat.

Had the four insurgents, as he had now begun to think of them, perished in the fire, either from above or from below? There was no conceivable way they could have escaped with all the exits blocked. Or was there?

Copella had never entered the building, but he had, however, examined the building from the outside, building a picture of what had transpired. Slowly, he realised they had used the river to get away. He had underestimated them, plain and simple.

This was confirmed by the deep tracks in the mud between the palace complex and the now scuffed-up jetty. It was further confirmed when he requested a report of sightings of any civilian or military craft on the river and was informed of the three rafts that had been encountered by a US Marine gunship.

He sat down on the jetty, deep in thought. The river had been a stroke of genius on their part, not just because it enabled them to escape the palace complex when all roads had been blocked, but also because it was the only viable way to transport bulky items out of the country.

Over the last few days, it had become clear that the Iraqi Republican Guard, or what remained of the fraction that hadn't deserted, no longer used military vehicles or uniforms – these were instantly identified and bombed by US forces from the sky. Instead, they had adapted their strategy by eschewing their uniforms for civilian garb and their military vehicles for civilian trucks and cars.

As a result, satellites and unseen reconnaissance planes now tracked every vehicle on every highway. If the unfortunate occupants were positively identified as a potential threat, for example, if a truck seemed to carry a number of males exclusively of military age, or if any sort of arms were detected, a kill order was conveyed to the Air Force.

All other vehicles had to be stopped and thoroughly searched. The focus was on the highways – Copella did not know of any arrangements made to monitor the meandering and fast-flowing riverways, aside from the odd military patrol boats that had been put out as an afterthought and had reported little so far.

Copella took out a map from one of the many pockets of his fatigues and laid it out on the jetty. He placed a finger on the Tigris in Baghdad and traced it south, taking in the names of the villages, towns and cities as it made its way to the sea. Immediately, one name stood out – Kut. It was the first settlement along the river that could be classified as a city, and one in which he knew there was a significant US military presence following a battle just days ago.

Kut, with an airfield and a suspected chemical weapons plant, was strategically important, and the Fedayeen had put up a fight to try and defend it. An air strike had been called and the B-52s eventually decimated the Iraqi resistance, but not before one American life was lost to Iraqi machine gun fire. Many of the Marines had then proceeded to the Battle of Baghdad which had finished two days ago. But a residual force from the 1st Marine Division had been maintained at Al Kut.

Copella did not command any boats or amphibious vehicles that could intercept the thieves. At this stage, he didn't want to borrow any either – the fewer people that knew about the cars, the less he would have to cut people into the deal to keep it quiet. He pulled out his radio and switched it to the channel that transmitted to Joint Mission Control. He chose his words carefully.

'This is First Lieutenant Copella of the 1st Marine Division, 1st Recon. Please be aware – we have sighted a small group of militants on the Tigris, transporting a large quantity of unknown material disguised as a burial party. I repeat – the three large craft have been covered with tarpaulin hiding potential weapons that could be chemical or biological in nature. Possible WMD. Suggested action – ambush or intercept the craft using deadly force at all costs. Suggested point of ambush – Al Kut City. ETA of insurgents is approximately sixty minutes.' He then switched off his radio.

Next, he commandeered one of the Humvees present at the scene, kicking out a couple of the Marines under his command. There was still time to get there before the rafts, and thus before the fireworks. He would find a way to take control of the rafts once his adversaries had been eliminated by the Marines at Al Kut.

He was confident of one thing – given the message he had just transmitted, there was simply no way the rafts would be allowed to continue their journey unhindered. In fact, the thieves would be heading directly into a well-armed ambush set expressly for them, courtesy of the US military.

Copella just hoped the people on the rafts gave the ambushing party an excuse to open fire.

37. Abdul / Ava / Rafan / Sofia

It had been some time since their encounter with the armed boat, but they still couldn't believe that their ploy had worked. All of their energy was now spent keeping the raft stable and afloat in the fast-flowing river. All of them looked forward to reaching Kut – Rafan had arranged for their rafts to be temporarily hidden in a large warehouse on the riverbanks, a facility that belonged to one of the suppliers to his factory, someone he considered quite reliable and had worked with for over ten years.

Then they could catch up on some much-needed sleep and have a bite to eat before getting back on the river and continuing their journey to the Persian Gulf, where they would be met by a boat that Ava had arranged – this would take them and the cars wherever they wished.

The plan was to get to Iran or Yemen where many hiding places for the cars could be found, at least for the short term. This would give them the chance to decide how best to liquidate the cars. They had two possible options, generally speaking.

The first involved finding a private buyer for the cars as soon as possible. There were many collectors in developing nations or small countries who wouldn't ask too many questions about the provenance of the cars. Some were even the rulers of said countries. However, as the buyers or their agents would realise immediately that the cars were 'hot', so to speak, this would likely result in more vigorous negotiations, and they would get less than top dollar for the cars.

The other route would involve the barn-find method that Ava usually employed, where she hid the car away for many years and then sold it to an agent who would pretend it was an authentic barn find, restored perfectly to its former glory for sale at auction, legally, for a much larger payout. However, in this case, that route might prove difficult. These cars were one of a kind, too famous to pass off as barn finds. Also, the value of the cars lay in their provenance – they were worth much more if their previous owners, particularly Saddam, could be traced back. But these were problems for another day.

All of them, besides Ali and his fellow boatman Hamza, were exhausted. They clung on to consciousness by sheer force of will. It helped that if any of them lost focus, even for a second, there was a good chance their raft would meet with an accident.

Rafan had been slightly perturbed by the fact that he couldn't reach his associate in Al Kut on the radio or the phone. He was aware, of course, that a major battle between Fedayeen and US forces had taken place there only last week, and things were just about returning to normalcy. It was said that small pockets of Fedayeen still existed in the region, hiding in the forests nearby, biding their time, waiting for an opportunity to sabotage or attack the allied forces again. There could be any number of reasons why his friend didn't answer.

It was Ali who mentioned they had reached the outskirts of the city and would reach the first of the three bridges in Kut in a few minutes. Rafan still had an uneasy feeling in the pit of his stomach, and he suggested a halt so that they could take stock of their situation and make a joint decision on whether to continue into Al Kut.

With some difficulty, they managed to steer the rafts toward the shore and tether them to trees along the muddy towpath. The spot that they had chosen was thankfully deserted.

After some deliberation, Abdul decided to take Rafan's binoculars and climb up a tree to see if he could spot anything.

At first, he could not see anything out of place, but the ominous feeling in the pit of his stomach persisted. Then he realised what it was. The streets were far too quiet – he could not see anyone at all. Then, he noticed something that made his blood freeze. From behind the arches of the first bridge of Kut, he could see the barrel of a mounted gun sticking out. Was it just a routine precaution taken by US troops? Or was it something more sinister than that? He decided to keep his eyes trained on the bridge.

Only a few minutes later, he noticed a Marine, in full combat uniform, approaching the bridge. The man was running, crouched over as if he did not want to be seen from the river. He disappeared behind one of the arches of the bridge and did not re-emerge on the other side.

Abdul scanned the banks of the river near the bridge. Several boats seemed to be tethered to the bank, some of them with engines, but none of them seemingly military in nature. They were all empty. Then, he noticed an arm, clad in military fatigues, stretch out above the rim of one of the seemingly unoccupied boats, only to be quickly retracted within as if the owner of the arm had realised he might have been at risk of being noticed.

It was clearly an ambush – and it was quite likely that they were the target. He wondered if they had already been detected by the US forces' 'eyes in the sky'. Probably not, he figured, as all the resources of the army were now focused north of Baghdad where the last remaining territories not yet occupied by coalition forces lay.

But what in the world could they do? They had to get past Al Kut in order to continue downriver – there was simply no other way. Even if they could somehow lay their hands on a couple of trucks, the roads were far too dangerous to use. Was this the end of the road for them, so to speak? Abdul could not bear the thought of abandoning the cars after they had been through so much.

His elevated position gave him the ability to scan more of the city. Not knowing what else to do, Abdul looked around, scanning the dusty and crumbling single-story buildings that formed much of the city. If Al Kut had been struggling before the invasion, it had now been totally decimated. It bore the marks of a city that had recently been under siege – bombed-out infrastructure, charred and crater-filled streets, and what could only be described as the smell of death in the air, perceptible even at the distance that Abdul currently was.

Then, he noticed some more movement, further afield, well behind the first bridge. More soldiers? No, these didn't look like any sort of allied troops. They were dressed in civilian clothes. A couple of them wore traditional robes but most of them were in jeans or sweats with sandals on their feet. They did have one thing in common – all of them were armed with AK-type weapons and lots of ammunition. They seemed to be approaching the bridge where the ambush had been laid extremely cautiously and quietly. They looked like they had some military training, expertly running towards and sheltering behind a building or parked truck while their colleagues covered them with their weapons, then leap-frogging closer and closer to the bridge where the ambush had been laid.

In a flash, Abdul realised what was happening – the US troops were lying in wait for something or someone travelling on the river, possibly them. In their eagerness to conduct a successful ambush, they were totally focused on whatever was approaching from upriver, without necessarily covering their rear.

The Fedayeen had seized upon the opportunity to ambush the ambushers.

It wouldn't have taken much – perhaps a short radio message from a river dweller to the contingent of Fedayeen still living in the forests outside the town, telling them US troops seemed exposed and vulnerable. It was rumoured that approximately 250 Iraqis had been killed in the battle of Kut last week, with another thousand injured. The Fedayeen were probably eager for payback.

Not for the first time, Abdul felt a wave of nausea due to the impending loss of life. He would have gladly given up the cars if it meant a stop to the massacre that was about to ensue. He didn't really care whether the lives being lost belonged to Iraqis, Americans or any other nationality – a life was a life. But he couldn't see any way to save the people he saw through the binoculars.

And then, out of the silence, a cacophony of gunfire erupted.

38. Copella

As First Lieutenant Copella's Humvee sped away from the palace towards Kut, he reflected on how much one could get away with amidst the chaos, confusion and fog of war.

Of course, many of their missions were planned with the precision that the military was so famous for. However, once the shit hit the fan, Copella found he could usually slink away on one of his solo missions. Due to his rank, no questions were asked of him. Even if they were, he always had a good excuse for his absence ready and prepared – preferably one that highlighted quick thinking and a cool head under fire.

The other thing he enjoyed was the awesome firepower ready and available to him. One could accomplish so much in the absence of law and order. In fact, to the world, they were supposed to *be* the law and order in Iraq. That would come later. Right now, their primary mission was to capture or kill Saddam, his two offspring, and the inner circle of the Baath Party. They had been told not to interfere with looting, rioting or any form of civil unrest unless it helped with their primary mission.

Well, thought Copella, he wouldn't tolerate looting on his watch – unless, of course, he was the one doing the looting. He felt a bit like what he imagined a sheriff might feel like in the Wild West.

He had been driving for two hours with his foot pressed firmly on the gas. His radio was switched off and if the eyes in the sky had picked him up, they must have dismissed him as yet another US military vehicle running some errand.

He turned a corner and, looking at the GPS on the dashboard, realised he was only about five minutes away from the city.

At first, he thought there was something wrong with the car but, as he drew nearer, he realised that it was the sound of distant gunfire that he heard. When he was nearer still, he realised that there was a full-blown gunbattle in progress.

He stomped on the brakes and the Humvee came to a screeching halt on the dusty tarmac. What in the world was going on? Did the thieves have the firepower to fight back with such ferocity?

Copella secretly had a motto, to which he attributed the fact that he was still alive: When in doubt, stay the fuck out. He took his own advice and pulled the Humvee into a thicket of trees by the side of the road and hunkered down to wait.

After about half an hour, the sound of the gunfire reduced from being a constant barrage to sporadic bursts. Then, occasional bursts. Finally, silence.

He waited for a good two hours before getting back onto the road and slowly, cautiously, driving towards Kut. When he entered the city, he could immediately tell there had been a gunbattle, but whether it was related to the thieves, he did not know. The smell of cordite was in the air and a medical tent had been set up. Groans and screams could be heard from within it. Several Marines had their rifles in hand and were on full alert.

He decided to ask someone what was going on and managed to corner a Lance Corporal, a man called McCoy.

'We were ambushed, plain and simple. We received an alert about some insurgents coming downriver on a raft, code red. So, we formed a welcoming party, large fireworks included. Well, we never saw any raft but some of the Hajis certainly saw us, that's for sure. We were so absorbed in keeping a lookout for the rafts, we weren't keeping an eye on our own six. Took us by surprise. Man, if I could find the bastard that put in the code red about the insurgents on the river, I could think of a few things I would like to say and do to him.'

'Any losses?'

'No losses, not yet anyway. Just injuries, about three of them career-ending and another four critical. Not sure if they are going to make it. Might be touch and go for a couple of them.', he said looking anxious. 'Where are you coming in from, anyway?'

'Just passing through, heading towards Amarah. So, those insurgents never turned up, eh?'

'No, they didn't. What did you say your name was?'

'I didn't. OK, gotta dash, amigo, on a schedule and all that. Nice chatting. All the best to your boys there.'

Copella rolled up the window and stomped on the gas, in a hurry to escape the Lance Corporal with his cover intact. He parked the Humvee in a side alley, threw on his helmet and body armour and checked his sidearm, before shouldering his rifle and getting out. It looked like McCoy's team had the area back under control, but one never knew – they were, after all, in a warzone. In fact, the area was a bit hotter than Copella would have liked. One never knew who was still lurking around.

He stopped a Marine passing by, who looked at the rank on his shoulders and stiffened, standing at attention and saluting.

'Hi,' said Copella, 'I'm leading the investigation into what happened around here. Did you see any insurgents on a raft, soldier?'

'No, sir. Just the ones who attacked us.'

'So, nothing came downriver recently?'

'Couldn't say, sir. Once the battle started, we were too preoccupied with engaging the enemy on land. It's a miracle we didn't take any losses, sir, seeing as we were so exposed. So far, that is.'

'I see…'

'Now that you mention it, sir, we didn't see any rafts, but we did see a reasonably sized boat leave the metalwork factory at the edge of the town, shortly after the battle was over.'

'Did you check it out?'

'Yes, sir.'

'Who was on it?'

'There were two men and two women on the boat, sir. They were transporting goods downriver. Said they were late to make a delivery at Al Qunah. The manager at the factory is known to us and corroborated this. Folks in this country seen so much war, they don't give a shit how hot it gets. They just do their business.'

'Did you check the cargo?'

'Guy from my team had a peek into the hold of the boat, sir. Large boxes covered with tarps. They said they were metal handles for various types of boxes, safes and cabinets.'

'But no one looked under the tarps?'

'Not that I recall, sir. They seemed fine. Particularly as we had no reason to suspect them.'

'OK. Thanks. On your way, soldier.'

Copella was now almost certain the people he was looking for were on that ship, and that the cargo might have held fewer metal handles and a few more vintage cars than the Marines might have noticed. Were the staff of the factory in cahoots with the thieves?

He decided to walk over to the factory. No one noticed yet another soldier in military fatigues and body armour walking around.

He knocked on the door, which was answered by the manager of the factory. There did not seem to be any other staff around. The manager was friendly and welcomed him inside, despite having been interviewed already. At first, Copella almost doubted his own suspicions. He was offered tea, along with the manager's sorrow at the recent gunfight.

Copella feigned interest in the factory's workings and asked if he could look around. It was obvious they were both aware Copella was there to investigate the factory to check if it was connected to the recent ambush, but the manager politely accepted his reasons and showed him around.

The factory wasn't large, and it took them only ten minutes to explore it. Besides the lobby in which they had drunk tea, there was one large warehouse-sized room and a small office they had walked through. Copella noticed that part of the river had cleverly been diverted under the roof of the factory to provide the flowing water required for the manufacture of the products. Not necessarily eco-friendly, but effective. However, there was one locked door that he had not been shown into. When he asked for access, he was told that it contained some old stock and the key had been lost.

Copella made up his mind. In one swift motion, he lifted up his rifle and fired a short burst at the lock on the door. The manager nearly jumped out of his skin, but he wasn't about to argue with a heavily armed Marine who seemed intent on going in.

Copella then kicked in the door and entered the room, which indeed looked like a place to store excess stock. He looked around.

Sure enough, behind a pile of cardboard boxes, he saw several blue plastic barrels, the sort that might have held up a raft, and the sort that had been described by the captain of the gunboat that had seen the thieves.

'What are these?'

'Barrels for storing chemicals used in manufacturing process.'

Copella looked closely. The icons on the barrels did indicate they were chemicals used in factories. He rubbed his chin, wondering what to make of it all when, from the corner of his eye, he saw what looked like the rudder of a ship. That confirmed it for him. He pointed his gun straight at the manager.

'The truth. Did you help a bunch of people escape with two cars?'

'No, sir, I promise, I don't know what you talk about.'

Copella shot the man in one of his kneecaps.

The manager fell to the floor in agony and Copella asked him about the thieves again.

But the man did not diverge from his story. Copella decided there was no point in killing him, as he did not want to risk a military investigation into the killing of an unarmed civilian.

'OK. I don't believe you. But I'm leaving. I will spare your life but at least you have a little reminder of what happens to people who don't tell the truth. Don't speak to anyone about meeting me unless you want me to come back for the other knee, followed by your head.'

He walked out of the factory, leaving the man writhing in a pool of blood on the floor.

He lit a cigarette outside the factory and exhaled a long plume of blue smoke. He was angry at being deceived. He was angry that his plan hadn't worked. But it was far from over.

Those cars would be his. Perhaps it was good that the thieves had done all the hard work and planning to smuggle them out of the country. Hell, maybe he ought to let them get all the way downriver to Amarah or Al Qunah. Then he could swoop in and grab them there. He would have to strike hard and fast, leaving all four individuals dead, so there was nothing and no one to connect him with the cars. He would relish it.

There was no other way for it, thought Copella as he strode away from the factory. I'm going to have to call in all my favours. He walked back to the Humvee and switched on the radio. He had a terse conversation with someone at the other end. His tone of voice went from friendly to cajoling to pleading and finally threatening. Finally, the two men came to some form of agreement.

Copella then switched off the radio, lit a cigarette and waited for the helicopter gunship to arrive.

39. Abdul / Ava / Rafan / Sofia

There are only so many times one can get lucky, thought Abdul to himself. There had been a few moments in the last 24 hours that he had found far too close for comfort. He had decided in Kut that he wouldn't bank on luck anymore – their planning needed to be more precise if they were to get away with the cars.

Sofia, Rafan and Ava had agreed.

When the fighting in Kut began, they decided to make the best of the distraction and sneak the rafts into Rafan's friend's factory, which was a mile or so away from the bridge where the ambush had happened.

The factory had been visible from the bridge where the fighting was taking place, but only if one were to focus on that part of the river. There had been a good chance they could sneak in unnoticed while the Marines had their hands full, and they had decided to take the gamble.

It had paid off, and both rafts managed to get into the tributary leading to the factory without incident.

Once inside, Rafan's friend had suggested they take one of his boats, the one big enough to hold two cars, usually used to ferry around goods between Kut and Baghdad – the rafts were now too 'hot' to use. Ava, Abdul, Sofia and Rafan agreed – they paid the raftsmen of Baghdad, along with a generous bonus, and let them make their way back. They could manage the factory boat themselves.

When the gunfire abated, they cautiously cast off downriver. The factory's boats were a common sight, and the Marines based at Kut had seen them go up and down the Tigris over the last couple of days. In fact, the owner of the factory, one of the more prosperous businessmen in Kut, had offered the coalition forces supplies and tasked his workers to help wounded Marines after the battle a week ago. They thought highly of him and were also impressed by his ability to keep his business running despite the war.

Of course, what the Marines weren't aware of, was the businessman had also treated some of the wounded Fedayeen, hidden from view in the factory. When it came to aid for those who were suffering, he did not discriminate. Besides, as all good businessmen know, it pays to keep both sides happy. One never knew who would form the next administration of Kut or that of Iraq. He knew he would be rewarded for his kindness, either in this life or the next, although he sincerely hoped it would be this one.

However, the boat had been stopped and searched by a few weary Marines regardless – the Captain on the scene wanted to ensure no one could fault him for letting insurgents escape – be it some of the group who had attacked them, or the supposed group of dangerous insurgents who they had been told were on rafts.

After the cursory search of the boat by the Marines was over, and they were on their way, they all heaved a huge sigh of relief – hugs were exchanged, tea was brewed and bread was broken. Sofia collapsed into Abdul's arms and Abdul collapsed onto the deck of the boat.

Ava and Rafan decided to take the first shift, inviting Abdul and Sofia to rest in the small cabin while they steered the boat and kept watch on the path ahead with binoculars.

Abdul and Sofia gratefully accepted; they were totally exhausted. Scarcely had they disrobed and gotten under the sheets of the narrow bunk when they started to doze off. Abdul had his arm around Sofia.

As he drifted off to sleep, he realised he didn't really care about the cars so much anymore. They would make him wealthy, but when had he cared about being wealthy?

He didn't really care about the invasion anymore either. How many times had Baghdad seen war in the past? And the politics – who really knew if they were better off with or without Saddam?

Even though it was what Baghdad had needed at the time, he realised he didn't really care for the lonely role he played as Whistler.

He was very happy holding Sofia close, and he didn't really care about much else.

Sofia had similar thoughts as she drifted off to sleep. The past few days had been the most traumatic ones in her short and, until recently, very closeted life that her father had carefully curated for her.

She thought back to the risks she had taken – stealing the memo from her father's office, escaping Uday not once but twice, planning her departure from Baghdad and trusting her life to Abdul and his friends. It was also ironic that it was during such upheaval that she felt more in control of her own destiny than ever. It was also ironic that surrounded by death, she had never felt more alive.

Then, of course, there was the sex.

The newness of being physically intimate, particularly with someone as sensitive and gentle as Abdul, had not only been a welcome diversion from the war, it had been a complete revelation. They had virtually lived in each other's arms since he had carried her out of the fire.

Throughout her life, Sofia had never considered herself to be a girl who needed a man to be happy, to feel safe or to get what she wanted. Even though they had been overly protective of her, her parents had always been preoccupied – her father with politics and her mother with a very active social life. Early on, she had learnt to depend only on herself, and what she learnt about life from the books on Al-Mutanabbi Street and, later, the internet.

Now she couldn't believe how incredibly lucky she was to have Abdul in her life. She loved how different he was from everyone else she had met: his savant-level skill with anything mechanical, his shy but earnest personality, his resourcefulness, his friends, his moral outlook, his political beliefs and their shared passion for a good book. There was an almost naive honesty about him that she found incredibly attractive. And, of course, she loved that he loved her.

They must have been asleep for ten minutes when they heard a pounding on their door.

Abdul sat bolt upright, banging his temple on the bunk above. He opened the door, rubbing his head. At the back of his mind, he realised the boat was no longer in motion. Sofia groggily awakened and drew the blanket to her chest.

'We have a problem,' said Ava, who was at the door looking grim. 'The engine's fucked. We aren't going to make it.'

40. Copella

Copella stared out of the helicopter at the meandering river below. The sliding door of the aircraft was open so that it did not hinder his field of vision, and he was strapped into his seat. A headset and mic covered his ears so that he could communicate with the pilot, and he had a pair of field glasses with which to scan the river.

He had called in every favour he was owed to get to the vintage cars.

A convoy of armoured light vehicles and transport trucks, as well as an entire battalion of Marines, were already en route towards Kut to help capture or kill the 'insurgents' and secure the cargo.

He thought back to the conversation he had with central command an hour ago.

He had decided that his best chances of success were, initially, to be honest. He told central command that insurgents were stealing a cargo of two of the most prized symbols of absolute power in Iraq – Saddam Hussein's parade cars.

As Saddam's main state vehicles, he had been seen in them during military parades and prestigious televised state functions. Whoever claimed those cars, say for example, one of the handful of senior Baathist leaders still on the loose, would be seen as the rightful heir to Saddam's rule. This would provide a tremendous morale boost to the Iraqi forces.

For good measure, he blamed the thieves for shooting and injuring his troops when his team had tried to apprehend them. Central Command was aware of shots fired and soldiers injured there a short while ago but what they did not know was that it was actually due to friendly fire when they had been attacked by a lion. His troops would stick to his script, he had made sure of that. The familiar US standard-issue bullets in their bodies had been explained to medics by saying the insurgents had used captured US weaponry.

His plan was to use the resources of the military – who were now trigger-happy and feeling rather vengeful when they heard the target had almost killed a few of their own – to capture the cars and then put his own unit in charge of transporting them back to base, where they would disappear into the massive chaos of the military administration.

He would spread rumours that they had been dispatched to Jordan for analysis when really he would put them on a ship bound for the US, where he would sell them to a dealer he knew. Their loss would be put down to yet another misplaced item in the hazy fog of war. Not that Central Command would care too much, as long as Iraqi leadership were not seen or filmed in the cars.

Central Command did, however, care about wasting precious military resources. He had been asked several times about the veracity of his information and the accuracy of his claim. Even though he had not officially been blamed for the firefight at Kut, the fact that no raft had been seen had cast a shadow over his claims. He was told in no uncertain terms that he had better be certain – the unexpected cost of the military invasion was only exceeded by the unexpected cost of civilian casualties, and Central Command was trying to be good.

No matter, he thought, the cars would be seen by all and sundry in the hold of the boat very soon.

They had just taken off in the Black Hawk and he expected to see the boat in a few minutes. The satellites were also being used to look for the boat as a backup to his physical search. The radio crackled in his ear – it said the armoured vehicles and troops would pass Kut in the next ten minutes and were tracking his helicopter, travelling on the road that ran parallel to the river. A hundred highly armed troops to capture four thieves.

Sometimes, he thought, smiling, he surprised himself with his own cunning.

'What's the plan, sir?' the pilot asked over the headset.

'We are looking for a craft travelling along the Tigris, it's got a red hull and it is big enough to store two cars in its cargo hold. There are four armed and dangerous insurgents aboard: two male and two female. We have to stop them. Tell me, can we use force to stop the boat without damaging the cargo? We do not have to take them alive. Repeat, they can be killed.'

The pilot thought for a while before answering into the microphone. 'Depends on how fast they are going and what the acceptable margin of error is. Obviously, would be much easier to shoot them if they are slow or stationary. We could target the bridge of the boat where the pilot's nest is likely to be. Either way, you won't get them all – if they are smart, they will go into the hold with the cargo.'

'That's fine. Once we disable the boat, we can wait for the troops to arrive. Wait… OK. I see the boat. It isn't moving for some reason. Fly past and strafe the deck. Fuck up everyone aboard as much as possible'.

The pilot looked through his helmet mounted display and lined up the impact point of the M60 machine guns, aiming directly at the man steering the boat.

Then, he pulled the trigger.

41. Abdul / Ava / Rafan / Sofia

Abdul and Ava looked at the engine while Rafan sat in the captain's nest, turning on and off the ignition. The smell of something burning filled the air.

But it was no good – they would have to remove the engine from its bay altogether and get it to a workshop to fix it, which, of course, wouldn't be possible under the circumstances.

They were all exhausted, pushed almost to the limit of their endurance. 'Bloody rafts were more reliable,' grumbled Ava. 'Nice of Rafan's mate to lend us the boat but looks like his generosity exceeds his basic maintenance ability.'

'Is there a dinghy aboard? For safety?' asked Abdul.

'I'd be surprised,' snorted Ava. 'If the boat came with a dinghy, I'm sure it has been sold or repurposed long ago. In emergencies, the crew would probably just radio ahead and swim the short distance to the shore of the river. But it's worth looking around in the hold, just in case.'

They were about to descend into the hold when they heard the unmistakable sound of a helicopter approaching. The two men looked up to scan the horizon and, sure enough, the predatory silhouette of a Black Hawk emerged.

It drew nearer and nearer.

Then, without warning, a fusillade of bullets hit the deck. The massive 50-calibre rounds decimated the poorly constructed boat – each bullet created a big hole in the cheap planks that covered the deck.

Abdul and Ava dived instinctively, headfirst, into the hatch that led below deck but Rafan was still in the captain's nest.

Over the gunfire, Abdul and Ava heard the glass of the captain's nest shatter, followed by an anguished scream from Rafan. Abdul immediately made for the ladder leading up to the deck but Ava pulled him back down. 'Wait. They will need to reload or cool down in a second. We can't deal with two casualties.'

Thankfully, as Ava predicted, there was a pause in the gunfire. Neither of them hesitated – they rushed over to Rafan, who lay slumped over the controls of the boat.

His right arm was mangled and bloody above the elbow. The bullet had gone straight through and shattered the floor of the captain's nest below. The blood splatter was tremendous – it dripped from his arm to the control panel and then onto the floor, forming a small, red puddle.

But they had no time to wonder what to do. The machine gun might open up again any second – the priority was to get Rafan below deck as soon as possible.

Ava grabbed Rafan's good arm and slung it over her shoulder. Abdul caught hold of his friend at the waistband of his trousers. Rafan screamed again as they moved him but his two friends continued to half drag, half walk to the hatch. Abdul went in first and grabbed Rafan as Ava lowered him in. The gunfire resumed just after Ava scrambled in and shut the hatch.

As soon as Rafan lay on the floor, Ava's basic first-aid training kicked in. She tore off his shirt and tied it tightly above the wound to slow the blood loss. Sofia found a medical kit aboard and gave Rafan a few morphine tablets they found inside.

When they took a closer look at the arm, they realised it was no good – Rafan needed to get to a medical facility. This could not be fixed with a small first aid kit on a boat.

From outside, they heard the sound of a man on a bullhorn, speaking in Arabic. 'Lay down your weapons, raise your hands and come above deck. This is your final warning before we storm the boat.'

Sofia climbed up the stairs to the deck and popped her head out of the hatch. She scanned both banks of the river – one of them was empty but the other held what looked like dozens of US soldiers – all heavily armed, all with their guns pointed directly at the boat.

She came back down. When she stepped off the last stair and put her foot on the floor of the boat, it was immediately soaked.

Looking down, she realised that the floor of the boat was covered in two inches of water and rising steadily.

42. Copella

Copella scanned the scene below him with the binoculars.

He had been pleased when he managed to hit one of the thieves. He hoped the wound would be mortal. There certainly seemed to be enough blood to suggest that.

Then, when he was reloading, two of the others had scrambled up onto the deck and taken the wounded man below. He had tried to gun them down but they had been too quick. Furious, he had loosened a barrage of gunfire at the hatch. Then, when he noticed the craft listing to one side, he realised he had been overzealous and immediately stopped. He did not want to risk losing the precious cargo any more than he already had.

Thankfully, the ground forces had caught up. From his vantage point above, he could see the convoy had stopped on the road parallel to the river and had made their way, on foot, to the bank near the boat.

He established radio contact with the leader of the ground forces and asked him to board immediately to secure the cargo, warning him not to take any chances with the people aboard the craft – they had wounded his men and would shoot to kill.

A military craft was launched onto the river. A curious machine, it had a big open deck with a crane attached to one side of it, specifically for logistical operations on the water. Several soldiers kneeled on the deck with their guns trained firmly on the damaged red boat.

As they drew nearer, they saw what looked like a white flag on a stick emerging from the hatch, followed by, to their immense surprise, what looked like a Caucasian female. Then, to their continued surprise, she shouted over the water in what sounded like a British accent.

'Hold your fire! What on earth is going on? Why are you shooting at us?'

'Keep your hands up. Identify yourself', came the response from the military craft.

'Jane Carr, reporter. I'm doing a story on trade and commerce during the invasion. You've wounded my subject quite badly, need to get him to a hospital, stat. And we're taking on water. Again, why on earth did you shoot at us?'

'Bullshit. I really don't know what story they fed you, or whether you're working with them, but there's stolen merchandise aboard, and those subjects of yours have a history of violence towards coalition forces. Keep those hands where I can see them, we're coming aboard.'

The craft drew alongside the red cargo boat, and some of the soldiers jumped nimbly aboard, all the time keeping their weapons trained at Ava.

Her hands and feet were efficiently secured with plastic zip ties and two soldiers were left with their guns trained on her as the others descended into the hold.

An Iraqi man and woman stood with their hands up. Another man, wounded quite badly, lay on the table, away from the rising water levels, at least temporarily.

The radio connection was left open so that Copella could hear what was going on aboard the boat while he hovered in the sky above. Of course, he could no longer see what was going on below the deck but at least he could hear the proceedings on the radio.

The leader of the ground forces had asked for, and was observing, the white female's identification, which seemed legitimate.

The boat was now listing quite badly to one side. 'You better hurry,' Copella mumbled to himself, then shouted into the radio, 'Secure the cargo, that's the main priority.'

'Main priority is the insurgents, Commander, once they are secured, we will grab their illicit cargo.'

The ground leader sounded firm. Then, a few moments later, he provided an update. 'OK. All the insurgents have been secured, two males and two females. Gotta say they don't look like your typical insurgents. They're clearly well-educated urban youngsters.'

'Trust me, they shot several of my men, they are dangerous.'

'Well, you better be right. We have come a long way for this, even though we were needed at Basra. Let's get Saddam's cars and get out of here.'

'What do you see down there?'

'Two pieces of cargo, secured with tarps and webbing to the lower cargo deck. Our own cargo craft is in place outside the boat with winches. Gotta act quickly if we want to open this boat's cargo door, the bottom of it is probably underwater already. I'm risking the safety of my men for these damned cars. May as well let the bloody things sink. No one can get them if they do. Problem solved.'

'Don't you dare! I have reason to believe the cars may be a source of further intel. They must, I repeat, must be secured.'

'OK, we'll do our best. Cutting the ropes holding down the tarps now.'

Copella waited anxiously, hoping the water levels wouldn't already be too high to salvage the cars. He had already decided what to do with the money he would get for the cars. A new house. That state-of-the-art hunting rifle he had always wanted. A new Ducati.

In his head, they were as good as his.

Some rustling sounds came over his earpiece. The tarp being removed he imagined.

The sound of something being pried open and some metal banging against metal.

Then silence.

'What's going on?' he asked.

There was no reply from the commander, just more sounds of metal against metal.

Then, finally, the leader came back on the radio. He sounded like he was making some effort to restrain his anger.

'There are no cars here. Under either tarp. Just boxes. Lots of boxes. They contain what look like metal handles of all sizes. We're getting out of here now.' Then, not quite succeeding at staying professional, he added, 'Central's going to have your head for this. And if they don't, I'm going to knock it off your shoulders, you fucking waste of space.'

And with that, the radio went dead.

Despite the pain, a glimmer of a smile passed over the wounded man's face.

Epilogue I

The four men and one woman had travelled some distance to meet. They stood in a circle inside the darkened building.

One of them was an Iraqi government official, he had driven over from the city personally. His expression was one of anticipation as he stood in the dust of the factory, elegant in his dark suit. His driver, who also served as an armed bodyguard, waited outside. Even though it had been over ten years since the US invasion of Iraq, the power vacuum left in Saddam's absence had never quite been filled. Danger lurked everywhere as various factions were constantly vying for power.

The other person present was the owner of the factory, who stood with the aid of crutches. He had been shot in the knee over 10 years ago by a rogue American commander. Despite his old wound, which often flared up and pained him, he maintained a cheery disposition – amidst the invasion and the unrest that followed, his factory had gone from strength to strength, now even exporting metal door handles to America. He was adored by the people of his city, Kut, by the coalition forces and by any faction that happened to garner political power within the region at the time. Indeed, he had been urged to go into politics himself but firmly refused.

The third person was a woman, dressed in traditional robes. However, if you looked closely, you could see a pair of Levis poking out from underneath her abaya, and English features under the peak of her hat. She had travelled to the factory from London. She was not displeased to be back in Iraq, she had rather fallen in love with the food and the people when she was there last, over 10 years ago now. Life had been kind to her in the interim. She now operated a chain of workshops and garages across the United Kingdom in partnership with a young Iraqi man and woman who had travelled back to England with her, as refugees, after her stint as a reporter in Iraq.

The Iraqi (now British) woman had stayed back in London, looking after their business while they were away, and also looking after the ten-year-old girl she had with the Iraqi man. She couldn't have come – the little girl had a poetry recital, and the couple had decided at least one of them would attend.

The father of the little girl stood next to the Englishwoman. He was Iraqi but had mixed feelings about being back in the country. On one hand, it had felt nice to be home, near the water of the Tigris, where he could hear the familiar call of the birds and smell the familiar scents of the river. On the other hand, it pained him to see his countrymen still struggling with the ongoing conflict, more than 10 years after the invasion. Would there ever be peace in Iraq? He wasn't sure. He continued to write about Iraq while living in London, often contributing articles to the *Guardian.* An anthology of his blogs had even been published as a book.

The fifth and final man who stood in the building was a Baghdadi businessman. If one were to pull up the sleeve of his right arm, one would notice a latticework of scars and stitches, remnants of the surgery he had undergone a decade ago. They had managed to save the arm but, unfortunately, its function was very limited. That, however, seldom stopped him from getting things done. Indeed, it was this man who was directing the operations of the crane that stood before them, its business end currently being lowered slowly into the mud floor of the factory. A notepad with calculations lay on the floor in front of him.

Also on display, were two very large holes in the ground, created with the help of an excavating machine and 10 factory workers with pickaxes and shovels.

Finally, one of the workers jumped down into the first hole and secured the head of the crane to the tethers on the crate that seemed to have been buried underground many years ago. The worker had joined the factory only six years ago and had no idea these crates had been buried under his feet as he toiled above, powder-coating metal door handles. But he was just happy to help – he would have walked through fire for the owner of the factory if need be. Generous bosses were very hard to find in the war-torn country.

Finally, the two massive crates were painstakingly and carefully pulled from the rubble, set down on the factory floor and opened. The graceful lines of the objects within were obvious, despite the debris they had gathered from being underground for some time.

Memories from 10 years ago came rushing back to the Iraqi man. He was very glad he and his friends had decided not to proceed with the cars after their pit stop in the factory, choosing instead to hide them and leave them behind in the factory itself.

The Iraqi government official, who had been holding his breath, finally exhaled – a low whistle emerged from his mouth.

'So, it's true. The true Ghazi car has been in Iraq all this time. Incredible. Gentlemen, the nation of Iraq owes you a great debt for preserving a part of our heritage. The car belonged to King Ghazi, then to Saddam Hussein. Now, it shall pass to the next rulers of Iraq, hopefully the people themselves.'

The Englishwoman replied, 'Yup. Should be fairly easy to prove this is the original car, too. There's a museum in Germany that claims they have the original car, which is actually a replica created in the 1980s by Wagner Restorations in Landshut, lower Bavaria. Although both are built on authentic 540k platforms, this is the car that actually belonged to King Ghazi and Saddam, and briefly also belonged to King Hussein of Jordan.'

The government official smiled. 'Miss Ava, I've looked you up. Our government's intelligence arm, although newly instated, is not entirely useless. I know about your former occupation. Tell me. Why didn't you and your friends keep the car? It would have been easy enough to ship it back to England and sell it. I have personally received lucrative offers from a few wealthy and very private individuals in search of this particular car, not that I would have ever let it part ways with the ministry, even if I had it. Surely you didn't go through all the trouble of 'liberating' it from Al Sijood, just to give it back to the Iraqi people?'

'Well, we won't lie. Initially, we did want to keep the cars,' Abdul replied on behalf of them all. 'But look around. Much of what Iraq has created over the years has been taken away. At least, this way, we can feel proud that we have helped to retain a small part of Iraq's heritage. All that we ask is that the car is protected and displayed to the public as *their* car.'

'It will be,' resolved the official. 'And whatever the reason is for you removing these two cars from the palace, thank goodness you did. All the remaining cars have been destroyed or genuinely stolen. But this one is the jewel in the crown. It always has been.'

Rafan, Ava and Abdul looked at the car, one last time. Each of them nodded at the official from the ministry. He nodded back at them.

Then, without another word, they left the building.

Epilogue II

The Schwarzwald Hochstrasse is one of the most beautiful, elevated sections of highway in the Black Forest region. The initial stretch is fast and smooth; the views are as spectacular on either side as they are straight ahead.

One needs to watch one's speed, however, as it's certainly easy to get carried away amidst the stunning landscape.

The next part of the road takes the driver through a dense forest, but the road always remains wide, sweeping and incredible to drive. Then comes its highest point, around Hornisgrinde, where there are panoramic views. For its final stretch, the Hochstrasse drops down towards Baden Baden and one feels as if one is on a racetrack all the way through.

Abdul pressed down on the accelerator, and the demonic howl of the 1930s Mercedes supercharger emerged instantly from beneath the huge bonnet of the car. The car shot ahead through the light morning mist. Even though the car itself was a behemoth – 1.8 metres wide and extremely heavy – it felt light and nimble on the turns. Created only five years after the road had originally been built, the car was in its element and surged forward, consuming mile after mile with an appetite to match its size.

He thought of all the people who had occupied the seat he was in. Saddam and Uday Hussein, King Hussein of Jordan and, of course, King Ghazi, the first owner of the car.

Everyone seemed to have forgotten that when King Ghazi had fallen in love at the Barcelona Automobile Show, three lifetimes ago, it had been with a car that had a much smaller engine – albeit one that still had the spectacular Erdmann & Rossi coachwork. As a consummate petrolhead, he made enquiries immediately.

Mercedes could not bring themselves to sell the car with the smaller engine to the King – they knew of his passion for speed, the same passion that would eventually lead to his death behind the wheel of a 1939 Buick convertible. So, they had offered to build him another, identical Mercedes in partnership with Erdman & Rossi, except with a far bigger engine and a supercharger. As someone who did not buy cars to merely store them in a showcase, the King had agreed to this immediately. But then what happened to the original car with the smaller engine? What did Mercedes do with it?

In her past life, when Ava had stolen vintage automobiles that were very famous, she had managed to offload them to an agent he had in Germany. These cars, in legitimate circumstances, always led to a far greater selling price. However, on the black market, far less so – what use was a famous car if you could not tell anyone you owned it for fear of legal repercussions? However, this agent worked for a German billionaire who always remained unnamed but had been only too happy to receive the famous cars and pay full price for them, including a premium for famous previous owners. Sure, he did not have bragging rights, but he was a man who did not care to brag to anyone. That he drove a car previously owned by a famous actor, a mob boss or indeed a dictator was a source of constant amusement to him. He did not need anyone else to know.

The same German had always had his eye on the 540k and knew of its history intimately. In his advanced years, it had become an obsession on which he had focussed his considerable resources to try and procure it in order to complete his collection. Like King Ghazi many years ago, he too had fallen in love. However, the owner of the car, the dictator of Iraq, was the one person who could not be convinced to part with it in exchange for mere wealth. Saddam, after all, considered the car to be chief among all his symbols of power. There are things that money simply cannot buy.

So, the billionaire told himself that some things were not meant to be. He tracked down and procured the original car that had been displayed at the Barcelona Automobile Show, the one with the smaller engine. He told himself he would make do with this car instead. After all, it was, in every way identical to its Iraqi cousin, save for the engine.

But alas, after procuring it, he realised the car was no fun to drive at all. The small engine was incapable of moving the bulk of the car with any level of expediency. Further, he did not feel any sense of history or occasion while driving it. As a result, he became even more frustrated and doubled his resolve to obtain the Ghazi car. He had not reached where he was in life by giving up. But he understood the value of patience.

A few years later, in the run-up to 2003, he watched the political developments with the greatest of interest. When, finally, Bush announced the invasion would be going ahead, he knew this would be his best chance. He put out the word that he would part with a king's ransom to obtain the car.

Alas, for the longest time, nothing happened.

Then, to his surprise, years after the invasion, his agent phoned him up and mentioned that they had a chance to buy the car – but it came with a very unexpected condition. The seller of the car, a woman called Ava, whom they had done business with several times in the past, would only deliver the car to Germany if they would deliver its lower-powered cousin to Iraq. It became clear to all involved that Ava had the opportunity to do a swap, one in which no one would be any the wiser. The payment for this swap was astronomical and, in addition, the German would also have to part with the car he already owned.

He did not hesitate. In fact, the idea of conducting the swap, unbeknownst to anyone else, amused him no end and enhanced the value of the deal for him.

Then it had simply been a matter of logistics. The low-powered car – externally, in every way identical to the one that King Ghazi had taken home – was transported to Iraq. Of course, now that commerce and trade had commenced again in the region, despite continued terrorism, it had not been too hard – with the right connections – to swap it for the more powerful King Ghazi/Hussein/Saddam car that lay buried in the warehouse in Kut. The car with the low-powered engine was buried in the warehouse, and the original Ghazi car was transported to Germany.

They say a car does not get to choose its owner. But this car certainly seemed to enjoy its constant proximity to great power. Its next owner would be just as powerful. It would be the German's final reward to himself in his old age, for a life well lived. A deserving owner. But Ava and Abdul still had a few miles to go till they got there.

For that time, the car was theirs to drive.

Because not driving it would have been a far greater crime.

Epilogue III

The little boy's father was trying to inculcate in his son the habit of reading.

So, as his father had done when he was young, and his father before him, he took his son for a walk down Al-Mutanabbi Street.

'Did you know, son, that when I used to work for Saddam, I hated being in the palaces? This is where I came for solace. I would drink tea in that café or just purchase a book and sit on the pavement and read. When I escaped, I left Iraq for a few years. But I couldn't stay away. I love it too much.' He inhaled deeply, drinking in the smell of paper that seemed to envelop the street.

The little boy knew his father's past had been difficult, and that he had experienced unspeakable horrors at the hands of Saddam Hussein's family. His father had been in charge of their cars and their zoo, among other things. He had seen pictures of Saddam on the internet. Smiling. Friendly. Big moustache. But he also knew that sometimes, people weren't who they seemed to be.

'Did you know, son, the booksellers always used to pretend to sell books that praised the rulers? When I used to come here, there were books praising Saddam and his family. When the Americans killed Saddam, the booksellers did not have to pretend anymore. Now, again, we are back to an era in which there are some who prefer that you don't read whatever you want.'

'A couple of years ago, they even planted a bomb, right here, on Al-Mutanabbi Street – they killed many people and many booksellers. But the booksellers eventually came back, as did the readers, as they had done for centuries gone past.'

They walked towards a very grand-looking building and walked into its courtyard.

'Since we are here, son, I thought we should have a look at this exhibition. I hear there are some beautiful cars on display. Some of which I cared for, with my own two hands. I have not seen them for a while.'

They walked in.

In the courtyard of the restored Ottoman-era military college that served as a temporary cultural centre, were two gleaming vintage Mercedes automobiles: a 770k and a 540k.

Any Baghdadi worth her or his salt knew of these two cars and had seen them in parades, on the TV or in the papers throughout their lifetimes. More precious than the people who rode inside them, the cars had been there before many regimes and would be there long after, a symbol of continuity and familiarity in a constantly changing country.

There was a lot of hustle and bustle. Many Baghdadis had come to view the exhibition, whatever their politics or opinions on past regimes.

The man's son wandered up to the 540k, awestruck by its sweeping curves and gigantic dimensions. What would it be like to ride inside it, he thought? Would it even work? That such a large object was built expressly for the purpose of creating motion seemed beyond belief.

He was about to ask about this when he noticed his father was very deep in thought, staring intently at the car. The expression on his face was the same one he wore when the fish seller tried to assure him that the more fragrant elements of his offering had truly been caught that morning.

An Iraqi government official stood beside the car, dressed in a dark suit despite the warm weather. There were a few military police around, doing their best to provide an air of security to the proceedings. The official noticed the little boy and pulled out a picture from the pocket of his suit. It was a black-and-white image of a very smart young man, posing next to that very car. 'Do you know who this is son?' he asked.

The little boy shook his head.

'That's King Ghazi. He used to rule Iraq many years ago. He bought this car. And this,' he said, producing another photograph, 'is his little son, King Faisal II. Look, he's about your age in this picture. He also ruled Iraq.'

Then a third picture, again featuring the 540k. 'This,' said the old man, 'is King Faisal II's friend, King Hussein of Jordan, who also owned the car for a while. A friend of our people.

'And finally,' he said, producing a fourth picture of a man in the car, 'this is Saddam Hussein. He also ruled his country for a while. In the end, he and his sons stole a lot of money from everyone and ran away! No one even found the money!

'So, you see – this car – it's been many places, and had many masters. Where are those masters today? Gone! But see how beautiful she still looks?'

The boy looked again at the car with a newfound respect in his eyes. She was beautiful, there was no denying that!

He was quiet for a few minutes, holding his father's hand and reflecting on what the man had said.

Come to think of it, thought the boy, the car seemed to be a little like the people of Iraq – dignified and strong despite many decades of turmoil. Living through years of setbacks, difficulties and upheavals. Sometimes hiding, sometimes getting a bit rusty and a bit dirty. But always picking themselves up, dusting themselves off and retaining the inner luminescence that makes them who they are.

Sometimes ruled and, yes, sometimes fooled by many who have come and gone through the ages.

Through invasions and bomb blasts, through sanctions and war, they had continued to live, determinedly reading their books and sipping their tea.

Still standing proud. Still there.

At that moment, the little boy wanted to read more about the history of his country.

But more than that, he realised, he wanted to write it too.

After a while, the father looked away from the car and glanced down at the expression on his son's face. He saw pride. He saw curiosity. He saw determination.

The father shrugged.

After some ice cream, they made their way home.

AUTHOR'S NOTE

This is first and foremost a work of fiction – not history. Even though this novel is a culmination of 10 years' worth of on-and-off research, some characters have been made up entirely, and some loosely inspired by people who lived during this time. All dialogue, thoughts and actions attributed to any character have been entirely made up.

That being said, some of the strangest parts of this book are true. For example, the car in question – the Erdmann & Rossi Mercedes 540k Roadster was purchased by King Ghazi of Iraq and briefly owned by the King of Jordan before landing in Saddam's collection. Research shows there has been lots of mystery surrounding this valuable automobile. Oh, and Uday did own lions that were said to have escaped during the bombing.

ACKNOWLEDGEMENTS

Zainab Karachiwala for the wonderful cover art. My parents Behram and Shernaz for the encouragement. Kian for the inspiration. Nikhil Vijayan for one of the earliest beta reads. Vishad Sanghvi for one of the later ones. Lucy Hamilton and the folks from The Spun Yarn - Johnny, Sara and Daisy – for helping to take the novel to the next level with their suggestions and beta reads. The Gully Gang for providing great feedback that night in Bali, and for, well, being the Gully Gang. Zarin Virji for being an example. Gaia Martinelli-Bunzl for the insightful feedback. Matt & Emily for the support and the lovely book on writing. Jordan Mulligan for being an amazing copy editor. Rod Stewart from Tide for the amazing video trailer.

All of my brilliant beta readers.

All the wonderful authors whose books made me who I am today and provided me with countless hours of joy. Particularly, Ken Follett and Stephen King for going a step further and sharing their writing tips.

Printed in Dunstable, United Kingdom

75717844R00180